TO THE LIGHTHOUSE

Virginia Woolf

COLLINS
CLASSICS

Harper Press
An imprint of HarperCollins*Publishers*
1 London Bridge Street
London SE1 9GF

This Harper Press paperback edition published 2013

A catalogue record for this book is available from the British Library

ISBN: 978-0-00-793441-6

Printed and bound by CPI Group (UK) Ltd, Croydon, CR0 4YY

MIX
Paper from
responsible sources
FSC™ C007454
www.fsc.org

FSC™ is a non-profit international organisation established to promote the
responsible management of the world's forests. Products carrying the FSC label
are independently certified to assure consumers that they come
from forests that are managed to meet the social, economic and
ecological needs of present and future generations.

Find out more about HarperCollins and the environment at
www.harpercollins.co.uk/green

Life & Times section © HarperCollins*Publishers* Ltd
Gerard Cheshire asserts his moral rights as author of the Life & Times section
Classic Literature: Words and Phrases adapted from
Collins English Dictionary
Typesetting in Kalix by Palimpsest Book Production Limited,
Falkirk, Stirlingshire

History of Collins

In 1819, millworker William Collins from Glasgow, Scotland, set up a company for printing and publishing pamphlets, sermons, hymn books, and prayer books. That company was Collins and was to mark the birth of HarperCollins Publishers as we know it today. The long tradition of Collins dictionary publishing can be traced back to the first dictionary William published in 1824, *Greek and English Lexicon*. Indeed, from 1840 onwards, he began to produce illustrated dictionaries and even obtained a licence to print and publish the Bible.

Soon after, William published the first Collins novel, *Ready Reckoner*; however, it was the time of the Long Depression, where harvests were poor, prices were high, potato crops had failed, and violence was erupting in Europe. As a result, many factories across the country were forced to close down and William chose to retire in 1846, partly due to the hardships he was facing.

Aged 30, William's son, William II, took over the business. A keen humanitarian with a warm heart and a generous spirit, William II was truly 'Victorian' in his outlook. He introduced new, up-todate steam presses and published affordable editions of Shakespeare's works and *The Pilgrim's Progress*, making them available to the masses for the first time. A new demand for educational books meant that success came with the publication of travel books, scientific books, encyclopedias, and dictionaries. This demand to be educated led to the later publication of atlases, and Collins also held the monopoly on scripture writing at the time.

In the 1860s Collins began to expand and diversify

and the idea of 'books for the millions' was developed. Affordable editions of classical literature were published, and in 1903 Collins introduced 10 titles in their Collins Handy Illustrated Pocket Novels. These proved so popular that a few years later this had increased to an output of 50 volumes, selling nearly half a million in their year of publication. In the same year, The Everyman's Library was also instituted, with the idea of publishing an affordable library of the most important classical works, biographies, religious and philosophical treatments, plays, poems, travel, and adventure. This series eclipsed all competition at the time, and the introduction of paperback books in the 1950s helped to open that market and marked a high point in the industry.

HarperCollins is and has always been a champion of the classics, and the current Collins Classics series follows in this tradition – publishing classical literature that is affordable and available to all. Beautifully packaged, highly collectible, and intended to be reread and enjoyed at every opportunity.

Life & Times

Mental Health and Creativity

It would be fair to say that Virginia Woolf was an intense and complex personality. Some might describe her as highly imaginative, sensitive and creative, while others might use the words high-maintenance, introspective and obsessive. In truth, she was all of the above, which meant that she was highly regarded as a novelist by many and entirely disregarded by others.

The central sticking point with the latter was that she came from a highly privileged, upper-middle-class background, yet she viewed the world in quite a negative light. Untroubled by the daily pressures of most, her time was spent in deep analysis of life – or rather, her own life and that of her friends and family. Her literature, therefore, could occasionally disconnect with the lay reader, because her concerns could be seen as self-indulgent and focused on a rarified environment to which most people were not privy.

As a human specimen, Woolf was not a very robust figure. She was prone to bouts of depression and breakdown, in part possibly brought on by the lack of any necessity to just get on with activities that were positive for her mental and physical constitution. In the absence of responsibilities to toughen the character, she lived in a world of ever-decreasing circles until, one day, her horizons closed in so tight that she chose suicide as a means of escape. She filled the pockets of her overcoat with pebbles and walked head-long into a river to drown her sorrows, quite literally. Her life was ended by her own thoughts and actions at the age of 59.

Woolf is a classic case of an artist whose creative

expression was bad for their health. Had she abandoned writing in favour of an occupation that took her mind away from her obsessive thoughts, she would undoubtedly have lived a happier and more fulfilled life, but instead she became the author of her own undoing. So, a weighty question remains: was it worth all the pain and suffering? Inevitably those with similar leanings will say *yes*, because they are able to identify with Woolf's desire to commit her thoughts to the written word as a kind of catharsis. Inevitably those who cannot identify will say *no*, because her work offers nothing to which they can relate as they have no need of therapy. It may be that there has never been a more divisive novelist in the history of English literature, and this is probably Woolf's most interesting aspect.

Woolf's main influence on modern literature was her 'stream of consciousness' approach to prose. Her novels were really vehicles for the copious current of thoughts and emotions to flow without parameters. She was an aesthete and intelligentsium, investing all of her mental capacity into understanding and disseminating the minutiae of human nature, human society, human culture and the human condition. Woolf and her set could be seen as looking down on those who chose not to analyse human existence in such microscopic detail, but realistically this was probably the result of insecurities about one's own talent, context and significance. The one thing that is certain about belief systems is that believing things doesn't make them true. This is certainly not to say that Woolf's portfolio has no value – far from it – but that we do well to remember the context of the author. After all, it was precisely because she existed in her particular milieu that she produced her pioneering style of literature. Moreover, had she been born into a more typical, lower-middle or working class background, she would probably not have had the wherewithal to dissect humanity to such a level.

Mrs Dalloway and To the Lighthouse

Virginia Woolf's prolific patch continued in 1925 and 1927, when she published *Mrs Dalloway* and then *To the Lighthouse*. In these two novels, she displays the kind of original approach to prose that would forge her reputation as a literary genius. Woolf experimented with innovative approaches to writing that set her apart from her contemporaries by largely abandoning plot in favour of psychological exploration. She made it her mission to delve into the human condition – something most people took so much for granted that they failed to consider its importance.

Of course, this approach didn't make her books easy to read, but the whole point of the method was to challenge literary norms. Just as one needed to apply effort to understand the work of the Cubist artistic movement, which was prevalent at that time, so Woolf published literature with a similar requirement for analysis. She had turned the novel into high art. This wasn't to everyone's taste, but it would inevitably prove very influential. It was a sea change in defining the purpose of the novel, as the author was no longer expected to take the work to the reader. Instead, the reader was expected to do their own work and accept the challenge of interpreting a text's meaning. It was an intellectual workout on offer, rather than an unthinking stroll. Inevitably, this catalysed a division within the realm of the novel, as it divided into the 'literary novel' and the 'commercial novel'. The landscape of fiction publishing had been irreversibly altered by progress, and Woolf was at the forefront of the march to modernity.

The surface plot for *Mrs Dalloway* is simply that Clarissa Dalloway is preparing to host a party in the evening. But beyond the surface, Woolf explores the thought processes of Mrs Dalloway as she is prompted to reflect on her life and past events. Central to the novel is reference to the effect of World War I on British society in the post-war years and, in particular, the loss of loved ones and the altering fate of those left behind. The consequences of this included the physical and psychological damage done to those who fought and survived, as well as to those who survived despite never having set foot on the battlefield. It all adds up to an odd juxtaposition of people carrying on their lives, with parties, families and friends, while an unspoken suffering erodes their happiness.

The chronology of *To the Lighthouse* brackets World War I, examining the societal transformation caused by the conflict. The eponymous lighthouse is the summer home of the Ramsay family, on the Isle of Sky, in the Hebrides archipelago, off Scotland. The dynamic of the social environment inevitably changes year after year, but the war causes an abrupt change, due in part to the hiatus, but also due to three deaths – one from old age, one from combat and one from complications in childbirth. The use of the lighthouse is, of course, symbolic as a metaphorical guiding light that leads people to safety in life's travels. Despite the turbulence that life has wrought on the surviving members of the family, they manage to maintain the notion that meeting at the island provides them with a sense of insight and contentment that their world would otherwise lack.

Woolf's general take on society and the individual lives of her characters has an air of the upper-middle class about it, as those are the people seen to throw parties and have holiday homes, but this doesn't detract from the weight of her prose or to remove her meaning from the reaches of other readers. This is because she uses these characters as devices to bring protagonists together in order to investigate the interaction of personality with great skill.

The Bloomsbury Set

Virginia Woolf came from a background of intellectualism, however, this was largely cemented by her family's relocation from Kensington to Bloomsbury, where she became part of an intellectual elite known as the Bloomsbury Set. Together, they were all goldfish in the same bowl, looking out at the world around them with a similar artistic palette.

The pretentions of her social group actually allowed her to blossom as a writer, because she was given the encouragement and freedom she needed to experiment with her prose. In short, she was allowed to think of herself as an author and she was told what she wanted to hear. This was vitally important to someone with nagging self-doubt, so she developed deep and lasting bonds with those who saw and nurtured her potential. Indeed, she married one of them – Leonard Woolf – and remained devoted to him.

In time, of course, the pretentions of the Bloomsbury Set transcended into success, as they were undoubtedly intelligent, talented and well educated. This process of ascendance was, in part, aided by a number of stunts designed to draw public attention. One stunt in particular has become famous for its daring and humour: the Dreadnought Hoax. This was an elaborate plan to gain egress to the battleship *HMS Dreadnought* for no other reason than to have a good look around. A number of the Bloomsbury Set, including Woolf, disguised themselves as Abyssinian princes. They wore the appropriate garb of robes and turbans, but they also 'blacked-up' and sported fake beards. With escort and interpreter in tow, they boarded a VIP coach and took a train from Paddington to Weymouth, where they were received as genuine royalty with honour guard and allowed to inspect Royal Navy fleet. All the while, they pretended to communicate in a foreign tongue by uttering gibberish furnished with Greek and Latin, which the interpreter duly pretended to understand and translate.

Having returned to London, a photograph of the Bloomsbury Set, still in character, was sent to the *Daily Mirror* newspaper and the hoax was revealed. Not surprisingly, the affair turned into a scandal. The Foreign Office and the Royal Navy were the target of a great deal of finger-pointing, partly in fun and partly in seriousness for allowing such a blatant lapse in national security. The situation wasn't helped by the fact that the Bloomsbury Set were pacifists, which only served to rub salt into the wound. When the Navy high command pushed to have the perpetrators punished, they found themselves powerless to do anything. For one thing, no laws were broken, and secondly the consensus was that they themselves should be punished for allowing themselves to be beguiled by such a lame practical joke.

Needless to say, the Dreadnought Hoax planted the Bloomsbury Set in the public consciousness once and for all, as the oxygen of publicity was theirs to breathe in and enjoy. The hoax occurred on 7 February, 1910. Woolf's first novel was begun the same year, although she did not publish until 1915, by which time she was already a minor celebrity.

Despite her subsequent success, Woolf was never particularly contented, however, for she had such a troubled soul and indefatigable mind. Today her malady would, doubtless, be described as a bipolar condition, for she oscillated from exuberant mood highs to despairing clinical lows. In the end, she was convinced that she would never come full circle again, so she decided to cut her loses while in the grip of a crushing depression that rendered her unable to see any light at the end of the tunnel. Virginia Woolf died in 1941, leaving behind a highly respected, progressive and considerable canon of essays, critique and novels.

TO THE
LIGHTHOUSE

CONTENTS

Bibliographical Note

The following is a list of abbreviated titles used in this edition.

MS: *To the Lighthouse: The Original Holograph Draft*, transcribed and ed. Susan Dick (Toronto University Press, 1982; Hogarth Press, 1983). Square brackets are used to indicate words deleted in original draft.

TL: *To the Lighthouse*, first British edn (Hogarth Press, 5 May 1927).

Moments of Being: *Moments of Being: Unpublished Autobiographical Writings of Virginia Woolf*, ed. Jeanne Schulkind (Chatto & Windus, 1976).

Diary: *The Diary of Virginia Woolf*, 5 vols., ed. Anne Olivier Bell (Hogarth Press, 1977; Penguin Books, 1979).

Letters: *The Letters of Virginia Woolf*, 6 vols., ed. Nigel Nicolson and Joanne Trautmann (Hogarth Press, 1975–80).

Essays: *The Essays of Virginia Woolf*, 3 vols. (to be 6 vols.), ed. Andrew McNeillie (Hogarth Press, 1986).

CE: *Collected Essays*, 4 vols., ed. Leonard Woolf (Chatto & Windus, 1966, 1967).

Mausoleum: *Sir Leslie Stephen's Mausoleum Book* (1895), introduced by Alan Bell (OUP, 1977).

CHAPTER 1

The Window

I

'Yes, of course, if it's fine tomorrow,' said Mrs Ramsay. 'But you'll have to be up with the lark,' she added.

To her son these words conveyed an extraordinary joy, as if it were settled the expedition were bound to take place, and the wonder to which he had looked forward, for years and years it seemed, was, after a night's darkness and a day's sail, within touch. Since he belonged, even at the age of six, to that great clan which cannot keep this feeling separate from that, but must let future prospects, with their joys and sorrows, cloud what is actually at hand, since to such people even in earliest childhood any turn in the wheel of sensation has the power to crystallise and transfix the moment upon which its gloom or radiance rests, James Ramsay, sitting on the floor cutting out pictures from the illustrated catalogue of the Army and Navy Stores, endowed the picture of a refrigerator as his mother spoke with heavenly bliss. It was fringed with joy. The wheel-barrow, the lawn-mower, the sound of poplar trees, leaves whitening before rain, rooks cawing, brooms knocking, dresses rustling – all these were so coloured and distinguished in his mind that he had already his private code, his secret language, though he appeared the image of stark and uncompromising severity, with his high forehead and his fierce blue eyes, impeccably candid and pure, frowning slightly at the sight of human frailty, so that his mother, watching him guide his scissors neatly round the refrigerator, imagined him all red and ermine on the Bench or directing a stern and momentous enterprise in some crisis of public affairs.

'But,' said his father, stopping in front of the drawing-room window, 'it won't be fine.'

Had there been an axe handy, a poker, or any weapon that would have gashed a hole in his father's breast and killed him, there and then, James would have seized it. Such were the extremes of emotion that Mr Ramsay excited in his children's breasts by his mere presence; standing, as now, lean as a knife, narrow as the blade of one, grinning sarcastically, not only with the pleasure of disillusioning his son and casting ridicule upon his wife, who was ten thousand times better in every way than he was (James thought), but also with some secret conceit at his own accuracy of judgement. What he said was true. It was always true. He was incapable of untruth; never tampered with a fact; never altered a disagreeable word to suit the pleasure or convenience of any mortal being, least of all of his own children, who, sprung from his loins, should be aware from childhood that life is difficult; facts uncompromising; and the passage to that fabled land where our brightest hopes are extinguished, our frail barks founder in darkness (here Mr Ramsay would straighten his back and narrow his little blue eyes upon the horizon), one that needs, above all, courage, truth, and the power to endure.

'But it may be fine – I expect it will be fine,' said Mrs Ramsay, making some little twist of the reddish-brown stocking she was knitting, impatiently. If she finished it tonight, if they did go to the Lighthouse after all, it was to be given to the Lighthouse keeper for his little boy, who was threatened with a tuberculous hip; together with a pile of old magazines, and some tobacco, indeed whatever she could find lying about, not really wanted, but only littering the room, to give those poor fellows who must be bored to death sitting all day with nothing to do but polish the lamp and trim the wick and rake about on their scrap of garden, something to amuse them. For how would you like to be shut up for a whole month at a time, and possibly more in stormy weather, upon a rock the size of a tennis lawn? she would ask; and to have no letters or newspapers, and to see nobody; if you were married, not to see your wife, not to know how your children were, – if they were ill, if they had fallen down and broken their legs or arms; to see the same dreary waves breaking week after week, and then a dreadful storm coming, and the windows covered with spray, and birds dashed against the lamp, and the whole place rocking, and not be able to put your nose out of doors for fear of being swept into the sea? How would you like that? she asked, addressing herself particularly to her daughters. So she added, rather differently, one must take them whatever comforts one can.

'It's due west,' said the atheist Tansley, holding his bony fingers spread so that the wind blew through them, for he was sharing Mr Ramsay's evening walk up and down, up and down the terrace. That is to say, the wind blew from the worst possible direction for landing at the Lighthouse. Yes, he did say disagreeable things, Mrs Ramsay admitted; it was odious of him to rub this in, and make James still more disappointed; but at the same time, she would not let them laugh at him. 'The atheist', they called him; 'the little atheist'. Rose mocked him; Prue mocked him; Andrew, Jasper, Roger mocked him; even old Badger without a tooth in his head had bit him, for being (as Nancy put it) the hundred and tenth young man to chase them all the way up to the Hebrides when it was ever so much nicer to be alone.

'Nonsense,' said Mrs Ramsay, with great severity. Apart from the habit of exaggeration which they had from her, and from the implication (which was true) that she asked too many people to stay, and had to lodge some in the town, she could not bear incivility to her guests, to young men in particular, who were poor as church mice, 'exceptionally able', her husband said, his great admirers, and come there for a holiday. Indeed, she had the whole of the other sex under her protection; for reasons she could not explain, for their chivalry and valour, for the fact that they negotiated treaties, ruled India, controlled finance; finally for an attitude towards herself which no woman could fail to feel or to find agreeable, something trustful, childlike, reverential; which an old woman could take from a young man without loss of dignity, and woe betide the girl – pray Heaven it was none of her daughters! – who did not feel the worth of it, and all that it implied, to the marrow of her bones.

She turned with severity upon Nancy. He had not chased them, she said. He had been asked.

They must find a way out of it all. There might be some simpler way, some less laborious way, she sighed. When she looked in the glass and saw her hair grey, her cheek sunk, at fifty, she thought, possibly she might have managed things better – her husband; money; his books. But for her own part she would never for a single second regret her decision, evade difficulties, or slur over duties. She was now formidable to behold, and it was only in silence, looking up from their plates, after she had spoken so severely about Charles Tansley, that her daughters – Prue, Nancy, Rose – could sport with infidel ideas which they had brewed for themselves of a life different from hers; in Paris, perhaps; a wilder life; not always taking care of some man or other; for there was in all their minds a mute questioning of deference and chivalry, of the Bank of England and the Indian Empire, of ringed fingers and lace, though to them all there was something in this of the essence of beauty, which called out the manliness in their girlish hearts, and made them, as they sat at table beneath their mother's eyes, honour her strange severity, her extreme courtesy, like a Queen's raising from the mud a beggar's dirty foot and washing it, when she thus admonished them so very severely about that wretched atheist who had chased them to – or, speaking accurately, been invited to stay with them in – the Isle of Skye.

'There'll be no landing at the Lighthouse tomorrow,' said Charles Tansley, clapping his hands together as he stood at the window with her husband. Surely, he had said enough. She wished they would both leave her and James alone and go on talking. She looked at him. He was such a miserable specimen, the children said, all humps and hollows. He couldn't play cricket; he poked; he shuffled. He was a sarcastic brute, Andrew said. They knew what he liked best – to be for ever walking up and down, up and down, with Mr Ramsay, and saying who had won this, who had won that, who was a 'first-rate man' at Latin verses, who was 'brilliant but I think fundamentally unsound', who was undoubtedly the 'ablest fellow in Balliol', who had buried his light temporarily at Bristol or Bedford, but was bound to be heard of later when his Prolegomena, of which Mr Tansley had the first pages in proof with him if Mr Ramsay would like to see them, to some branch of mathematics or philosophy saw the light of day. That was what they talked about.

She could not help laughing herself sometimes. She said, the other day, something about 'waves mountains high'. Yes, said Charles Tansley, it was a little rough. 'Aren't you drenched to the skin?' she had said. 'Damp, not wet through,' said Mr Tansley, pinching his sleeve, feeling his socks.

But it was not that they minded, the children said. It was not his face; it was not his manners. It was him – his point of view. When they talked about something interesting, people, music, history, anything, even said it was a fine evening so why not sit out of doors, then what they complained of about Charles Tansley was that until he had turned the whole thing round and made it somehow reflect himself and disparage them, put them all on edge somehow with his acid way of peeling the flesh and blood off everything, he was not satisfied. And he would go to picture galleries, they said, and he would ask one, did one like his tie? God knows, said Rose, one did not.

Disappearing as stealthily as stags from the dinner-table directly the meal was over, the eight sons and daughters of Mr and Mrs Ramsay sought their bedrooms, their fastnesses in a house where there was no other privacy to debate anything, everything; Tansley's tie; the passing of the Reform Bill; sea-birds and butterflies; people; while the sun poured into those attics, which a plank alone separated from each other so that every footstep could be plainly heard and the Swiss girl sobbing for her father who was dying of cancer in a valley of the Grisons, and lit up bats, flannels, straw hats, ink-pots, paint-pots, beetles, and the skulls of small birds, while it drew from the long frilled strips of seaweed pinned to the wall a smell of salt and weeds, which was in the towels too, gritty with sand from bathing.

Strife, divisions, difference of opinion, prejudices twisted into the very fibre of being, oh that they should begin so early, Mrs Ramsay deplored. They were so critical, her children. They talked such nonsense. She went from the dining-room, holding James by the hand, since he would not go with the others. It seemed to her such nonsense – inventing differences, when people, heaven knows, were different enough without that. The real differences, she thought, standing by the drawing-room window, are enough, quite enough. She had in mind at the moment, rich and poor, high and low; the great in birth receiving from her, half grudging, some respect, for had she not in her veins the blood of that very noble, if slightly mythical, Italian house, whose daughters, scattered about English drawing-rooms in the nineteenth century, had lisped so charmingly, had stormed so wildly, and all her wit and her bearing and her temper came from them, and not from the sluggish English, or the cold Scotch; but more profoundly she ruminated the other problem, of rich and poor, and the things she saw with her own eyes, weekly, daily, here or in London, when she visited this widow, or that struggling wife in person with a bag on her arm, and a note-book and pencil with which she wrote down in columns carefully ruled for the purpose wages and spendings, employment and unemployment, in the hope that thus she would cease to be a private woman whose charity was half a sop to her own indignation, half a relief to her own curiosity, and become, what with her untrained mind she greatly admired, an investigator, elucidating the social problem.

Insoluble questions they were, it seemed to her, standing there, holding James by the hand. He had followed her into the drawing-room, that young man they laughed at; he was standing by the table, fidgeting with something, awkwardly, feeling himself out of things, as she knew without looking round. They had all gone – the children; Minta Doyle and Paul Rayley; Augustus Carmichael; her husband – they had all gone. So she turned with a sigh and said, 'Would it bore you to come with me, Mr Tansley?'

She had a dull errand in the town; she had a letter or two to write; she would be ten minutes perhaps; she would put on her hat. And, with her basket and her parasol, there she was again, ten minutes later, giving out a sense of being ready, of being equipped for a jaunt, which, however, she must interrupt for a moment, as they passed the tennis lawn, to ask Mr Carmichael, who was basking with his yellow cat's eyes ajar, so that like a cat's they seemed to reflect the branches moving or the clouds passing, but to give no inkling of any inner thoughts or emotion whatsoever, if he wanted anything.

For they were making the great expedition, she said, laughing. They were going to the town. 'Stamps, writing-paper, tobacco?' she suggested, stopping by his side. But no, he wanted nothing. His hands clasped themselves over his capacious paunch, his eyes blinked, as if he would have liked to reply kindly to these blandishments (she was seductive but a little nervous) but could not, sunk as he was in a grey-green somnolence which embraced them all, without need of words, in a vast and benevolent lethargy of well-wishing; all the house; all the world; all the people in it, for he had slipped into his glass at lunch a few drops of something, which accounted, the children thought, for the vivid streak of canary-yellow in moustache and beard that were otherwise milk-white. He wanted nothing, he murmured.

He should have been a great philosopher, said Mrs Ramsay, as they went down the road to the fishing village, but he had made an unfortunate marriage. Holding her black parasol very erect, and moving with an indescribable air of expectation, as if she were going to meet someone round the corner, she told the story; an affair at Oxford with some girl; an early marriage; poverty; going to India; translating a little poetry 'very beautifully, I believe', being willing to teach the boys Persian or Hindustanee, but what really was the use of that? – and then lying, as they saw him, on the lawn.

It flattered him; snubbed as he had been, it soothed him that Mrs Ramsay should tell him this. Charles Tansley revived. Insinuating, too, as she did the greatness of man's intellect, even in its decay, the subjection of all wives – not that she blamed the girl, and the marriage had been happy enough, she believed – to their husband's labours, she made him feel better pleased with himself than he had done yet, and he would have liked, had they taken a cab, for example, to have paid the fare. As for her little bag, might he not carry that? No, no, she said, she always carried *that* herself. She did too. Yes, he felt that in her. He felt many things, something in particular that excited him and disturbed him for reasons which he could not give. He would like her to see him, gowned and hooded, walking in a procession. A fellowship, a professorship, – he felt capable of anything and saw himself – but what was she looking at? At a man pasting a bill. The vast flapping sheet flattened itself out, and each shove of the brush revealed fresh legs, hoops, horses, glistening reds and blues, beautifully smooth, until half the wall was covered with the advertisement of a circus; a hundred horsemen, twenty performing seals, lions, tigers . . . Craning forwards, for she was short-sighted, she read out how it . . . 'will visit this town.' It was terribly dangerous work for a one-armed man, she exclaimed, to stand on top of a ladder like that – his left arm had been cut off in a reaping machine two years ago.

'Let us all go!' she cried, moving on, as if all those riders and horses had filled her with child-like exultation and made her forget her pity.

'Let's go,' he said, repeating her words, clicking them out, however, with a self-consciousness that made her wince. 'Let us go to the Circus.' No. He could not say it right. He could not feel it right. But why not? she wondered. What was wrong with him then? She liked him warmly, at the moment. Had they not been taken, she asked, to circuses when they were children? Never, he answered, as if she asked the very thing he wanted to reply to; had been longing all these days to say, how they did not go to circuses. It was a large family, nine brothers and sisters, and his father was a working man; 'My father is a chemist, Mrs Ramsay. He keeps a shop.' He himself had paid his own way since he was thirteen. Often he went without a greatcoat in winter. He could never 'return hospitality' (those were his parched stiff words) at college. He had to make things last twice the time other people did; he smoked the cheapest tobacco; shag; the same the old men smoked on the quays. He worked hard – seven hours a day; his subject was now the influence of something upon somebody – they were walking on and Mrs Ramsay did not quite catch the meaning, only the words, here and there . . . dissertation . . . fellowship . . . readership . . . lectureship. She could not follow the ugly academic jargon, that rattled itself off so glibly, but said to herself that she saw now why going to the circus had knocked him off his perch, poor little man, and why he came out, instantly, with all that about his father and mother and brothers and sisters, and she would see to it that they didn't laugh at him any more; she would tell Prue about it. What he would have liked, she supposed, would have been to say how he had been to Ibsen with the Ramsays. He was an awful prig – oh yes, an insufferable bore. For, though they had reached the town now and were in the main street, with carts grinding past on the cobbles, still he went on talking, about settlements, and teaching, and working men, and helping our own class, and lectures, till she gathered that he had got back entire self-confidence, had recovered from the circus, and was about (and now again she liked him warmly) to tell her – but here, the houses falling away on both sides, they came out on the quay, and the whole bay spread before them and Mrs Ramsay could not help exclaiming, 'Oh, how beautiful!' For the great plateful of blue water was before her; the hoary Lighthouse, distant austere, in the midst; and on the right, as far as the eye could see, fading and falling, in soft low pleats, the green sand dunes with the wild flowing grasses on them, which always seemed to be running away into some moon country, uninhabited of men.

That was the view, she said, stopping, growing greyer-eyed, that her husband loved.

She paused a moment. But now, she said, artists had come here. There indeed, only a few paces off, stood one of them, in Panama hat and yellow boots, seriously, softly, absorbedly, for all that he was watched by ten little boys, with an air of profound contentment on his round red face, gazing, and then, when he had gazed, dipping; imbuing the tip of his brush in some soft mound of green or pink. Since Mr Paunceforte had been there, three years before, all the pictures were like that she said, green and grey, with lemon-coloured sailing-boats, and pink women on the beach.

But her grandmother's friends, she said, glancing discreetly as they passed, took the greatest pains; first they mixed their own colours, and then they ground them, and then they put damp cloths on them to keep them moist.

So Mr Tansley supposed she meant him to see that that man's picture was skimpy, was that what one said? The colours weren't solid? Was that what one said? Under the influence of that extraordinary emotion which had been growing all the walk, had begun in the garden when he had wanted to take her bag, had increased in the town when he had wanted to tell her everything about himself, he was coming to see himself and everything he had ever known gone crooked a little. It was awfully strange.

There he stood in the parlour of the poky little house where she had taken him, waiting for her, while she went upstairs a moment to see a woman. He heard her quick step above; heard her voice cheerful, then low; looked at the mats, tea-caddies, glass shades; waited quite impatiently; looked forward eagerly to the walk home, determined to carry her bag; then heard her come out; shut a door; say they must keep the windows open and the doors shut, ask at the house for anything they wanted (she must be talking to a child), when, suddenly, in she came, stood for a moment silent (as if she had been pretending up there, and for a moment let herself be now), stood quite motionless for a moment against a picture of Queen Victoria wearing the blue ribbon of the Garter; and all at once he realised that it was this: it was this: – she was the most beautiful person he had ever seen.

With stars in her eyes and veils in her hair, with cyclamen and wild violets – what nonsense was he thinking? She was fifty at least; she had eight children. Stepping through fields of flowers and taking to her breast buds that had broken and lambs that had fallen; with the stars in her eyes and the wind in her hair – He took her bag.

'Good-bye, Elsie,' she said, and they walked up the street,

she holding her parasol erect and walking as if she expected to meet someone round the corner, while for the first time in his life Charles Tansley felt an extraordinary pride; a man digging in a drain stopped digging and looked at her; let his arm fall down and looked at her; Charles Tansley felt an extraordinary pride; felt the wind and the cyclamen and the violets for he was walking with a beautiful woman for the first time in his life. He had hold of her bag.

II

'No going to the Lighthouse, James,' he said, as he stood by the window, speaking awkwardly, but trying in deference to Mrs Ramsay to soften his voice into some semblance of geniality at least.

Odious little man, thought Mrs Ramsay, why go on saying that?

III

'Perhaps you will wake up and find the sun shining and the birds singing,' she said compassionately, smoothing the little boy's hair, for her husband, with his caustic saying that it would not be fine, had dashed his spirits she could see. This going to the Lighthouse was a passion of his, she saw, and then, as if her husband had not said enough, with his caustic saying that it would not be fine tomorrow, this odious little man went and rubbed it in all over again.

'Perhaps it will be fine tomorrow,' she said, smoothing his hair.

All she could do now was to admire the refrigerator, and turn the pages of the Stores list in the hope that she might come upon something like a rake, or a mowing-machine, which, with its prongs and its handles, would need the greatest skill and care in cutting out. All these young men parodied her husband, she reflected; he said it would rain; they said it would be a positive tornado.

But here, as she turned the page, suddenly her search for the picture of a rake or a mowing-machine was interrupted. The gruff murmur, irregularly broken by the taking out of pipes and the putting in of pipes which had kept on assuring her, though she could not hear what was said (as she sat in the window), that the men were happily talking; this sound, which had lasted now half an hour and had taken its place soothingly in the scale of sounds pressing on top of her, such as the tap of balls upon bats, the sharp, sudden bark now and then, 'How's that? How's that?' of the children playing cricket, had ceased; so that the monotonous fall of the waves on the beach, which for the most part beat a measured and soothing tattoo to her thoughts and seemed consolingly to repeat over and over again as she sat with the children the words of some old cradle song, murmured by nature, 'I am guarding you – I am your support', but at other times suddenly and unexpectedly, especially when her mind raised itself slightly from the task actually in hand, had no such kindly meaning, but like a ghostly roll of drums remorselessly beat the measure of life, made one think of the destruction of the island and its engulfment in the sea, and warned her whose day had slipped past in one quick doing after another that it was all ephemeral as a rainbow – this sound which had been obscured and concealed under the other sounds suddenly thundered hollow in her ears and made her look up with an impulse of terror.

They had ceased to talk; that was the explanation. Falling in one second from the tension which had gripped her to the other extreme which, as if to recoup her for her unnecessary expense of emotion, was cool, amused, and even faintly malicious, she concluded that poor Charles Tansley had been shed. That was of little account to her. If her husband required sacrifices (and indeed he did) she cheerfully offered up to him Charles Tansley, who had snubbed her little boy.

One moment more, with her head raised, she listened, as if she waited for some habitual sound, some regular mechanical sound; and then, hearing something rhythmical, half said, half chanted, beginning in the garden, as her husband beat up and down the terrace, something between a croak and a song, she was soothed once more, assured again that all was well, and looking down at the book on her knee found the picture of a pocket knife with six blades which could only be cut out if James was very careful.

Suddenly a loud cry, as of a sleep-walker, half roused, something about

Stormed at with shot and shell

sung out with the utmost intensity in her ear, made her turn apprehensively to see if any one heard him. Only Lily Briscoe, she was glad to find; and that did not matter. But the sight of the girl standing on the edge of the lawn painting reminded her; she was supposed to be keeping her head as much in the same position as possible for Lily's picture. Lily's picture! Mrs Ramsay smiled. With her little Chinese eyes and her puckered-up face she would never marry; one could not take her painting very seriously; but she was an independent little creature, Mrs Ramsay liked her for it, and so remembering her promise, she bent her head.

IV

Indeed, he almost knocked her easel over, coming down upon her with his hands waving, shouting out 'Boldly we rode and well', but, mercifully, he turned sharp, and rode off, to die gloriously she supposed upon the heights of Balaclava. Never was anybody at once so ridiculous and so alarming. But so long as he kept like that, waving, shouting, she was safe; he would not stand still and look at her picture. And that was what Lily Briscoe could not have endured. Even while she looked at the mass, at the line, at the colour, at Mrs Ramsay sitting in the window with James, she kept a feeler on her surroundings lest someone should creep up, and suddenly she should find her picture looked at. But now, with all her senses quickened as they were, looking, straining, till the colour of the wall and the jacmanna beyond burnt into her eyes, she was aware of someone coming out of the house, coming towards her; but somehow divined, from the footfall, William Bankes, so that though her brush quivered, she did not, as she would have done had it been Mr Tansley, Paul Rayley, Minta Doyle, or practically anybody else, turn her canvas upon the grass, but let it stand. William Bankes stood beside her.

They had rooms in the village, and so, walking in, walking out, parting late on door-mats, had said little things about the soup, about the children, about one thing and another which made them allies; so that when he stood beside her now in his judicial way (he was old enough to be her father too, a botanist, a widower, smelling of soap, very scrupulous and clean) she just stood there. He just stood there. Her shoes were excellent, he observed. They allowed the toes their natural expansion. Lodging in the same house with her, he had noticed too, how orderly she was, up before breakfast and off to paint, he believed, alone: poor, presumably, and without the complexion or the allurement of Miss Doyle certainly, but with a good sense which made her in his eyes superior to that young lady. Now, for instance, when Ramsay bore down on them, shouting, gesticulating, Miss Briscoe, he felt certain, understood.

Someone had blundered.

Mr Ramsay glared at them. He glared at them without seeming to see them. That did make them both vaguely uncomfortable. Together they had seen a thing they had not been meant to see. They had encroached upon a privacy. So, Lily thought, it was probably an excuse of his for moving, for getting out of earshot, that made Mr Bankes almost immediately say something about its being chilly and suggest taking a stroll. She would come, yes. But it was with difficulty that she took her eyes off her picture.

The jacmanna was bright violet; the wall staring white. She would not have considered it honest to tamper with the bright violet and the staring white, since she saw them like that, fashionable though it was, since Mr Paunceforte's visit, to see everything pale, elegant, semi-transparent. Then beneath the colour there was the shape. She could see it all so clearly, so commandingly, when she looked: it was when she took her brush in hand that the whole thing changed. It was in that moment's flight between the picture and her canvas that the demons set on her who often brought her to the verge of tears and made this passage from conception to work as dreadful as any down a dark passage for a child. Such she often felt herself – struggling against terrific odds to maintain her courage; to say: 'But this is what I see; this is what I see', and so to clasp some miserable remnant of her vision to her breast, which a thousand forces did their best to pluck from her. And it was then too, in that chill and windy way, as she began to paint, that there forced themselves upon her other things, her own inadequacy, her insignificance, keeping house for her father off the Brompton Road, and had much ado to control her impulse to fling herself (thank Heaven she had always resisted so far) at Mrs Ramsay's knee and say to her – but what could one say to her? 'I'm in love with you?' No, that was not true. 'I'm in love with this all', waving her hand at the hedge, at the house, at the children? It was absurd, it was impossible. One could not say what one meant. So now she laid her brushes neatly in the box, side by side, and said to William Bankes:

'It suddenly gets cold. The sun seems to give less heat,' she said, looking about her, for it was bright enough, the grass still a soft deep green, the house starred in its greenery with purple passion flowers, and rooks dropping cool cries from the high blue. But something moved, flashed, turned a silver wing in the air. It was September after all, the middle of September, and past six in the evening. So off they strolled down the garden in the usual direction, past the tennis lawn, past the pampas grass, to that break in the thick hedge, guarded by red-hot pokers like brasiers of clear burning coal, between which the blue waters of the bay looked bluer than ever.

They came there regularly every evening drawn by some need. It was as if the water floated off and set sailing thoughts which had grown stagnant on dry land, and gave to their bodies even some sort of physical relief. First, the pulse of colour flooded the bay with blue, and the heart expanded with it and the body swam, only the next instant to be checked and chilled by the prickly blackness on the ruffled waves. Then, up behind the great black rock, almost every evening spurted irregularly, so that one had to watch for it and it was a delight when it came, a fountain of white water; and then, while one waited for that, one watched, on the pale semi-circular beach, wave after wave shedding again and again smoothly a film of mother-of-pearl.

They both smiled, standing there. They both felt a common hilarity, excited by the moving waves; and then by the swift cutting race of a sailing boat, which, having sliced a curve in the bay, stopped; shivered; let its sail drop down; and then, with a natural instinct to complete the picture, after this swift movement, both of them looked at the dunes far away, and instead of merriment felt come over them some sadness – because the thing was completed partly, and partly because distant views seem to outlast by a million years (Lily thought) the gazer and to be communing already with a sky which beholds an earth entirely at rest.

Looking at the far sandhills, William Bankes thought of Ramsay: thought of a road in Westmorland, thought of Ramsay striding along a road by himself hung round with that solitude which seemed to be his natural air. But this was suddenly interrupted, William Bankes remembered (and this must refer to some actual incident), by a hen, straddling her wings out in protection of a covey of little chicks, upon which Ramsay, stopping, pointed his stick and said 'Pretty – pretty,' an odd illumination into his heart, Bankes had thought it, which showed his simplicity, his sympathy with humble things; but it seemed to him as if their friendship had ceased, there, on that stretch of road. After that, Ramsay had married. After that, what with one thing and another, the pulp had gone out of their friendship. Whose fault it was he could not say, only, after a time, repetition had taken the place of newness. It was to repeat that they met. But in this dumb colloquy with the sand dunes he maintained that his affection for Ramsay had in no way diminished; but there, like the body of a young man laid up in peat for a century, with the red fresh on his lips, was his friendship, in its acuteness and reality laid up across the bay among the sandhills.

He was anxious for the sake of this friendship and perhaps too in order to clear himself in his own mind from the imputation of having dried and shrunk – for Ramsay lived in a welter of children, whereas Bankes was childless and a widower – he was anxious that Lily Briscoe should not disparage Ramsay (a great man in his own way) yet should understand how things stood between them. Begun long years ago, their friendship had petered out on a Westmorland road, where the hen spread her wings before her chicks; after which Ramsay had married, and their paths lying different ways, there had been, certainly for no one's fault, some tendency, when they met, to repeat.

Yes. That was it. He finished. He turned from the view. And, turning to walk back the other way, up the drive, Mr Bankes was alive to things which would not have struck him had not those sandhills revealed to him the body of his friendship lying with the red on its lips laid up in peat – for instance, Cam, the little girl, Ramsay's youngest daughter. She was picking Sweet Alice on the bank. She was wild and fierce. She would not 'give a flower to the gentleman' as the nursemaid told her. No! no! no! she would not! She clenched her fist. She stamped. And Mr Bankes felt aged and saddened and somehow put into the wrong by her about his friendship. He must have dried and shrunk.

The Ramsays were not rich, and it was a wonder how they managed to contrive it all. Eight children! To feed eight children on philosophy! Here was another of them, Jasper this time, strolling past, to have a shot at a bird, he said, nonchalantly, swinging Lily's hand like a pump-handle as he passed, which caused Mr Bankes to say, bitterly, how *she* was a favourite. There was education now to be considered (true, Mrs Ramsay had something of her own perhaps) let alone the daily wear and tear of shoes and stockings which those 'great fellows', all well grown, angular, ruthless youngsters, must require. As for being sure which was which, or in what order they came, that was beyond him. He called them privately after the Kings and Queens of England; Cam the Wicked, James the Ruthless, Andrew the Just, Prue the Fair – for Prue would have beauty, he thought, how could she help it? – and Andrew brains. While he walked up the drive and Lily Briscoe said yes and no and capped his comments (for she was in love with them all, in love with this world) he weighed Ramsay's case, commiserated him, envied him, as if he had seen him divest himself of all those glories of isolation and austerity which crowned him in youth to cumber himself definitely with fluttering wings and clucking domesticities. They gave him something – William Bankes acknowledged that; it would have been pleasant if Cam had stuck a flower in his coat or clambered over his shoulder, as over her father's, to look at a picture of Vesuvius in eruption; but they had also, his old friends could not but feel, destroyed something. What would a stranger think now? What did this Lily Briscoe think? Could one help noticing that habits grew on him? eccentricities, weaknesses perhaps? It was astonishing that a man of his intellect could stoop so low as he did – but that was too harsh a phrase – could depend so much as he did upon people's praise.

'Oh but,' said Lily, 'think of his work!'

Whenever she 'thought of his work' she always saw clearly before her a large kitchen table. It was Andrew's doing. She asked him what his father's books were about. 'Subject and object and the nature of reality', Andrew had said. And when she said Heavens, she had no notion what that meant, 'Think of a kitchen table then', he told her, 'when you're not there'.

So she always saw, when she thought of Mr Ramsay's work, a scrubbed kitchen table. It lodged now in the fork of a pear tree, for they had reached the orchard. And with a painful effort of concentration, she focused her mind, not upon the silver-bossed bark of the tree, or upon its fish-shaped leaves, but upon a phantom kitchen table, one of those scrubbed board tables, grained and knotted, whose virtue seems to have been laid bare by years of muscular integrity, which stuck there, its four legs in air. Naturally, if one's days were passed in this seeing of angular essences, this reducing of lovely evenings, with all their flamingo clouds and blue and silver to a white deal four-legged table (and it was a mark of the finest minds so to do), naturally one could not be judged like an ordinary person.

Mr Bankes liked her for bidding him 'think of his work'. He had thought of it, often and often. Times without number, he had said, 'Ramsay is one of those men who do their best work before they are forty'. He had made a definite contribution to philosophy in one little book when he was only five and twenty; what came after was more or less amplification, repetition. But the number of men who make a definite contribution to anything whatsoever is very small, he said, pausing by the pear tree, well brushed, scrupulously exact, exquisitely judicial. Suddenly, as if the movement of his hand had released it, the load of her accumulated impressions of him tilted up, and down poured in a ponderous avalanche all she felt about him. That was one sensation. Then up rose in a fume the essence of his being. That was another. She felt herself transfixed by the intensity of her perception; it was his severity; his goodness. I respect you (she addressed him silently) in every atom; you are not vain; you are entirely impersonal; you are finer than Mr Ramsay; you are the finest human being that I know; you have neither wife nor child (without any sexual feeling, she longed to cherish that loneliness), you live for science (involuntarily, sections of potatoes rose before her eyes); praise would be an insult to you; generous, pure-hearted, heroic man! But simultaneously, she remembered how he had brought a valet all the way up here; objected to dogs on chairs; would prose for hours (until Mr Ramsay slammed out of the room) about salt in vegetables and the iniquity of English cooks.

How then did it work out, all this? How did one judge people, think of them? How did one add up this and that and conclude that it was liking one felt, or disliking? And to those words, what meaning attached, after all? Standing now, apparently transfixed, by the pear tree, impressions poured in upon her of those two men, and to follow her thought was like following a voice which speaks too quickly to be taken down by one's pencil, and the voice was her own voice saying without prompting undeniable, everlasting, contradictory things, so that even the fissures and humps on the bark of the pear tree were irrevocably fixed there for eternity. You have greatness, she continued, but Mr Ramsay has none of it. He is petty, selfish, vain, egotistical; he is spoilt; he is a tyrant; he wears Mrs Ramsay to death; but he has what you (she addressed Mr Bankes) have not; a fiery unworldliness; he knows nothing about trifles; he loves dogs and his children. He has eight. You have none. Did he not come down in two coats the other night and let Mrs Ramsay trim his hair into a pudding basin? All of this danced up and down, like a company of gnats, each separate, but all marvellously controlled in an invisible elastic net – danced up and down in Lily's mind, in and about the branches of the pear tree, where still hung in effigy the scrubbed kitchen table, symbol of her profound respect for Mr Ramsay's mind, until her thought which had spun quicker and quicker exploded of its own intensity; she felt released; a shot went off close at hand, and there came, flying from its fragments, frightened, effusive, tumultuous, a flock of starlings.

'Jasper!' said Mr Bankes. They turned the way the starlings flew, over the terrace. Following the scatter of swift-flying birds in the sky they stepped through the gap in the high hedge straight into Mr Ramsay, who boomed tragically at them, 'Someone had blundered!'

His eyes, glazed with emotion, defiant with tragic intensity, met theirs for a second, and trembled on the verge of recognition; but then, raising his hand half-way to his face as if to avert, to brush off, in an agony of peevish shame, their normal gaze, as if he begged them to withhold for a moment what he knew to be inevitable, as if he impressed upon them his own child-like resentment of interruption, yet even in the moment of discovery was not to be routed utterly, but was determined to hold fast to something of this delicious emotion, this impure rhapsody of which he was ashamed, but in which he revelled – he turned abruptly, slammed his private door on them; and Lily Briscoe and Mr Bankes, looking uneasily up into the sky, observed that the flock of starlings which Jasper had routed with his gun had settled on the tops of the elm trees.

V

'And even if it isn't fine tomorrow,' said Mrs Ramsay, raising her eyes to glance at William Bankes and Lily Briscoe as they passed, 'it will be another day. And now,' she said, thinking that Lily's charm was her Chinese eyes, aslant in her white, puckered little face, but it would take a clever man to see it, 'and now stand up, and let me measure your leg,' for they might go to the Lighthouse after all, and she must see if the stocking did not need to be an inch or two longer in the leg.

Smiling, for an admirable idea had flashed upon her this very second – William and Lily should marry – she took the heather mixture stocking, with its criss-cross of steel needles at the mouth of it, and measured it against James's leg.

'My dear, stand still,' she said, for in his jealousy, not liking to serve as measuring-block for the Lighthouse keeper's little boy, James fidgeted purposely; and if he did that, how could she see, was it too long, was it too short? she asked.

She looked up – what demon possessed him, her youngest, her cherished? – and saw the room, saw the chairs, thought them fearfully shabby. Their entrails, as Andrew said the other day, were all over the floor; but then what was the point, she asked herself, of buying good chairs to let them spoil up here all through the winter when the house, with only one old woman to see to it, positively dripped with wet? Never mind: the rent was precisely twopence halfpenny; the children loved it; it did her husband good to be three thousand, or if she must be accurate, three hundred miles from his library and his lectures and his disciples; and there was room for visitors. Mats, camp beds, crazy ghosts of chairs and tables whose London life of service was done – they did well enough here; and a photograph or two, and books. Books, she thought, grew of themselves. She never had time to read them. Alas! even the books that had been given her, and inscribed by the hand of the poet himself: 'For her whose wishes must be obeyed' . . . 'The happier Helen of our days' . . . disgraceful to say, she had never read them. And Croom on the Mind and Bates on the Savage Customs of Polynesia ('My dear, stand still,' she said) – neither of those could one send to the Lighthouse. At a certain moment, she supposed, the house would become so shabby that something must be done. If they could be taught to wipe their feet and not bring the beach in with them – that would be something. Crabs, she had to allow, if Andrew really wished to dissect them, or if Jasper believed that one could make soup from seaweed, one could not prevent it; or Rose's objects – shells, reeds, stones; for they were gifted, her children, but all in quite different ways. And the result of it was, she sighed, taking in the whole room from floor to ceiling, as she held the stocking against James's leg, that things got shabbier and got shabbier summer after summer. The mat was fading; the wall-paper was flapping. You couldn't tell any more that those were roses on it. Still, if every door in a house is left perpetually open, and no lockmaker in the whole of Scotland can mend a bolt, things must spoil. What was the use of flinging a green Cashmere shawl over the edge of a picture frame? In two weeks it would be the colour of pea soup. But it was the doors that annoyed her; every door was left open. She listened. The drawing-room door was open; the hall door was open; it sounded as if the bedroom doors were open; and certainly the window on the landing was open, for that she had opened herself. That windows should be open, and doors shut – simple as it was, could none of them remember it? She would go into the maids' bedrooms at night and find them sealed like ovens, except for Marie's, the Swiss girl, who would rather go without a bath than without fresh air, but then at home, she had said, 'the mountains are so beautiful.' She had said that last night looking out of the window with tears in her eyes. 'The mountains are so beautiful.' Her father was dying there, Mrs Ramsay knew. He was leaving them fatherless. Scolding and demonstrating (how to make a bed, how to open a window, with hands that shut and spread like a Frenchwoman's) all had folded itself quietly about her, when the girl spoke, as, after a flight through the sunshine the wings of a bird fold themselves quietly and the blue of its plumage changes from bright steel to soft purple. She had stood there silent for there was nothing to be said. He had cancer of the throat. At the recollection – how she had stood there, how the girl had said 'At home the mountains are so beautiful', and there was no hope, no hope whatever, she had a spasm of irritation, and speaking sharply, said to James:

'Stand still. Don't be tiresome,' so that he knew instantly that her severity was real, and straightened his leg and she measured it.

The stocking was too short by half an inch at least, making allowance for the fact that Sorley's little boy would be less well grown than James.

'It's too short,' she said, 'ever so much too short.'

Never did anybody look so sad. Bitter and black, half-way down, in the darkness, in the shaft which ran from the sunlight to the depths, perhaps a tear formed; a tear fell; the waters swayed this way and that, received it, and were at rest. Never did anybody look so sad.

But was it nothing but looks? people said. What was there behind it – her beauty, her splendour? Had he blown his brains out, they asked, had he died the week before they were married – some other, earlier lover, of whom rumours reached one? Or was there nothing? nothing but an incomparable beauty which she lived behind, and could do nothing to disturb? For easily though she might have said at some moment of intimacy when stories of great passion, of love foiled, of ambition thwarted came her way how she too had known or felt or been through it herself, she never spoke. She was silent always. She knew then – she knew without having learnt. Her simplicity fathomed what clever people falsified. Her singleness of mind made her drop plumb like a stone, alight exact as a bird, gave her, naturally, this swoop and fall of the spirit upon truth which delighted, eased, sustained – falsely perhaps.

('Nature has but little clay', said Mr Bankes once, hearing her voice on the telephone, and much moved by it though she was only telling him a fact about a train, 'like that of which she moulded you.' He saw her at the end of the line,

Greek, blue-eyed, straight-nosed. How incongruous it seemed to be telephoning to a woman like that. The Graces assembling seemed to have joined hands in meadows of asphodel to compose that face. Yes, he would catch the 10.30 at Euston.

'But she's no more aware of her beauty than a child,' said Mr Bankes, replacing the receiver and crossing the room to see what progress the workmen were making with an hotel which they were building at the back of his house. And he thought of Mrs Ramsay as he looked at that stir among the unfinished walls. For always, he thought, there was something incongruous to be worked into the harmony of her face. She clapped a deer-stalker's hat on her head; she ran across the lawn in goloshes to snatch a child from mischief. So that if it was her beauty merely that one thought of, one must remember the quivering thing, the living thing (they were carrying bricks up a little plank as he watched them), and work it into the picture; or if one thought of her simply as a woman, one must endow her with some freak of idiosyncrasy; or suppose some latent desire to doff her royalty of form as if her beauty bored her and all that men say of beauty, and she wanted only to be like other people, insignificant. He did not know. He did not know. He must go to his work.)

Knitting her reddish-brown hairy stocking, with her head outlined absurdly by the gilt frame, the green shawl which she had tossed over the edge of the frame, and the authenticated masterpiece by Michael Angelo, Mrs Ramsay smoothed out what had been harsh in her manner a moment before, raised his head, and kissed her little boy on the forehead. 'Let's find another picture to cut out,' she said.

VI

But what had happened?

Someone had blundered.

Starting from her musing she gave meaning to words which she had held meaningless in her mind for a long stretch of time. 'Someone had blundered' – Fixing her short-sighted eyes upon her husband, who was now bearing down upon her, she gazed steadily until his closeness revealed to her (the jingle mated itself in her head) that something had happened, someone had blundered. But she could not for the life of her think what.

He shivered; he quivered. All his vanity, all his satisfaction in his own splendour, riding fell as a thunderbolt, fierce as a hawk at the head of his men through the valley of death, had been shattered, destroyed. Stormed at by shot and shell, boldly we rode and well, flashed through the valley of death, volleyed and thundered – straight into Lily Briscoe and William Bankes. He quivered; he shivered.

Not for the world would she have spoken to him, realising, from the familiar signs, his eyes averted, and some curious gathering together of his person, as if he wrapped himself about and needed privacy in which to regain his equilibrium, that he was outraged and anguished. She stroked James's head; she transferred to him what she felt for her husband, and, as she watched him chalk yellow the white dress shirt of a gentleman in the Army and Navy Stores catalogue, thought what a delight it would be to her should he turn out a great artist; and why should he not? He had a splendid forehead. Then, looking up, as her husband passed her once more, she was relieved to find that the ruin was veiled; domesticity triumphed; custom crooned its soothing rhythm, so that when stopping deliberately, as his turn came round again, at the window he bent quizzically and whimsically to tickle James's bare calf with a sprig of something, she twitted him for having dispatched 'that poor young man', Charles Tansley. Tansley had had to go in and write his dissertation, he said.

'James will have to write *his* dissertation one of these days,' he added ironically, flicking his sprig.

Hating his father, James brushed away the tickling spray

with which in a manner peculiar to him, compound of severity and humour, he teased his youngest son's bare leg.

She was trying to get these tiresome stockings finished to send to Sorley's little boy tomorrow, said Mrs Ramsay.

There wasn't the slightest possible chance that they could go to the Lighthouse tomorrow, Mr Ramsay snapped out irascibly.

How did he know? she asked. The wind often changed.

The extraordinary irrationality of her remark, the folly of women's minds enraged him. He had ridden through the valley of death, been shattered and shivered; and now she flew in the face of facts, made his children hope what was utterly out of the question, in effect, told lies. He stamped his foot on the stone step. 'Damn you,' he said. But what had she said? Simply that it might be fine tomorrow. So it might.

Not with the barometer falling and the wind due west.

To pursue truth with such astonishing lack of consideration for other people's feelings, to rend the thin veils of civilisation so wantonly, so brutally, was to her so horrible an outrage of human decency that, without replying, dazed and blinded, she bent her head as if to let the pelt of jagged hail, the drench of dirty water, bespatter her unrebuked. There was nothing to be said.

He stood by her in silence. Very humbly, at length, he said that he would step over and ask the Coastguards if she liked.

There was nobody whom she reverenced as she reverenced him.

She was quite ready to take his word for it, she said. Only then they need not cut sandwiches – that was all. They came to her, naturally, since she was a woman, all day long with this and that; one wanting this, another that; the children were growing up; she often felt she was nothing but a sponge sopped full of human emotions. Then he said, Damn you. He said, It must rain. He said, It won't rain; and instantly a

Heaven of security opened before her. There was nobody she reverenced more. She was not good enough to tie his shoe strings, she felt.

Already ashamed of that petulance, of that gesticulation of the hands when charging at the head of his troops, Mr Ramsay rather sheepishly prodded his son's bare legs once more, and then, as if he had her leave for it, with a movement which oddly reminded his wife of the great sealion at the Zoo tumbling backwards after swallowing his fish and walloping off so that the water in the tank washes from side to side, he dived into the evening air which already thinner was taking the substance from leaves and hedges but, as if in return, restoring to roses and pinks a lustre which they had not had by day.

'Someone had blundered,' he said again, striding off, up and down the terrace.

But how extraordinarily his note had changed! It was like the cuckoo; 'in June he gets out of tune'; as if he were trying over, tentatively seeking, some phrase for a new mood, and having only this at hand, used it, cracked though it was. But it sounded ridiculous – 'Someone had blundered' – said like that, almost as a question, without any conviction, melodiously. Mrs Ramsay could not help smiling, and soon, sure enough, walking up and down, he hummed it, dropped it, fell silent.

He was safe, he was restored to his privacy. He stopped to light his pipe, looked once at his wife and son in the window, and as one raises one's eyes from a page in an express train and sees a farm, a tree, a cluster of cottages as an illustration, a confirmation of something on the printed page to which one returns, fortified, and satisfied, so without his distinguishing either his son or his wife, the sight of them fortified him and satisfied him and consecrated his effort to arrive at a perfectly clear understanding of the problem which now engaged the energies of his splendid mind.

It was a splendid mind. For if thought is like the keyboard of a piano, divided into so many notes, or like the alphabet is ranged in twenty-six letters all in order, then his splendid mind had no sort of difficulty in running over those letters one by one, firmly and accurately, until it had reached, say, the letter Q. He reached Q. Very few people in the whole of England ever reach Q. Here, stopping for one moment by the stone urn which held the geraniums, he saw, but now far far away, like children picking up shells, divinely innocent and occupied with little trifles at their feet and somehow entirely defenceless against a doom which he perceived, his wife and son, together, in the window. They needed his protection; he gave it them. But after Q? What comes next? After Q there are a number of letters the last of which is scarcely visible to mortal eyes, but glimmers red in the distance. Z is only reached once by one man in a generation. Still, if he could reach R it would be something. Here at least was Q. He dug his heels in at Q. Q he was sure of. Q he could demonstrate. If Q then is Q – R – Here he knocked his pipe out, with two or three resonant taps on the ram's horn which made the handle of the urn, and proceeded. 'Then R . . .' He braced himself. He clenched himself.

Qualities that would have saved a ship's company exposed on a broiling sea with six biscuits and a flask of water – endurance and justice, foresight, devotion, skill, came to his help. R is then – what is R?

A shutter, like the leathern eyelid of a lizard, flickered over the intensity of his gaze and obscured the letter R. In that flash of darkness he heard people saying – he was a failure – that R was beyond him. He would never reach R. On to R, once more. R—

Qualities that in a desolate expedition across the icy solitudes of the Polar region would have made him the leader, the guide, the counsellor, whose temper, neither sanguine nor despondent, surveys with equanimity what is to be and faces it, came to his help again. R—

The lizard's eye flickered once more. The veins on his forehead bulged. The geranium in the urn became startlingly visible and, displayed among its leaves, he could see, without wishing it, that old, that obvious distinction between the two classes of men; on the one hand the steady goers of superhuman strength who, plodding and persevering, repeat the whole alphabet in order, twenty-six letters in all, from start to finish; on the other the gifted, the inspired who, miraculously, lump all the letters together in one flash – the way of genius. He had not genius; he laid no claim to that: but he had, or might have had, the power to repeat every letter of the alphabet from A to Z accurately in order. Meanwhile, he stuck at Q. On, then, on to R.

Feelings that would not have disgraced a leader who, now that the snow has begun to fall and the mountain-top is covered in mist, knows that he must lay himself down and die before morning comes, stole upon him, paling the colour of his eyes, giving him, even in the two minutes of his turn on the terrace, the bleached look of withered old age. Yet he would not die lying down; he would find some crag of rock, and there, his eyes fixed on the storm, trying to the end to pierce the darkness, he would die standing. He would never reach R.

He stood stock still, by the urn, with the geranium flowing over it. How many men in a thousand million, he asked himself, reach Z after all? Surely the leader of a forlorn hope may ask himself that, and answer, without treachery to the expedition behind him, 'One perhaps'. One in a generation. Is he to be blamed then if he is not that one? provided he has toiled honestly, given to the best of his power, till he has no more left to give? And his fame lasts how long? It is permissible even for a dying hero to think before he dies how men will speak of him hereafter. His fame lasts perhaps two thousand years. And what are two thousand years? (asked Mr Ramsay ironically, staring at the hedge). What, indeed, if you look from a mountain-top down the long wastes of the ages?

The very stone one kicks with one's boot will outlast Shakespeare. His own little light would shine, not very brightly, for a year or two, and would then be merged in some bigger light, and that in a bigger still. (He looked into the darkness, into the intricacy of the twigs.) Who then could blame the leader of that forlorn party which after all has climbed high enough to see the waste of the years and the perishing of stars, if before death stiffens his limbs beyond the power of movement he does a little consciously raise his numbed fingers to his brow, and square his shoulders, so that when the search party comes they will find him dead at his post, the fine figure of a soldier? Mr Ramsay squared his shoulders and stood very upright by the urn.

Who shall blame him, if, so standing for a moment, he dwells upon fame, upon search parties, upon cairns raised by grateful followers over his bones? Finally, who shall blame the leader of the doomed expedition, if, having adventured to the uttermost, and used his strength wholly to the last ounce and fallen asleep not much caring if he wakes or not, he now perceives by some pricking in his toes that he lives, and does not on the whole object to live, but requires sympathy, and whisky, and someone to tell the story of his suffering to at once? Who shall blame him? Who will not secretly rejoice when the hero puts his armour off, and halts by the window and gazes at his wife and son, who very distant at first, gradually come closer and closer, till lips and book and head are clearly before him, though still lovely and unfamiliar from the intensity of his isolation and the waste of ages and the perishing of the stars, and finally putting his pipe in his pocket and bending his magnificent head before her – who will blame him if he does homage to the beauty of the world?

VII

But his son hated him. He hated him for coming up to them, for stopping and looking down on them; he hated him for interrupting them; he hated him for the exaltation and sublimity of his gestures; for the magnificence of his head; for his exactingness and egotism (for there he stood, commanding them to attend to him); but most of all he hated the twang and twitter of his father's emotion which, vibrating round them, disturbed the perfect simplicity and good sense of his relations with his mother. By looking fixedly at the page, he hoped to make him move on; by pointing his finger at a word, he hoped to recall his mother's attention, which, he knew angrily, wavered instantly his father stopped. But no. Nothing would make Mr Ramsay move on. There he stood, demanding sympathy.

Mrs Ramsay, who had been sitting loosely, folding her son in her arm, braced herself, and, half turning, seemed to raise herself with an effort, and at once to pour erect into the air a rain of energy, a column of spray, looking at the same time animated and alive as if all her energies were being fused into force, burning and illuminating (quietly though she sat, taking up her stocking again), and into this delicious fecundity, this fountain and spray of life, the fatal sterility of the male plunged itself, like a beak of brass, barren and bare. He wanted sympathy. He was a failure, he said. Mrs Ramsay flashed her needles. Mr Ramsay repeated, never taking his eyes from her face, that he was a failure. She blew the words back at him. 'Charles Tansley . . .' she said. But he must have more than that. It was sympathy he wanted, to be assured of his genius, first of all, and then to be taken within the circle of life, warmed and soothed, to have his senses restored to him, his barrenness made fertile, and all the rooms of the house made full of life – the drawing-room; behind the drawing-room the kitchen; above the kitchen the bedrooms; and beyond them the nurseries; they must be furnished, they must be filled with life.

Charles Tansley thought him the greatest metaphysician of the time, she said. But he must have more than that. He must have sympathy. He must be assured that he too lived in the heart of life; was needed; not here only, but all over the world. Flashing her needles, confident, upright, she created drawing-room and kitchen, set them all aglow; bade him take his ease there, go in and out, enjoy himself. She laughed, she knitted. Standing between her knees, very stiff, James felt all her strength flaring up to be drunk and quenched by the beak of brass, the arid scimitar of the male, which smote mercilessly, again and again, demanding sympathy.

He was a failure, he repeated. Well, look then, feel then. Flashing her needles, glancing round about her, out of the window, into the room, at James himself, she assured him, beyond a shadow of a doubt, by her laugh, her poise, her competence (as a nurse carrying a light across a dark room assures a fractious child), that it was real; the house was full; the garden blowing. If he put implicit faith in her, nothing should hurt him; however deep he buried himself or climbed high, not for a second should he find himself without her. So boasting of her capacity to surround and protect, there was scarcely a shell of herself left for her to know herself by; all was so lavished and spent; and James, as he stood stiff between her knees, felt her rise in a rosy-flowered fruit tree laid with leaves and dancing boughs into which the beak of brass, the arid scimitar of his father, the egotistical man, plunged and smote, demanding sympathy.

Filled with her words, like a child who drops off satisfied, he said, at last, looking at her with humble gratitude, restored, renewed, that he would take a turn; he would watch the children playing cricket. He went.

Immediately, Mrs Ramsay seemed to fold herself together, one petal closed in another, and the whole fabric fell in exhaustion upon itself, so that she had only strength enough to move her finger, in exquisite abandonment to exhaustion, across the page of Grimm's fairy story, while there throbbed through her, like the pulse in a spring which has expanded to its full width and now gently ceases to beat, the rapture of successful creation.

Every throb of this pulse seemed, as he walked away, to enclose her and her husband, and to give to each that solace which two different notes, one high, one low, struck together, seem to give each other as they combine. Yet, as the resonance died, and she turned to the Fairy Tale again, Mrs Ramsay felt not only exhausted in body (afterwards, not at the time, she always felt this) but also there tinged her physical fatigue some faintly disagreeable sensation with another origin. Not that, as she read aloud the story of the Fisherman's Wife, she knew precisely what it came from; nor did she let herself put into words her dissatisfaction when she realised, at the turn of the page when she stopped and heard dully, ominously, a wave fall, how it came from this: she did not like, even for a second, to feel finer than her husband; and further, could not bear not being entirely sure, when she spoke to him, of the truth of what she said. Universities and people wanting him, lectures and books and their being of the highest import-ance – all that she did not doubt for a moment; but it was their relation, and his coming to her like that, openly, so that anyone could see, that discomposed her; for then people said he depended on her, when they must know that of the two he was infinitely the more important, and what she gave the world, in comparison with what he gave, negligible. But then again, it was the other thing too – not being able to tell him the truth, being afraid, for instance, about the greenhouse roof and the expense it would be, fifty pounds perhaps, to mend it; and then about his books, to be afraid that he might guess, what she a little suspected, that his last book was not quite his best book (she gathered that from William Bankes); and then to hide small daily things, and the children seeing it, and the burden it laid on them – all this diminished the entire joy, the pure joy, of the two notes sounding together, and let the sound die on her ear now wth a dismal flatness.

A shadow was on the page; she looked up. It was Augustus Carmichael shuffling past, precisely now, at the very moment when it was painful to be reminded of the inadequacy of human relationships, that the most perfect was flawed, and could not bear the examination which, loving her husband, with her instinct for truth, she turned upon it; when it was painful to feel herself convicted of unworthiness, and impeded in her proper function by these lies, these exaggerations, – it was at this moment when she was fretted thus ignobly in the wake of her exaltation, that Mr Carmichael shuffled past, in his yellow slippers, and some demon in her made it necessary for her to call out, as he passed,

'Going indoors, Mr Carmichael?'

VIII

He said nothing. He took opium. The children said he had stained his beard yellow with it. Perhaps. What was obvious to her was that the poor man was unhappy, came to them every year as an escape; and yet every year, she felt the same thing; he did not trust her. She said, 'I am going to the town. Shall I get you stamps, paper, tobacco?' and she felt him wince. He did not trust her. It was his wife's doing. She remembered that iniquity of his wife's towards him, which had made her turn to steel and adamant there, in the horrid little room in St John's Wood, when with her own eyes she had seen that odious woman turn him out of the house. He was unkempt; he dropped things on his coat; he had the tiresomeness of an old man with nothing in the world to do; and she turned him out of the room. She said, in her odious way, 'Now, Mrs Ramsay and I want to have a little talk together,' and Mrs Ramsay could see, as if before her eyes, the innumerable miseries of his life. Had he money enough to buy tobacco? Did he have to ask her for it? half a crown? eighteenpence? Oh, she could not bear to think of the little indignities she made him suffer. And always now (why, she could not guess, except that it came probably from that woman somehow) he shrank from her. He never told her anything. But what more could she have done? There was a sunny room given up to him. The children were good to him. Never did she show a sign of not wanting him. She went out of her way indeed to be friendly. Do you want stamps, do you want tobacco? Here's a book you might like and so on. And after all – after all (here insensibly she drew herself together, physically, the sense of her own beauty becoming, as it did so seldom, present to her) – after all, she had not generally any difficulty in making people like her; for instance, George Manning; Mr Wallace; famous as they were, they would come to her of an evening, quietly, and talk alone over her fire. She bore about with her, she could not help knowing it, the torch of her beauty; she carried it erect into any room that she entered; and after all, veil it as she might, and shrink from the monotony of bearing that it imposed on her, her beauty was apparent. She had been admired. She had been loved. She had entered rooms where mourners sat. Tears had flown in her presence. Men, and women too, letting go the multiplicity of things, had allowed themselves with her the relief of simplicity. It injured her that he should shrink. It hurt her. And yet not cleanly, not rightly. That was what she minded, coming as it did on top of her discontent with her husband; the sense she had now when Mr Carmichael shuffled past, just nodding to her question, with a book beneath his arm, in his yellow slippers, that she was suspected; and that all this desire of hers to give, to help, was vanity. For her own self-satisfaction was it that she wished so instinctively to help, to give, that people might say of her, 'O Mrs Ramsay! dear Mrs Ramsay . . . Mrs Ramsay, of course!' and need her and send for her and admire her? Was it not secretly this that she wanted, and therefore when Mr Carmichael shrank away from her, as he did at this moment, making off to some corner where he did acrostics endlessly, she did not feel merely snubbed back in her instinct, but made aware of the pettiness of some part of her, and of human relations, how flawed they are, how despicable, how self-seeking, at their best. Shabby and worn out, and not presumably (her cheeks were hollow, her hair was white) any longer a sight that filled the eyes with joy, she had better devote her mind to the story of the Fisherman and his Wife and so pacify that bundle of sensitiveness (none of her children was as sensitive as he was) her son James.

'The man's heart grew heavy,' she read aloud, 'and he would not go. He said to himself, "It is not right," and yet he went. And when he came to the sea the water was quite purple and dark blue, and grey and thick, and no longer so green and yellow, but it was still quiet. And he stood there and said—'

Mrs Ramsay could have wished that her husband had not chosen that moment to stop. Why had he not gone as he said to watch the children playing cricket? But he did not speak; he looked; he nodded; he approved; he went on. He slipped seeing before him that hedge which had over and over again rounded some pause, signified some conclusion, seeing his wife and child, seeing again the urns with the trailing red geraniums which had so often decorated processes of thought, and bore, written up among their leaves, as if they were scraps of paper on which one scribbles notes in the rush of reading – he slipped, seeing all this, smoothly into speculation suggested by an article in *The Times* about the number of Americans who visit Shakespeare's house every year. If Shakespeare had never existed, he asked, would the world have differed much from what it is today? Does the progress of civilisation depend upon great men? Is the lot of the average human being better now than in the time of the Pharaohs? Is the lot of the average human being, however, he asked himself, the criterion by which we judge the measure of civilisation? Possibly not. Possibly the greatest good requires the existence of a slave class. The liftman in the Tube is an eternal necessity. The thought was distasteful to him. He tossed his head. To avoid it, he would find some way of snubbing the predominance of the arts. He would argue that the world exists for the average human being; that the arts are merely a decoration imposed on the top of human life; they do not express it. Nor is Shakespeare necessary to it. Not knowing precisely why it was that he wanted to disparage Shakespeare and come to the rescue of the man who stands eternally in the door of the lift, he picked a leaf sharply from the hedge. All this would have to be dished up for the young men at Cardiff next month, he thought; here, on his terrace, he was merely foraging and picnicking (he threw away the leaf that he had picked so peevishly) like a man who reaches from his horse to pick a bunch of roses, or stuffs his pockets with nuts as he ambles at his ease through the lanes and fields of a country known to him from boyhood. It was all familiar; this turning, that stile, that cut across the fields. Hours he would spend thus, with his pipe, of an evening, thinking up and down and in and out of the old familiar lanes and commons, which were all stuck about with the history of that campaign there, the life of this statesman here, with poems and with anecdotes, with figures too, this thinker, that soldier; all very brisk and clear; but at length the lane, the field, the common, the fruitful nut-tree and the flowering hedge led him on to that further turn of the road where he dismounted always, tied his horse to a tree, and proceeded on foot alone. He reached the edge of the lawn and looked out on the bay beneath.

It was his fate, his peculiarity, whether he wished it or not, to come out thus on a spit of land which the sea is slowly eating away, and there to stand, like a desolate sea-bird, alone. It was his power, his gift, suddenly to shed all superfluities, to shrink and diminish so that he looked barer and felt sparer, even physically, yet lost none of his intensity of mind, and so to stand on his little ledge facing the dark of human ignorance, how we know nothing and the sea eats away the ground we stand on – that was his fate, his gift. But having thrown away, when he dismounted, all gestures and fripperies, all trophies of nuts and roses, and shrunk so that not only fame but even his own name was forgotten by him, he kept even in that desolation a vigilance which spared no phantom and luxuriated in no vision, and it was in this guise that he inspired in William Bankes (intermittently) and in Charles Tansley (obsequiously) and in his wife now, when she looked up and saw him standing at the edge of the lawn, profound reverence, and pity, and gratitude too, as a stake driven into the bed of a channel upon which the gulls perch and the waves beat inspires in merry boat-loads a feeling of gratitude for the duty it has taken upon itself of marking the channel out there in the floods alone.

'But the father of eight children has no choice. . . .' Muttering half aloud, so he broke off, turned, sighed, raised his eyes, sought the figure of his wife reading stories to the little boy; filled his pipe. He turned from the sight of human ignorance and human fate and the sea eating the ground we stand on, which, had he been able to contemplate it fixedly might have led to something; and found consolation in trifles so slight compared with the august theme just now before him that he was disposed to slur that comfort over, to deprecate it, as if to be caught happy in a world of misery was for an honest man the most despicable of crimes. It was true; he was for the most part happy; he had his wife; he had his children; he had promised in six weeks' time to talk 'some nonsense' to the young men of Cardiff about Locke, Hume, Berkeley, and the causes of the French Revolution. But this and his pleasure in it, in the phrases he made, in the ardour of youth, in his wife's beauty, in the tributes that reached him from Swansea, Cardiff, Exeter, Southampton, Kidderminster, Oxford, Cambridge – all had to be deprecated and concealed under the phrase 'talking nonsense,' because, in effect, he had not done the thing he might have done. It was a disguise; it was the refuge of a man afraid to own his own feelings, who could not say, This is what I like – this is what I am; and rather pitiable and distasteful to William Bankes and Lily Briscoe, who wondered why such concealments should be necessary; why he needed always praise; why so brave a man in thought should be so timid in life; how strangely he was venerable and laughable at one and the same time.

Teaching and preaching is beyond human power, Lily suspected. (She was putting away her things.) If you are exalted you must somehow come a cropper. Mrs Ramsay gave him what he asked too easily. Then the change must be so upsetting, Lily said. He comes in from his books and finds us all playing games and talking nonsense. Imagine what a change from the things he thinks about, she said.

He was bearing down upon them. Now he stopped dead and stood looking in silence at the sea. Now he had turned away again.

IX

Yes, Mr Bankes said, watching him go. It was a thousand pities. (Lily had said something about his frightening her – he changed from one mood to another so suddenly.) Yes, said Mr Bankes, it was a thousand pities that Ramsay could not behave a little more like other people. (For he liked Lily Briscoe; he could discuss Ramsay with her quite openly.) It was for that reason, he said, that the young don't read Carlyle. A crusty old grumbler who lost his temper if the porridge was cold, why should he preach to us? was what Mr Bankes understood that young people said nowadays. It was a thousand pities if you thought, as he did, that Carlyle was one of the great teachers of mankind. Lily was ashamed to say that she had not read Carlyle since she was at school. But in her opinion one liked Mr Ramsay all the better for thinking that if his little finger ached the whole world must come to an end. It was not *that* she minded. For who could be deceived by him? He asked you quite openly to flatter him, to admire him, his little dodges deceived nobody. What she disliked was his narrowness, his blindness, she said, looking after him.

'A bit of a hypocrite?' Mr Bankes suggested, looking, too, at Mr Ramsay's back, for was he not thinking of his friendship, and of Cam refusing to give him a flower, and of all those boys and girls, and his own house, full of comfort, but, since his wife's death, quiet rather? Of course, he had his work . . . All the same, he rather wished Lily to agree that Ramsay was, as he said, 'a bit of a hypocrite'.

Lily Briscoe went on putting away her brushes, looking up, looking down. Looking up, there he was – Mr Ramsay – advancing towards them, swinging, careless, oblivious, remote. A bit of a hypocrite? she repeated. Oh no – the most sincere of men, the truest (here he was), the best; but, looking down, she thought, he is absorbed in himself, he is tyrannical, he is unjust; and kept looking down, purposely, for only so could she keep steady, staying with the Ramsays. Directly one looked up and saw them, what she called 'being in love' flooded them. They became part of that unreal but penetrating and exciting universe which is the world seen through the eyes of love. The sky stuck to them; the birds sang through them. And, what was even more exciting, she felt, too, as she saw Mr Ramsay bearing down and retreating, and Mrs Ramsay sitting with James in the window and the cloud moving and the tree bending, how life, from being made up of little separate incidents which one lived one by one, became curled and whole like a wave which bore one up with it and threw one down with it, there, with a dash on the beach.

Mr Bankes expected her to answer. And she was about to say something criticising Mrs Ramsay, how she was alarming, too, in her way, high-handed, or words to that effect, when Mr Bankes made it entirely unnecessary for her to speak by his rapture. For such it was considering his age, turned sixty, and his cleanliness and his impersonality, and the white scientific coat which seemed to clothe him. For him to gaze as Lily saw him gazing at Mrs Ramsay was a rapture, equivalent, Lily felt, to the loves of dozens of young men (and perhaps Mrs Ramsay had never excited the loves of dozens of young men). It was love, she thought, pretending to move her canvas, distilled and filtered; love that never attempted to clutch its object; but, like the love which mathematicians bear their symbols, or poets their phrases, was meant to be spread over the world and become part of the human gain. So it was indeed. The world by all means should have shared it, could Mr Bankes have said why that woman pleased him so; why the sight of her reading a fairy tale to her boy had upon him precisely the same effect as the solution of a scientific problem, so that he rested in contemplation of it, and felt, as he felt when he had proved something absolute about the digestive system of plants, that barbarity was tamed, the reign of chaos subdued.

Such a rapture – for by what other name could one call it? – made Lily Briscoe forget entirely what she had been about to say. It was nothing of importance; something about Mrs Ramsay. It paled beside this 'rapture', this silent stare, for which she felt intense gratitude; for nothing so solaced her, eased her of the perplexity of life, and miraculously raised its burdens, as this sublime power, this heavenly gift, and one would no more disturb it, while it lasted, than break up the shaft of sunlight lying level across the floor.

That people should love like this, that Mr Bankes should feel this for Mrs Ramsay (she glanced at him musing) was helpful, was exalting. She wiped one brush after another upon a piece of old rag, menially, on purpose. She took shelter from the reverence which covered all women; she felt herself praised. Let him gaze; she would steal a look at her picture.

She could have wept. It was bad, it was bad, it was infinitely bad! She could have done it differently of course; the colour could have been thinned and faded; the shapes etherealised; that was how Paunceforte would have seen it. But then she did not see it like that. She saw the colour burning on a framework of steel; the light of a butterfly's wing lying upon the arches of a cathedral. Of all that only a few random marks scrawled upon the canvas remained. And it would never be seen; never be hung even, and there was Mr Tansley whispering in her ear, 'Women can't paint, women can't write . . .'

She now remembered what she had been going to say about Mrs Ramsay. She did not know how she would have put it; but it would have been something critical. She had been annoyed the other night by some high-handedness. Looking along the level of Mr Bankes' glance at her, she thought that no woman could worship another woman in the way he worshipped; they could only seek shelter under the shade which Mr Bankes extended over them both. Looking along his beam she added to it her different ray, thinking that she was unquestionably the loveliest of people (bowed over her book); the best perhaps; but also, different too from the perfect shape which one saw there. But why different, and how different? she asked herself, scraping her palette of all those mounds of blue and green which seemed to her like clods with no life in them now, yet she vowed, she would inspire them, force them to move, flow, do her bidding tomorrow. How did she differ? What was the spirit in her, the essential thing, by which, had you found a glove in the corner of a sofa, you would have known it, from its twisted finger, hers indisputably? She was like a bird for speed, an arrow for directness. She was wilful; she was commanding (of course, Lily reminded herself, I am thinking of her relations with women, and I am much younger, an insignificant person, living off the Brompton Road). She opened bedroom windows.

She shut doors. (So she tried to start the tune of Mrs Ramsay in her head.) Arriving late at night, with a light tap on one's bedroom door, wrapped in an old fur coat (for the setting of her beauty was always that – hasty, but apt), she would enact again whatever it might be – Charles Tansley losing his umbrella; Mr Carmichael snuffling and sniffing; Mr Bankes saying, 'the vegetable salts are lost'. All this she would adroitly shape; even maliciously twist; and, moving over to the window, in pretence that she must go, – it was dawn, she could see the sun rising, – half turn back, more intimately, but still always laughing, insist that she must, Minta must, they all must marry, since in the whole world, whatever laurels might be tossed to her (but Mrs Ramsay cared not a fig for her painting), or triumphs won by her (probably Mrs Ramsay had had her share of those), and here she saddened, darkened, and came back to her chair, there could be no disputing this: an unmarried woman (she lightly took her hand for a moment), an unmarried woman has missed the best of life. The house seemed full of children sleeping and Mrs Ramsay listening; of shaded lights and regular breathing.

Oh but, Lily would say, there was her father; her home; even, had she dared to say it, her painting. But all this seemed so little, so virginal, against the other. Yet, as the night wore on, and white lights parted the curtains, and even now and then some bird chirped in the garden, gathering a desperate courage she would urge her own exemption from the universal law; plead for it; she liked to be alone; she liked to be herself; she was not made for that; and so have to meet a serious stare from eyes of unparalleled depth, and confront Mrs Ramsay's simple certainty (and she was childlike now) that her dear Lily, her little Brisk, was a fool. Then, she remembered, she had laid her head on Mrs Ramsay's lap and laughed and laughed and laughed, laughed almost hysterically at the thought of Mrs Ramsay presiding with immutable calm over destinies which she completely failed to understand. There she sat, simple, serious. She had recovered her sense of her now – this was the glove's twisted finger. But into what sanctuary had one penetrated? Lily Briscoe had looked up at last, and there was Mrs Ramsay, unwitting entirely what had caused her laughter, still presiding, but now with every trace of wilfulness abolished, and in its stead, something clear as the space which the clouds at last uncover – the little space of sky which sleeps beside the moon.

Was it wisdom? Was it knowledge? Was it, once more, the deceptiveness of beauty, so that all one's perceptions, half-way to truth, were tangled in a golden mesh? or did she lock up within her some secret which certainly Lily Briscoe believed people must have for the world to go on at all? Every one could not be as helter skelter, hand to mouth as she was. But if they knew, could they tell one what they knew? Sitting on the floor with her arms round Mrs Ramsay's knees, close as she could get, smiling to think that Mrs Ramsay would never know the reason of that pressure, she imagined how in the chambers of the mind and heart of the woman who was, physically, touching her, were stood, like the treasures in the tombs of kings, tablets bearing sacred inscriptions, which if one could spell them out would teach one everything, but they would never be offered openly, never made public. What art was there, known to love or cunning, by which one pressed through into those secret chambers? What device for becoming, like waters poured into one jar, inextricably the same, one with the object one adored? Could the body achieve it, or the mind, subtly mingling in the intricate passages of the brain? or the heart? Could loving, as people called it, make her and Mrs Ramsay one? for it was not knowledge but unity that she desired, not inscriptions on tablets, nothing that could be written in any language known to men, but intimacy itself, which is knowledge, she had thought, leaning her head on Mrs Ramsay's knee.

Nothing happened. Nothing! Nothing! as she leant her

head against Mrs Ramsay's knee. And yet, she knew knowledge and wisdom were stored in Mrs Ramsay's heart. How then, she had asked herself, did one know one thing or another thing about people, sealed as they were? Only like a bee, drawn by some sweetness or sharpness in the air intangible to touch or taste, one haunted the dome-shaped hive, ranged the wastes of the air over the countries of the world alone, and then haunted the hives with their murmurs and their stirrings; the hives which were people. Mrs Ramsay rose. Lily rose. Mrs Ramsay went. For days there hung about her, as after a dream some subtle change is felt in the person one has dreamt of, more vividly than anything she said, the sound of murmuring and, as she sat in the wicker arm-chair in the drawing-room window she wore, to Lily's eyes, an august shape; the shape of a dome.

This ray passed level with Mr Bankes's ray straight to Mrs Ramsay sitting reading there with James at her knee. But now while she still looked, Mr Bankes had done. He had put on his spectacles. He had stepped back. He had raised his hand. He had slightly narrowed his clear blue eyes, when Lily, rousing herself, saw what he was at, and winced like a dog who sees a hand raised to strike it. She would have snatched her picture off the easel, but she said to herself, One must. She braced herself to stand the awful trial of someone looking at her picture. One must, she said, one must. And if it must be seen, Mr Bankes was less alarming than another. But that any other eyes should see the residue of her thirty-three years, the deposit of each day's living, mixed with something more secret than she had ever spoken or shown in the course of all those days was an agony. At the same time it was immensely exciting.

Nothing could be cooler and quieter. Taking out a penknife, Mr Bankes tapped the canvas with the bone handle. What did she wish to indicate by the triangular purple shape, 'just there?' he asked.

It was Mrs Ramsay reading to James, she said. She knew his objection – that no one could tell it for a human shape. But she had made no attempt at likeness, she said. For what reason had she introduced them then? he asked. Why indeed? – except that if there, in that corner, it was bright, here, in this, she felt the need of darkness. Simple, obvious, commonplace, as it was, Mr Bankes was interested. Mother and child then – objects of universal veneration, and in this case the mother was famous for her beauty – might be reduced, he pondered, to a purple shadow without irreverence.

But the picture was not of them, she said. Or, not in his sense. There were other senses, too, in which one might reverence them. By a shadow here and a light there, for instance. Her tribute took that form, if, as she vaguely supposed, a picture must be a tribute. A mother and child might be reduced to a shadow without irreverence. A light here required a shadow there. He considered. He was interested. He took it scientifically in complete good faith. The truth was that all his prejudices were on the other side, he explained. The largest picture in his drawing-room, which painters had praised, and valued at a higher price than he had given for it, was of the cherry trees in blossom on the banks of the Kennet. He had spent his honeymoon on the banks of the Kennet, he said. Lily must come and see that picture, he said. But now – he turned, with his glasses raised to the scientific examination of her canvas. The question being one of the relations of masses, of light and shadows, which, to be honest, he had never considered before, he would like to have it explained – what then did she wish to make of it? And he indicated the scene before them. She looked. She could not show him what she wished to make of it, could not see it even herself, without a brush in her hand. She took up once more her old painting position with the dim eyes and the absent-minded manner, subduing all her impressions as a woman to something much more general; becoming once more under the power of that vision which she had seen clearly once and must now grope for among hedges and houses and mothers and children – her picture. It was a question, she remembered, how to connect this mass on the right hand with that on the left. She might do it by bringing the line of the branch across so; or break the vacancy in the foreground by an object (James perhaps) so. But the danger was that by doing that the unity of the whole might be broken. She stopped; she did not want to bore him; she took the canvas lightly off the easel.

But it had been seen; it had been taken from her. This man had shared with her something profoundly intimate. And, thanking Mr Ramsay for it and Mrs Ramsay for it and the hour and the place, crediting the world with a power which she had not suspected, that one could walk away down that long gallery not alone any more but arm in arm with somebody – the strangest feeling in the world, and the most exhilarating – she nicked the catch of her paint-box to, more firmly than was necessary, and the nick seemed to surround in a circle for ever the paint-box, the lawn, Mr Bankes, and that wild villain, Cam, dashing past.

X

For Cam grazed the easel by an inch; she would not stop for Mr Bankes and Lily Briscoe; though Mr Bankes, who would have liked a daughter of his own, held out his hand; she would not stop for her father, whom she grazed also by an inch; nor for her mother, who called 'Cam! I want you a moment!' as she dashed past. She was off like a bird, bullet, or arrow, impelled by what desire, shot by whom, at what directed, who could say? What, what? Mrs Ramsay pondered, watching her. It might be a vision – of a shell, of a wheelbarrow, of a fairy kingdom on the far side of the hedge; or it might be the glory of speed; no one knew. But when Mrs Ramsay called 'Cam!' a second time, the projectile dropped in mid career, and Cam came lagging back, pulling a leaf by the way, to her mother.

What was she dreaming about, Mrs Ramsay wondered, seeing her engrossed, as she stood there, with some thought of her own, so that she had to repeat the message twice – ask Mildred if Andrew, Miss Doyle, and Mr Rayley have come back? – The words seemed to be dropped into a well, where, if the waters were clear, they were also so extraordinarily distorting that, even as they descended, one saw them twisting about to make Heaven knows what pattern on the floor of the child's mind. What message would Cam give the cook? Mrs Ramsay wondered. And indeed it was only by waiting patiently, and hearing that there was an old woman in the kitchen with very red cheeks, drinking soup out of a basin, that Mrs Ramsay at last prompted that parrot-like instinct which had picked up Mildred's words quite accurately and could now produce them, if one waited, in a colourless sing-song. Shifting from foot to foot, Cam repeated the words, 'No, they haven't, and I've told Ellen to clear away tea.'

Minta Doyle and Paul Rayley had not come back then. That could only mean, Mrs Ramsay thought, one thing. She must accept him, or she must refuse him. This going off after luncheon for a walk, even though Andrew was with them – what could it mean? except that she had decided, rightly, Mrs Ramsay thought (and she was very, very fond of Minta), to accept that good fellow, who might not be brilliant, but then, thought Mrs Ramsay, realising that James was tugging at her to make her go on reading aloud the Fisherman and his Wife, she did in her own heart infinitely prefer boobies to clever men who wrote dissertations; Charles Tansley for instance. Anyhow it must have happened, one way or the other, by now.

But she read, 'Next morning the wife awoke first, and it was just daybreak, and from her bed she saw the beautiful country lying before her. Her husband was still stretching himself . . .'

But how could Minta say now that she would not have him? Not if she agreed to spend whole afternoons trapesing about the country alone – for Andrew would be off after his crabs – but possibly Nancy was with them. She tried to recall the sight of them standing at the hall door after lunch. There they stood, looking at the sky, wondering about the weather, and she had said, thinking partly to cover their shyness, partly to encourage them to be off (for her sympathies were with Paul),

'There isn't a cloud anywhere within miles,' at which she could feel little Charles Tansley, who had followed them out, snigger. But she did it on purpose. Whether Nancy was there or not, she could not be certain, looking from one to the other in her mind's eye.

She read on: '"Ah, wife," said the man, "why should we be King? I do not want to be King." "Well," said the wife, "if you won't be King, I will; go to the Flounder, for I will be King."

'Come in or go out, Cam,' she said, knowing that Cam was attracted only by the word 'Flounder' and that in a moment she would fidget and fight with James as usual. Cam shot off. Mrs Ramsay went on reading, relieved, for she and James shared the same tastes and were comfortable together.

'And when he came to the sea, it was quite dark grey, and the water heaved up from below, and smelt putrid. Then he went and stood by it and said,

> "Flounder, flounder, in the sea,
> Come, I pray thee, here to me;
> For my wife, good Ilsabil,
> Wills not as I'd have her will."

"Well, what does she want then?" said the Flounder.' And where were they now? Mrs Ramsay wondered, reading and thinking, quite easily, both at the same time; for the story of the Fisherman and his Wife was like the bass gently accompanying a tune, which now and then ran up unexpectedly into the melody. And when should she be told? If nothing happened, she would have to speak seriously to Minta. For she could not go trapesing about all over the country, even if Nancy were with them (she tried again, unsuccessfully, to visualise their backs going down the path, and to count them). She was responsible to Minta's parents – the Owl and the Poker. Her nicknames for them shot into her mind as she read. The Owl and the Poker – yes, they would be annoyed if they heard – and they were certain to hear – that Minta, staying with the Ramsays, had been seen etcetera, etcetera, etcetera. 'He wore a wig in the House of Commons and she ably assisted him at the head of the stairs,' she repeated, fishing them up out of her mind by a phrase which, coming back from some party, she had made to amuse her husband. Dear, dear, Mrs Ramsay said to herself, how did they produce this incongruous daughter? this tomboy Minta, with a hole in her stocking? How did she exist in that portentous atmosphere where the maid was always removing in a dust-pan the sand that the parrot had scattered, and conversation was almost entirely reduced to the exploits – interesting perhaps, but limited after all – of that bird? Naturally, one had asked her to lunch, tea, dinner, finally to stay with them up at Finlay, which had resulted in some friction with the Owl, her mother, and more calling, and more conversation, and more sand, and really at the end of it, she had told enough lies about parrots to last her a lifetime (so she had said to her husband that night, coming back from the party). However, Minta came … Yes, she came, Mrs Ramsay thought, suspecting some thorn in the tangle of this thought; and disengaging it found it to be this: a woman had once accused her of 'robbing her of her daughter's affections'; something Mrs Doyle had said made her remember that charge again. Wishing to dominate, wishing to interfere, making people do what she wished – that was the charge against her, and she thought it most unjust. How could she help being 'like that' to look at? No one could accuse her of taking pains to impress. She was often ashamed of her own shabbiness. Nor was she domineering, nor was she tyrannical. It was more true about hospitals and drains and the dairy. About things like that she did feel passionately, and would, if she had had the chance, have liked to take people by the scruff of their necks and make them see. No hospital on the whole island. It was a disgrace. Milk delivered at your door in London positively brown with dirt. It should be made illegal. A model dairy and a hospital up here – those two things she would have liked to do, herself. But how? With all these children? When they were older, then perhaps she would have time; when they were all at school.

Oh, but she never wanted James to grow a day older or Cam either. These two she would have liked to keep for ever just as they were, demons of wickedness, angels of delight, never to see them grow up into long-legged monsters. Nothing made up for the loss. When she read just now to James, 'and there were numbers of soldiers with kettle-drums and trumpets', and his eyes darkened, she thought, why should they grow up, and lose all that? He was the most gifted, the most sensitive of her children. But all, she thought, were full of promise. Prue, a perfect angel with the others, and sometimes now, at night especially, she took one's breath away with her beauty. Andrew – even her husband admitted that his gift for mathematics was extraordinary. And Nancy and Roger, they were both wild creatures now, scampering about over the country all day long. As for Rose, her mouth was too big, but she had a wonderful gift with her hands. If they had charades, Rose made the dresses; made everything; liked best arranging tables, flowers, anything. She did not like it that Jasper should shoot birds; but it was only a stage; they all went through stages. Why, she asked, pressing her chin on James's head, should they grow up so fast? Why should they go to school? She would have liked always to have had a baby. She was happiest carrying one in her arms. Then people might say she was tyrannical, domineering, masterful, if they chose; she did not mind. And, touching his hair with her lips, she thought, he will never be so happy again, but stopped herself, remembering how it angered her husband that she should say that. Still, it was true. They were happier now than they would ever be again. A tenpenny tea set made Cam happy for days. She heard them stamping and crowing on the floor above her head the moment they woke. They came bustling along the passage. Then the door sprang open and in they came, fresh as roses, staring, wide awake, as if this coming into the dining-room after breakfast, which they did every day of their lives was a positive event to them; and so on, with one thing after another, all day long, until she went up to say good-night to them, and found them netted in their cots like birds among cherries and raspberries still making up stories about some little bit of rubbish – something they had heard, something they had picked up in the garden. They had all their little treasures . . . And so she went down and said to her husband, Why must they grow up and lose it all? Never will they be so happy again. And he was angry. Why take such a gloomy view of life? he said. It is not sensible. For it was odd; and she believed it to be true; that with all his gloom and desperation he was happier, more hopeful on the whole, than she was. Less exposed to human worries – perhaps that was it. He had always his work to fall back on. Not that she herself was 'pessimistic', as he accused her of being. Only she thought life – and a little strip of time presented itself to her eyes, her fifty years. There it was before her – life. Life: she thought but she did not finish her thought. She took a look at life, for she had a clear sense of it there, something real, something private, which she shared neither with her children nor with her husband. A sort of transaction went on between them, in which she was on one side, and life was on another, and she was always trying to get the better of it, as it was of her; and sometimes they parleyed (when she sat alone); there were, she remembered, great reconciliation scenes; but for the most part, oddly enough, she must admit that she felt this thing that she called life terrible, hostile, and quick to pounce on you if you gave it a chance. There were the eternal problems: suffering; death; the poor. There was always a woman dying of cancer even here. And yet she had said to all these children, You shall go through with it. To eight people she had said relentlessly that (and the bill for the greenhouse would be fifty pounds). For that reason, knowing what was before them – love and ambition and being wretched alone in dreary places – she had often the feeling, Why must they grow up and lose it all? And then she said to herself, brandishing her sword at life, nonsense. They will be perfectly happy. And here she was, she reflected, feeling life rather sinister again, making Minta marry Paul Rayley; because whatever she might feel about her own transaction and she had had experiences which need not happen to everyone (she did not name them to herself); she was driven on, too quickly she knew, almost as if it were an escape for her too, to say that people must marry; people must have children.

Was she wrong in this, she asked herself, reviewing her conduct for the past week or two, and wondering if she had indeed put any pressure upon Minta, who was only twenty-four, to make up her mind. She was uneasy. Had she not laughed about it? Was she not forgetting again how strongly she influenced people? Marriage needed – oh all sorts of qualities (the bill for the greenhouse would be fifty pounds); one – she need not name it – *that* was essential; the thing she had with her husband. Had they that?

'Then he put on his trousers and ran away like a madman,' she read. 'But outside a great storm was raging and blowing so hard that he could scarcely keep his feet; houses and trees toppled over, the mountains trembled, rocks rolled into the sea, the sky was pitch black, and it thundered and lightened, and the sea came in with black waves as high as church towers and mountains, and all with white foam at the top.'

She turned the page; there were only a few lines more, so that she would finish the story, though it was past bed-time. It was getting late. The light in the garden told her that; and the whitening of the flowers and something grey in the leaves conspired together to rouse in her a feeling of anxiety. What it was about she could not think at first. Then she remembered; Paul and Minta and Andrew had not come back. She summoned before her again the little group on the terrace in front of the hall door, standing looking up into the sky. Andrew had his net and basket. That meant he was going to catch crabs and things. That meant he would climb out on to a rock; he would be cut off. Or coming back single file on one of those little paths above the cliff one of them might slip. He would roll and then crash. It was growing quite dark.

But she did not let her voice change in the least as she finished the story, and added, shutting the book, and speaking the last words as if she had made them up herself, looking into James's eyes: 'And there they are living still at this very time.'

'And that's the end,' she said, and she saw in his eyes, as the interest of the story died away in them, something else take its place; something wondering, pale, like the reflection of a light, which at once made him gaze and marvel. Turning, she looked across the bay, and there, sure enough, coming regularly across the waves first two quick strokes and then one long steady stroke, was the light of the Lighthouse. It had been lit.

In a moment he would ask her, 'Are we going to the Lighthouse?' And she would have to say, 'No: not tomorrow; your father says not.' Happily, Mildred came in to fetch them, and the bustle distracted them. But he kept looking back over his shoulder as Mildred carried him out, and she was certain that he was thinking, we are not going to the Lighthouse tomorrow; and she thought, he will remember that all his life.

XI

No, she thought, putting together some of the pictures he had cut out – a refrigerator, a mowing machine, a gentleman in evening dress – children never forget. For this reason, it was so important what one said, and what one did, and it was a relief when they went to bed. For now she need not think about anybody. She could be herself, by herself. And that was what now she often felt the need of – to think; well not even to think. To be silent; to be alone. All the being and the doing, expansive, glittering, vocal, evaporated; and one shrunk, with a sense of solemnity, to being oneself, a wedge-shaped core of darkness, something invisible to others. Although she continued to knit, and sat upright, it was thus that she felt herself; and this self having shed its attachments was free for the strangest adventures. When life sank down for a moment, the range of experience seemed limitless. And to everybody there was always this sense of unlimited resources, she supposed; one after another, she, Lily, Augustus Carmichael, must feel, our apparitions, the things you know us by, are simply childish. Beneath it is all dark, it is all spreading, it is unfathomably deep; but now and again we rise to the surface and that is what you see us by. Her horizon seemed to her limitless. There were all the places she had not seen; the Indian plains; she felt herself pushing aside the thick leather curtain of a church in Rome. This core of darkness could go anywhere, for no one saw it. They could not stop it, she thought, exulting. There was freedom, there was peace, there was, most welcome of all, a summoning together, a resting on a platform of stability. Not as oneself did one find rest ever, in her experience (she accomplished here something dexterous with her needles), but as a wedge of darkness.

Losing personality, one lost the fret, the hurry, the stir; and there rose to her lips always some exclamation of triumph over life when things came together in this peace, this rest, this eternity; and pausing there she looked out to meet that stroke of the Lighthouse, the long steady stroke, the last of the three, which was her stroke, for watching them in this mood always at this hour one could not help attaching oneself to one thing especially of the things one saw; and this thing, the long steady stroke, was her stroke. Often she found herself sitting and looking, sitting and looking, with her work in her hands until she became the thing she looked at – that light for example. And it would lift up on it some little phrase or other which had been lying in her mind like that – 'Children don't forget, children don't forget' – which she would repeat and begin adding to it, It will end, It will end, she said. It will come, it will come, when suddenly she added, We are in the hands of the Lord.

But instantly she was annoyed with herself for saying that. Who had said it? not she; she had been trapped into saying something she did not mean. She looked up over her knitting and met the third stroke and it seemed to her like her own eyes meeting her own eyes, searching as she alone could search into her mind and her heart, purifying out of existence that lie, any lie. She praised herself in praising the light, without vanity, for she was stern, she was searching, she was beautiful like that light. It was odd, she thought, how if one was alone, one leant to things, inanimate things; trees, streams, flowers; felt they expressed one; felt they became one; felt they knew one, in a sense were one; felt an irrational tenderness thus (she looked at that long steady light) as for oneself. There rose, and she looked and looked with her needles suspended, there curled up off the floor of the mind, rose from the lake of one's being, a mist, a bride to meet her lover.

What brought her to say that: 'We are in the hands of the Lord'? she wondered. The insincerity slipping in among the truths roused her, annoyed her. She returned to her knitting again. How could any Lord have made this world? she asked. With her mind she had always seized the fact that there is no reason, order, justice: but suffering, death, the poor. There was no treachery too base for the world to commit; she knew that. No happiness lasted; she knew that. She knitted with firm composure, slightly pursing her lips and, without being aware of it, so stiffened and composed the lines of her face in a habit of sternness that when her husband passed, though he was chuckling at the thought that Hume, the philosopher, grown enormously fat, had stuck in a bog, he could not help noting, as he passed, the sternness at the heart of her beauty. It saddened him, and her remoteness pained him, and he felt, as he passed, that he could not protect her, and, when he reached the hedge, he was sad. He could do nothing to help her. He must stand by and watch her. Indeed, the infernal truth was, he made things worse for her. He was irritable – he was touchy. He had lost his temper over the Lighthouse. He looked into the hedge, into its intricacy, its darkness.

Always, Mrs Ramsay felt, one helped oneself out of solitude reluctantly by laying hold of some little odd or end, some sound, some sight. She listened, but it was all very still; cricket was over; the children were in their baths; there was only the sound of the sea. She stopped knitting; she held the long reddish-brown stocking dangling in her hands a moment. She saw the light again. With some irony in her interrogation, for when one woke at all, one's relations changed, she looked at the steady light, the pitiless, the remorseless, which was so much her, yet so little her, which had her at its beck and call (she woke in the night and saw it bent across their bed, stroking the floor), but for all that she thought, watching it with fascination, hypnotised, as if it were stroking with its silver fingers some sealed vessel in her brain whose bursting would flood her with delight, she had known happiness, exquisite happiness, intense happiness, and it silvered the rough waves a little more brightly, as daylight faded, and the blue went out of the sea and it rolled in waves of pure lemon which curved and swelled and broke upon the beach and the ecstasy burst in her eyes and waves of pure delight raced over the floor of her mind and she felt, It is enough! It is enough!

He turned and saw her. Ah! She was lovely, lovelier now than ever he thought. But he could not speak to her. He could not interrupt her. He wanted urgently to speak to her now that James was gone and she was alone at last. But he resolved, no; he would not interrupt her. She was aloof from him now in her beauty, in her sadness. He would let her be, and he passed her without a word, though it hurt him that she should look so distant, and he could not reach her, he could do nothing to help her. And again he would have passed her without a word had she not, at that very moment, given him of her own free will what she knew he would never ask, and called to him and taken the green shawl off the picture frame, and gone to him. For he wished, she knew, to protect her.

XII

She folded the green shawl about her shoulders. She took his arm. His beauty was so great, she said, beginning to speak of Kennedy the gardener at once; he was so awfully handsome, that she couldn't dismiss him. There was a ladder against the greenhouse, and little lumps of putty stuck about, for they were beginning to mend the green-house roof. Yes, but as she strolled along with her husband, she felt that that particular source of worry had been placed. She had it on the tip of her tongue to say, as they strolled, 'It'll cost fifty pounds', but instead, for her heart failed her about money, she talked about Jasper shooting birds, and he said, at once, soothing her instantly, that it was natural in a boy, and he trusted he would find better ways of amusing himself before long. Her husband was so sensible, so just. And so she said, 'Yes; all children go through stages,' and began considering the dahlias in the big bed, and wondering what about next year's flowers, and had he heard the children's nickname for Charles Tansley, she asked. The atheist, they called him, the little atheist. 'He's not a polished specimen,' said Mr Ramsay. 'Far from it,' said Mrs Ramsay.

She supposed it was all right leaving him to his own devices, Mrs Ramsay said, wondering whether it was any use sending down bulbs; did they plant them? 'Oh, he has his dissertation to write,' said Mr Ramsay. She knew all about *that*, said Mrs Ramsay. He talked of nothing else. It was about the influence of somebody upon something. 'Well, it's all he has to count on,' said Mr Ramsay. 'Pray Heaven he won't fall in love with Prue,' said Mrs Ramsay. He'd disinherit her if she married him, said Mr Ramsay. He did not look at the flowers, which his wife was considering, but at a spot about a foot or so above them. There was no harm in him, he added, and was just about to say that anyhow he was the only young man in England who admired his – when he choked it back. He would not bother her again about his books. These flowers seemed creditable, Mr Ramsay said, lowering his gaze and noticing something red, something brown. Yes, but then these she had put in with her own hands, said Mrs Ramsay. The question was, what happened if she sent bulbs down; did Kennedy plant them? It was his incurable laziness; she added, moving on. If she stood over him all day long with a spade in her hand, he did sometimes do a stroke of work. So they strolled along, towards the red-hot pokers. 'You're teaching your daughters to exaggerate,' said Mr Ramsay, reproving her. Her Aunt Camilla was far worse than she was, Mrs Ramsay remarked. 'Nobody ever held up your Aunt Camilla as a model of virtue that I'm aware of,' said Mr Ramsay. 'She was the most beautiful woman I ever saw,' said Mrs Ramsay. 'Somebody else was that,' said Mr Ramsay. Prue was going to be far more beautiful than she was, said Mrs Ramsay. He saw no trace of it, said Mr Ramsay. 'Well, then, look tonight,' said Mrs Ramsay.

They paused. He wished Andrew could be induced to work harder. He would lose every chance of a scholarship if he didn't. 'Oh scholarships!' she said. Mr Ramsay thought her foolish for saying that, about a serious thing, like a scholarship. He should be very proud of Andrew if he got a scholarship, he said. She would be just as proud of him if he didn't, she answered. They disagreed always about this, but it did not matter. She liked him to believe in scholarships, and he liked her to be proud of Andrew whatever he did. Suddenly she remembered those little paths on the edge of the cliffs.

Wasn't it late? she asked. They hadn't come home yet. He flicked his watch carelessly open. But it was only just past seven. He held his watch open for a moment, deciding that he would tell her what he had felt on the terrace. To begin with, it was not reasonable to be so nervous. Andrew could look after himself. Then, he wanted to tell her that when he was walking on the terrace just now – here he became uncomfortable, as if he were breaking into that solitude, that aloofness, that remoteness of hers . . . But she pressed him. What had he wanted to tell her, she asked, thinking it was about going to the Lighthouse; and that he was sorry he had said 'Damn you'. But no. He did not like to see her look so sad, he said. Only wool-gathering, she protested, flushing a little. They both felt uncomfortable, as if they did not know whether to go on or go back. She had been reading fairy tales to James, she said. No, they could not share that; they could not say that.

They had reached the gap between the two clumps of red-hot pokers, and there was the Lighthouse again, but she would not let herself look at it. Had she known that he was looking at her, she thought, she would not have let herself sit there, thinking. She disliked anything that reminded her that she had been seen sitting thinking. So she looked over her shoulder, at the town. The lights were rippling and running as if they were drops of silver water held firm in a wind. And all the poverty, all the suffering had turned to that, Mrs Ramsay thought. The lights of the town and of the harbour and of the boats seemed like a phantom net floating there to mark something which had sunk. Well, if he could not share her thoughts, Mr Ramsay said to himself, he would be off, then, on his own. He wanted to go on thinking, telling himself the story how Hume was stuck in a bog; he wanted to laugh. But first it was nonsense to be anxious about Andrew. When he was Andrew's age he used to walk about the country all day long, with nothing but a biscuit in his pocket and nobody bothered about him, or thought that he had fallen over a cliff. He said aloud he thought he would be off for a day's walk if the weather held. He had had about enough of Bankes and of Carmichael. He would like a little solitude. Yes, she said. It annoyed him that she did not protest. She knew that he would never do it. He was too old now to walk all day long with a biscuit in his pocket. She worried about the boys, but not about him. Years ago, before he had married, he thought, looking across the bay, as they stood between the clumps of red-hot pokers, he had walked all day. He had made a meal off bread and cheese in a public house. He had worked ten hours at a stretch; an old woman just popped her head in now and again and saw to the fire. That was the country he liked best, over there; those sandhills dwindling away into darkness. One could walk all day without meeting a soul. There was not a house scarcely, not a single village for miles on end. One could worry things out alone. There were little sandy beaches where no one had been since the beginning of time. The seals sat up and looked at you. It sometimes seemed to him that in a little house out there, alone – he broke off, sighing. He had no right. The father of eight children – he reminded himself. And he would have been a beast and a cur to wish a single thing altered. Andrew would be a better man than he had been. Prue would be a beauty, her mother said. They would stem the flood a bit. That was a good bit of work on the whole – his eight children. They showed he did not damn the poor little universe entirely, for on an evening like this, he thought, looking at the land dwindling away, the little island seemed pathetically small, half swallowed up in the sea.

'Poor little place,' he murmured with a sigh.

She heard him. He said the most melancholy things, but she noticed that directly he had said them he always seemed more cheerful than usual. All this phrase-making was a game, she thought, for if she had said half what he said, she would have blown her brains out by now.

It annoyed her, this phrase-making, and she said to him, in a matter-of-fact way, that it was a perfectly lovely evening. And what was he groaning about, she asked, half laughing, half complaining, for she guessed what he was thinking – he would have written better books if he had not married.

He was not complaining, he said. She knew that he did not complain. She knew that he had nothing whatever to complain of. And he seized her hand and raised it to his lips and kissed it with an intensity that brought the tears to her eyes, and quickly he dropped it.

They turned away from the view and began to walk up the path where the silver-green spear-like plants grew, arm in arm. His arm was almost like a young man's arm, Mrs Ramsay thought, thin and hard, and she thought with delight how strong he still was, though he was over sixty, and how untamed and optimistic, and how strange it was that being convinced, as he was, of all sorts of horrors, seemed not to depress him, but to cheer him. Was it not odd, she reflected? Indeed he seemed to her sometimes made differently from other people, born blind, deaf, and dumb, to the ordinary things, but to the extraordinary things, with an eye like an eagle's. His understanding often astonished her. But did he notice the flowers? No. Did he notice the view? No. Did he even notice his own daughter's beauty, or whether there was pudding on his plate or roast beef? He would sit at table with them like a person in a dream. And his habit of talking aloud, or saying poetry aloud, was growing on him, she was afraid; for sometimes it was awkward –

Best and brightest, come away!

poor Miss Giddings, when he shouted that at her, almost jumped out of her skin. But then, Mrs Ramsay, though instantly taking his side against all the silly Giddingses in the world, then, she thought, intimating by a little pressure on his arm that he walked up hill too fast for her, and she must stop for a moment to see whether those were fresh mole-hills on the bank, then, she thought, stooping down to look, a great mind like his must be different in every way from ours. All the great men she had ever known, she thought, deciding that a rabbit must have got in, were like that, and it was good for young men (though the atmosphere of lecture-rooms was stuffy and depressing to her beyond endurance almost) simply to hear him, simply to look at him. But without shooting rabbits, how was one to keep them down? she wondered. It might be a rabbit; it might be a mole. Some creature anyhow was ruining her evening primroses. And looking up, she saw above the thin trees the first pulse of the full-throbbing star, and wanted to make her husband look at it; for the sight gave her such keen pleasure. But she stopped herself. He never looked at things. If he did, all he would say would be, Poor little world, with one of his sighs.

At that moment, he said, 'Very fine', to please her, and pretended to admire the flowers. But she knew quite well that he did not admire them, or even realise that they were there. It was only to please her . . . Ah, but was that not Lily Briscoe strolling along with William Bankes? She focussed her short-sighted eyes upon the backs of a retreating couple. Yes, indeed it was. Did that not mean that they would marry? Yes, it must! What an admirable idea! They must marry!

XIII

He had been to Amsterdam, Mr Bankes was saying as he strolled across the lawn with Lily Briscoe. He had seen the Rembrandts. He had been to Madrid. Unfortunately, it was Good Friday and the Prado was shut. He had been to Rome. Had Miss Briscoe never been to Rome? Oh, she should— It would be a wonderful experience for her – the Sistine Chapel; Michael Angelo; and Padua, with its Giottos. His wife had been in bad health for many years, so that their sight-seeing had been on a modest scale.

She had been to Brussels; she had been to Paris, but only for a flying visit to see an aunt who was ill. She had been to Dresden; there were masses of pictures she had not seen; however, Lily Briscoe reflected, perhaps it was better not to see pictures: they only made one hopelessly discontented with one's own work. Mr Bankes thought one could carry that point of view too far. We can't all be Titians and we can't all be Darwins, he said; at the same time he doubted whether you could have your Darwin and your Titian if it weren't for humble people like ourselves. Lily would have liked to pay him a compliment; you're not humble, Mr Bankes, she would have liked to have said. But he did not want compliments (most men do, she thought), and she was a little ashamed of her impulse and said nothing while he remarked that perhaps what he was saying did not apply to pictures. Anyhow, said Lily, tossing off her little insincerity, she would always go on painting, because it interested her. Yes, said Mr Bankes, he was sure she would, and as they reached the end of the lawn he was asking her whether she had difficulty in finding subjects in London when they turned and saw the Ramsays. So that is marriage, Lily thought, a man and a woman looking at a girl throwing a ball. That is what Mrs Ramsay tried to tell me the other night, she thought. For she was wearing a green shawl, and they were standing close together watching Prue and Jasper throwing catches. And suddenly the meaning which, for no reason at all, as perhaps they are stepping out of the Tube or ringing a doorbell, descends on people, making them symbolical, making them representative, came upon them, and made them in the dusk standing, looking, the symbols of marriage, husband and wife. Then, after an instant, the symbolical outline which transcended the real figures sank down again, and they became, as they met them, Mr and Mrs Ramsay watching the children throwing catches. But still for a moment, though Mrs Ramsay greeted them with her usual smile (oh, she's thinking we're going to get married, Lily thought) and said, 'I have triumphed tonight,' meaning that for once Mr Bankes had agreed to dine with them and not run off to his own lodging where his man cooked vegetables properly; still, for one moment, there was a sense of things having been blown apart, of space, of irresponsibility as the ball soared high, and they followed it and lost it and saw the one star and the draped branches. In the failing light they all looked sharp-edged and ethereal and divided by great distances. Then, darting backwards over the vast space (for it seemed as if solidity had vanished altogether), Prue ran full tilt into them and caught the ball brilliantly high up in her left hand, and her mother said, 'Haven't they come back yet?' whereupon the spell was broken. Mr Ramsay felt free now to laugh out loud at Hume, who had stuck in a bog and an old woman rescued him on condition he said the Lord's Prayer, and chuckling to himself he strolled off to his study. Mrs Ramsay, bringing Prue back into the alliance of family life again, from which she had escaped, throwing catches, asked,

'Did Nancy go with them?'

XIV

(Certainly, Nancy had gone with them, since Minta Doyle had asked it with her dumb look, holding out her hand, as

Nancy made off, after lunch, to her attic, to escape the horror of family life. She supposed she must go then. She did not want to go. She did not want to be drawn into it all. For as they walked along the road to the cliff Minta kept on taking her hand. Then she would let it go. Then she would take it again. What was it she wanted? Nancy asked herself. There was something, of course, that people wanted; for when Minta took her hand and held it, Nancy, reluctantly, saw the whole world spread out beneath her, as if it were Constantinople seen through a mist, and then, however heavy-eyed one might be, one must needs ask, 'Is that Santa Sofia?' 'Is that the Golden Horn?' So Nancy asked, when Minta took her hand, 'What is it that she wants? Is it that?' And what was that? Here and there emerged from the mist (as Nancy looked down upon life spread beneath her) a pinnacle, a dome; prominent things, without names. But when Minta dropped her hand, as she did when they ran down the hillside, all that, the dome, the pinnacle, whatever it was that had protruded through the mist, sank down into it and disappeared.

Minta, Andrew observed, was rather a good walker. She wore more sensible clothes than most women. She wore very short skirts and black knickerbockers. She would jump straight into a stream and flounder across. He liked her rashness, but he saw that it would not do – she would kill herself in some idiotic way one of these days. She seemed to be afraid of nothing – except bulls. At the mere sight of a bull in a field she would throw up her arms and fly screaming, which was the very thing to enrage a bull of course. But she did not mind owning up to it in the least; one must admit that. She knew she was an awful coward about bulls, she said. She thought she must have been tossed in her perambulator when she was a baby. She didn't seem to mind what she said or did. Suddenly now she pitched down on the edge of the cliff and began to sing some song about

Damn your eyes, damn your eyes.

They all had to join in and sing the chorus, and shout out together:

Damn your eyes, damn your eyes,

but it would be fatal to let the tide come in and cover up all the good hunting-grounds before they got on to the beach.

'Fatal,' Paul agreed, springing up, and as they went slithering down, he kept quoting the guide-book about 'these islands being justly celebrated for their park-like prospects and the extent and variety of their marine curiosities'. But it would not do altogether, this shouting and damning your eyes, Andrew felt, picking his way down the cliff, this clapping him on the back, and calling him 'old fellow' and all that; it would not altogether do. It was the worst of taking women on walks. Once on the beach they separated, he going out on to the Pope's Nose, taking his shoes off, and rolling his socks in them and letting that couple look after themselves; Nancy waded out to her own rocks and searched her own pools and let that couple look after themselves. She crouched low down and touched the smooth rubber-like sea anemones, who were stuck like lumps of jelly to the side of the rock. Brooding, she changed the pool into the sea, and made the minnows into sharks and whales, and cast vast clouds over this tiny world by holding her hand against the sun, and so brought darkness and desolation, like God himself, to millions of ignorant and innocent creatures, and then took her hand away suddenly and let the sun stream down. Out on the pale criss-crossed sand, high-stepping, fringed, gauntletted, stalked some fantastic leviathan (she was still enlarging the pool), and slipped into the vast fissures of the mountain side. And then, letting her eyes slide imperceptibly above the pool and rest on that wavering line of sea and sky, on the tree trunks which the smoke of steamers made waver upon the horizon, she became with all that power sweeping savagely in and inevitably withdrawing, hypnotised, and the two senses of that vastness and this tininess (the pool had diminished again) flowering within it made her feel that she was bound hand and foot and unable to move by the intensity of feelings which reduced her own body, her own life, and the lives of all the people in the world, for ever, to nothingness. So listening to the waves, crouched over the pool, she brooded.

And Andrew shouted that the sea was coming in, so she leapt splashing through the shallow waves on to the shore and ran up the beach and was carried by her own impetuosity and her desire for rapid movement right behind a rock and there oh heavens! in each other's arms were Paul and Minta! kissing probably. She was outraged, indignant. She and Andrew put on their shoes and stockings in dead silence without saying a thing about it. Indeed they were rather sharp with each other. She might have called him when she saw the crayfish or whatever it was, Andrew grumbled. However, they both felt, it's not our fault. They had not wanted this horrid nuisance to happen. All the same it irritated Andrew that Nancy should be a woman, and Nancy that Andrew should be a man and they tied their shoes very neatly and drew the bows rather tight.

It was not until they had climbed right up on to the top of the cliff again that Minta cried out that she had lost her grandmother's brooch – her grandmother's brooch, the sole ornament she possessed – a weeping willow, it was (they must remember it) set in pearls. They must have seen it, she said, with the tears running down her cheeks, the brooch which her grandmother had fastened her cap with till the last day of her life. Now she had lost it. She would rather have lost anything than that! She would go back and look for it. They all went back. They poked and peered and looked. They kept their heads very low, and said things shortly and gruffly. Paul Rayley searched like a madman all about the rock where they had been sitting. All this pother about a brooch really didn't do at all, Andrew thought, as Paul told him to make a 'thorough search between this point and that'. The tide was coming in fast. The sea would cover the place where they had sat in a minute. There was not a ghost of a chance of their finding it now. 'We shall be cut off!' Minta shrieked, suddenly terrified. As if there were any danger of that! It was the same as the bulls all over again – she had no control over her emotions, Andrew thought. Women hadn't. The wretched Paul had to pacify her. The men (Andrew and Paul at once became manly, and different from usual) took counsel briefly and decided that they would plant Rayley's stick where they had sat and come back at low tide again. There was nothing more that could be done now. If the brooch was there, it would still be there in the morning, they assured her, but Minta still sobbed, all the way up to the top of the cliff. It was her grandmother's brooch; she would rather have lost anything but that, and yet Nancy felt, though it might be true that she minded losing her brooch, she wasn't crying only for that. She was crying for something else. We might all sit down and cry, she felt. But she did not know what for.

They drew ahead together, Paul and Minta, and he comforted her, and said how famous he was for finding things. Once when he was a little boy he had found a gold watch. He would get up at daybreak and he was positive he would find it. It seemed to him that it would be almost dark, and he would be alone on the beach, and somehow it would be rather dangerous. He began telling her, however, that he would certainly find it, and she said that she would not hear of his getting up at dawn: it was lost: she knew that: she had had a presentiment when she put it on that afternoon. And secretly he resolved that he would not tell her, but he would slip out of the house at dawn when they were all asleep and if he could not find it he would go to Edinburgh and buy her another, just like it but more beautiful. He would prove what he could do. And as they came out on the hill and saw the lights of the town beneath them, the lights coming out suddenly one by one seemed like things that were going to happen to him – his marriage, his children, his house; and again he thought, as they came out on to the high road, which was shaded with high bushes, how they would retreat into solitude together, and walk on and on, he always leading her, and she pressing close to his side (as she did now). As they turned by the cross roads he thought what an appalling experience he had been through, and he must tell some one – Mrs Ramsay of course, for it took his breath away to think what he had been and done. It had been far and away the worst moment of his life when he asked Minta to marry him. He would go straight to Mrs Ramsay, because he felt somehow that she was the person who had made him do it. She had made him think he could do anything. Nobody else took him seriously. But she made him believe that he could do whatever he wanted. He had felt her eyes on him all day today, following him about (though she never said a word) as if she were saying, 'Yes, you can do it. I believe in you. I expect it of you.' She had made him feel all that, and directly they got back (he looked for the lights of the house above the bay) he would go to her and say, 'I've done it, Mrs Ramsay; thanks to you.' And so turning into the lane that led to the house he could see lights moving about in the upper windows. They must be awfully late then. People were getting ready for dinner. The house was all lit up, and the lights after the darkness made his eyes feel full, and he said to himself, childishly, as he walked up the drive, Lights, lights, lights, and repeated in a dazed way, Lights, lights, lights, as they came into the house, staring about him with his face quite stiff. But, good heavens, he said to himself, putting his hand to his tie, I must not make a fool of myself.)

XV

'Yes,' said Prue, in her considering way, answering her mother's question, 'I think Nancy did go with them.'

XVI

Well then, Nancy had gone with them, Mrs Ramsay supposed, wondering, as she put down a brush, took up a comb, and said 'Come in' to a tap at the door (Jasper and Rose came in), whether the fact that Nancy was with them made it less likely or more likely that anything would happen; it made it less likely, somehow, Mrs Ramsay felt, very irrationally, except that after all holocaust on such a scale was not probable. They could not all be drowned. And again she felt alone in the presence of her old antagonist, life.

Jasper and Rose said that Mildred wanted to know whether she should wait dinner.

'Not for the Queen of England,' said Mrs Ramsay emphatically.

'Not for the Empress of Mexico,' she added, laughing at Jasper; for he shared his mother's vice: he, too, exaggerated.

And if Rose liked, she said, while Jasper took the message, she might choose which jewels she was to wear. When there are fifteen people sitting down to dinner, one cannot keep things waiting for ever. She was now beginning to feel annoyed with them for being so late; it was inconsiderate of them, and it annoyed her on top of her anxiety about them, that they should choose this very night to be out late, when, in fact, she wished the dinner to be particularly nice, since William Bankes had at last consented to dine with them; and they were having Mildred's masterpiece – *Bœuf en Daube*. Everything depended upon things being served up the precise moment they were ready. The beef, the bayleaf, and the wine – all must be done to a turn. To keep it waiting was out of the question. Yet of course tonight, of all nights, out they went, and they came in late, and things had to be sent out, things had to be kept hot; the *Bœuf en Daube* would be entirely spoilt.

Jasper offered her an opal necklace; Rose a gold necklace. Which looked best against her black dress? Which did indeed?

said Mrs Ramsay absent-mindedly, looking at her neck and shoulders (but avoiding her face), in the glass. And then, while the children rummaged among her things, she looked out of the window at a sight which always amused her – the rooks trying to decide which tree to settle on. Every time, they seemed to change their minds and rose up into the air again, because, she thought, the old rook, the father rook, old Joseph was her name for him, was a bird of a very trying and difficult disposition. He was a disreputable old bird, with half his wing feathers missing. He was like some seedy old gentleman in a top hat she had seen playing the horn in front of a public house.

'Look!' she said, laughing. They were actually fighting. Joseph and Mary were fighting. Anyhow they all went up again, and the air was shoved aside by their black wings and cut into exquisite scimitar shapes. The movement of the wings beating out, out, out – she could never describe it accurately enough to please herself – was one of the loveliest of all to her. Look at that, she said to Rose, hoping that Rose would see it more clearly than she could. For one's children so often gave one's own perceptions a little thrust forwards.

But which was it to be? They had all the trays of her jewel-case open. The gold necklace, which was Italian, or the opal necklace, which Uncle James had brought her from India; or should she wear her amethysts?

'Choose, dearests, choose,' she said, hoping that they would make haste.

But she let them take their time to choose: she let Rose, particularly, take up this and then that, and hold her jewels against the black dress, for this little ceremony of choosing jewels, which was gone through every night, was what Rose liked best, she knew. She had some hidden reason of her own for attaching great importance to this choosing what her mother was to wear. What was the reason, Mrs Ramsay wondered, standing still to let her clasp the necklace she had chosen, divining, through her own past, some deep, some buried, some quite speechless feeling that one had for one's mother at Rose's age. Like all feelings felt for oneself, Mrs Ramsay thought, it made one sad. It was so inadequate, what one could give in return; and what Rose felt was quite out of proportion to anything she actually was. And Rose would grow up; and Rose would suffer, she supposed, with these deep feelings, and she said she was ready now, and they would go down, and Jasper, because he was the gentleman, should give her his arm, and Rose, as she was the lady, should carry her handkerchief (she gave her the handkerchief), and what else? oh, yes, it might be cold: a shawl. Choose me a shawl, she said, for that would please Rose, who was bound to suffer so. 'There,' she said, stopping by the window on the landing, 'there they are again.' Joseph had settled on another tree-top. 'Don't you think they mind', she said to Jasper, 'having their wings broken?' Why did he want to shoot poor old Joseph and Mary? He shuffled a little on the stairs, and felt rebuked, but not seriously, for she did not understand the fun of shooting birds; that they did not feel; and being his mother she lived away in another division of the world, but he rather liked her stories about Mary and Joseph. She made him laugh. But how did she know that those were Mary and Joseph? Did she think the same birds came to the same trees every night? he asked. But here, suddenly, like all grown-up people, she ceased to pay him the least attention. She was listening to a clatter in the hall.

'They've come back!' she exclaimed, and at once she felt much more annoyed with them than relieved. Then she wondered, had it happened? She would go down and they would tell her – but no. They could not tell her anything, with all these people about. So she must go down and begin dinner and wait. And, like some queen who, finding her people gathered in the hall, looks down upon them, and descends among them, and acknowledges their tributes silently, and accepts their devotion and their prostration before her (Paul did not move a muscle but looked straight before him as she passed), she went down, and crossed the hall and bowed her head very slightly, as if she accepted what they could not say: their tribute to her beauty.

But she stopped. There was a smell of burning. Could they have let the Bœuf en Daube overboil, she wondered? pray heaven not! when the great clangour of the gong announced solemnly, authoritatively, that all those scattered about, in attics, in bedrooms, on little perches of their own, reading, writing, putting the last smooth to their hair, or fastening dresses, must leave all that, and the little odds and ends on their washing-tables and dressing-tables, and the novels on the bed-tables, and the diaries which were so private, and assemble in the dining-room for dinner.

XVII

But what have I done with my life? thought Mrs Ramsay, taking her place at the head of the table, and looking at all the plates making white circles on it. 'William, sit by me,' she said. 'Lily,' she said, wearily, 'over there.' They had that – Paul Rayley and Minta Doyle – she, only this – an infinitely long table and plates and knives. At the far end, was her husband, sitting down, all in a heap, frowning. What at? She did not know. She did not mind. She could not understand how she had ever felt any emotion or any affection for him. She had a sense of being past everything, through everything, out of everything, as she helped the soup, as if there was an eddy – there – and one could be in it, or one could be out of it, and she was out of it. It's all come to an end, she thought, while they came in one after another, Charles Tansley – 'Sit there, please,' she said – Augustus Carmichael – and sat down. And meanwhile she waited, passively, for someone to answer her, for something to happen. But this is not a thing, she thought, ladling out soup, that one says.

Raising her eyebrows at the discrepancy – that was what she was thinking, this was what she was doing – ladling out soup – she felt, more and more strongly, outside that eddy; or as if a shade had fallen, and, robbed of colour, she saw things truly. The room (she looked round it) was very shabby. There was no beauty anywhere. She forebore to look at Mr Tansley. Nothing seemed to have merged. They all sat separate. And the whole of the effort of merging and flowing and creating rested on her. Again she felt, as a fact without hostility, the sterility of men, for if she did not do it nobody would do it, and so, giving herself the little shake that one gives a watch that has stopped, the old familiar pulse began beating, as the watch begins ticking – one, two, three, one, two, three. And so on and so on, she repeated, listening to it, sheltering and fostering the still feeble pulse as one might guard a weak flame with a newspaper. And so then, she concluded, addressing herself by bending silently in his direction to William Bankes – poor man! who had no wife and no children, and dined alone in lodgings except for tonight; and in pity for him, life being now strong enough to bear her on again, she began all this business, as a sailor not without weariness sees the wind fill his sail and yet hardly wants to be off again and thinks how, had the ship sunk, he would have whirled round and round and found rest on the floor of the sea.

'Did you find your letters? I told them to put them in the hall for you,' she said to William Bankes.

Lily Briscoe watched her drifting into that strange no-man's land where to follow people is impossible and yet their going inflicts such a chill on those who watch them that they always try at least to follow them with their eyes as one follows a fading ship until the sails have sunk beneath the horizon.

How old she looks, how worn she looks, Lily thought, and how remote. Then when she turned to William Bankes, smiling, it was as if the ship had turned and the sun had struck its sails again, and Lily thought with some amusement because she was relieved, Why does she pity him? For that was the impression she gave, when she told him that his letters were in the hall. Poor William Bankes, she seemed to be saying, as if her own weariness had been partly pitying people, and the life in her, her resolve to live again, had been stirred by pity. And it was not true, Lily thought; it was one of those misjudgments of hers that seemed to be instinctive and to arise from some need of her own rather than of other people's. He is not in the least pitiable. He has his work, Lily said to herself. She remembered, all of a sudden as if she had found a treasure, that she too had her work. In a flash she saw her picture, and thought, Yes, I shall put the tree further in the middle; then I shall avoid that awkward space. That's what I shall do. That's what has been puzzling me. She took up the salt cellar and put it down again on a flower in the pattern in the table-cloth, so as to remind herself to move the tree.

'It's odd that one scarcely gets anything worth having by post, yet one always wants one's letters,' said Mr Bankes.

What damned rot they talk, thought Charles Tansley, laying down his spoon precisely in the middle of his plate, which he had swept clean, as if, Lily thought (he sat opposite to her with his back to the window precisely in the middle of the view), he were determined to make sure of his meals. Everything about him had that meagre fixity, that bare unloveliness. But nevertheless, the fact remained, it was almost impossible to dislike anyone if one looked at them. She liked his eyes; they were blue, deep set, frightening.

'Do you write many letters, Mr Tansley?' asked Mrs Ramsay, pitying him too, Lily supposed; for that was true of Mrs Ramsay – she pitied men always as if they lacked something – women never, as if they had something. He wrote to his mother; otherwise he did not suppose he wrote one letter a month, said Mr Tansley, shortly.

For he was not going to talk the sort of rot these people wanted him to talk. He was not going to be condescended to by these silly women. He had been reading in his room, and now he came down and it all seemed to him silly, superficial, flimsy. Why did they dress? He had come down in his ordinary clothes. He had not got any dress clothes. 'One never gets anything worth having by post' – that was the sort of thing they were always saying. They made men say that sort of thing. Yes, it was pretty well true, he thought. They never got anything worth having from one year's end to another. They did nothing but talk, talk, talk, eat, eat, eat. It was the women's fault. Women made civilisation impossible with all their 'charm', all their silliness.

'No going to the Lighthouse tomorrow, Mrs Ramsay,' he said asserting himself. He liked her; he admired her; he still thought of the man in the drain-pipe looking up at her; but he felt it necessary to assert himself.

He was really, Lily Briscoe thought, in spite of his eyes, the most uncharming human being she had ever met. Then why did she mind what he said? Women can't write, women can't paint – what did that matter coming from him, since clearly it was not true to him but for some reason helpful to him, and that was why he said it? Why did her whole being bow, like corn under a wind, and erect itself again from this abasement only with a great and rather painful effort? She must make it once more. There's the sprig on the table-cloth; there's my painting; I must move the tree to the middle; that matters – nothing else. Could she not hold fast to that, she asked herself, and not lose her temper, and not argue; and if she wanted a little revenge take it by laughing at him?

'Oh, Mr Tansley,' she said, 'do take me to the Lighthouse with you. I should so love it.'

She was telling lies he could see. She was saying what

she did not mean to annoy him, for some reason. She was laughing at him. He was in his old flannel trousers. He had no others. He felt very rough and isolated and lonely. He knew that she was trying to tease him for some reason; she didn't want to go to the Lighthouse with him; she despised him: so did Prue Ramsay; so did they all. But he was not going to be made a fool of by women, so he turned deliberately in his chair and looked out of the window and said, all in a jerk, very rudely, it would be too rough for her tomorrow. She would be sick.

It annoyed him that she should have made him speak like that, with Mrs Ramsay listening. If only he could be alone in his room working, he thought, among his books. That was where he felt at his ease. And he had never run a penny into debt; he had never cost his father a penny since he was fifteen; he had helped them at home out of his savings; he was educating his sister. Still, he wished he had known how to answer Miss Briscoe properly; he wished it had not come out all in a jerk like that. 'You'd be sick.' He wished he could think of something to say to Mrs Ramsay, something which would show her that he was not just a dry prig. That was what they all thought him. He turned to her. But Mrs Ramsay was talking about people he had never heard of to William Bankes.

'Yes, take it away,' she said briefly, interrupting what she was saying to Mr Bankes to speak to the maid. 'It must have been fifteen – no, twenty years ago – that I last saw her,' she was saying, turning back to him again as if she could not lose a moment of their talk, for she was absorbed by what they were saying. So he had actually heard from her this evening! And was Carrie still living at Marlow, and was everything still the same? Oh she could remember it as if it were yesterday – going on the river, feeling very cold. But if the Mannings made a plan they stuck to it. Never should she forget Herbert killing a wasp with a teaspoon on the bank!

And it was still going on, Mrs Ramsay mused, gliding like a ghost among the chairs and tables of that drawing-room on the banks of the Thames where she had been so very, very cold twenty years ago; but now she went among them like a ghost; and it fascinated her, as if, while she had changed, that particular day, now become very still and beautiful, had remained there, all these years. Had Carrie written to him herself? she asked.

'Yes. She says they're building a new billiard room,' he said. No! No! That was out of the question! Building a billiard room! It seemed to her impossible.

Mr Bankes could not see that there was anything very odd about it. They were very well off now. Should he give her love to Carrie?

'Oh,' said Mrs Ramsay with a little start, 'No,' she added, reflecting that she did not know this Carrie who built a new billiard room. But how strange, she repeated, to Mr Bankes's amusement, that they should be going on there still. For it was extraordinary to think that they had been capable of going on living all these years when she had not thought of them more than once all that time. How eventful her own life had been, during those same years. Yet perhaps Carrie Manning had not thought about her either. The thought was strange and distasteful.

'People soon drift apart,' said Mr Bankes, feeling, however, some satisfaction when he thought that after all he knew both the Mannings and the Ramsays. He had not drifted apart, he thought, laying down his spoon and wiping his clean-shaven lips punctiliously. But perhaps he was rather unusual, he thought, in this; he never let himself get into a groove. He had friends in all circles . . . Mrs Ramsay had to break off here to tell the maid something about keeping food hot. That was why he preferred dining alone. All these interruptions annoyed him. Well, thought William Bankes, preserving a demeanour of exquisite courtesy and merely spreading the fingers of his left hand on the table-cloth as a mechanic examines a tool beautifully polished and ready for use in an interval of leisure, such are the sacrifices one's friends ask of one. It would have hurt her if he had refused to come. But it was not worth it for him. Looking at his hand he thought that if he had been alone dinner would have been almost over now; he would have been free to work. Yes, he thought, it is a terrible waste of time. The children were dropping in still. 'I wish one of you would run up to Roger's room,' Mrs Ramsay was saying. How trifling it all is, how boring it all is, he thought, compared with the other thing – work. Here he sat drumming his fingers on the table-cloth when he might have been – he took a flashing bird's-eye view of his work. What a waste of time it all was to be sure! Yet, he thought, she is one of my oldest friends. I am by way of being devoted to her. Yet now, at this moment her presence meant absolutely nothing to him: her beauty meant nothing to him; her sitting with her little boy at the window – nothing, nothing. He wished only to be alone and to take up that book. He felt uncomfortable; he felt treacherous, that he could sit by her side and feel nothing for her. The truth was that he did not enjoy family life. It was in this sort of state that one asked oneself, What does one live for? Why, one asked oneself, does one take all these pains for the human race to go on? Is it so very desirable? Are we attractive as a species? Not so very, he thought, looking at those rather untidy boys. His favourite, Cam, was in bed, he supposed. Foolish questions, vain questions, questions one never asked if one was occupied. Is human life this? Is human life that? One never had time to think about it. But here he was asking himself that sort of question, because Mrs Ramsay was giving orders to servants, and also because it had struck him, thinking how surprised Mrs Ramsay was that Carrie Manning should still exist, that friendships, even the best of them, are frail things. One drifts apart. He reproached himself again. He was sitting beside Mrs Ramsay and he had nothing in the world to say to her.

'I'm so sorry,' said Mrs Ramsay, turning to him at last. He felt rigid and barren, like a pair of boots that has been soaked and gone dry so that you can hardly force your feet into them. Yet he must force his feet into them. He must make himself talk. Unless he were very careful, she would find out this treachery of his; that he did not care a straw for her, and that would not be at all pleasant, he thought. So he bent his head courteously in her direction.

'How you must detest dining in this bear garden,' she said, making use, as she did when she was distracted, of her social manner. So, when there is a strife of tongues at some meeting, the chairman, to obtain unity, suggests that every one shall speak in French. Perhaps it is bad French; French may not contain the words that express the speaker's thoughts; nevertheless speaking French imposes some order, some uniformity. Replying to her in the same language, Mr Bankes said, 'No, not at all,' and Mr Tansley, who had no knowledge of this language, even spoken thus in words of one syllable, at once suspected its insincerity. They did talk nonsense, he thought, the Ramsays; and he pounced on this fresh instance with joy, making a note which, one of these days, he would read aloud, to one or two friends. There, in a society where one could say what one liked he would sarcastically describe 'staying with the Ramsays' and what nonsense they talked. It was worth while doing it once, he would say; but not again. The women bored one so, he would say. Of course Ramsay had dished himself by marrying a beautiful woman and having eight children. It would shape itself something like that, but now, at this moment, sitting stuck there with an empty seat beside him nothing had shaped itself at all. It was all in scraps and fragments. He felt extremely, even physically, uncomfortable. He wanted somebody to give him a chance of asserting himself. He wanted it so urgently that he fidgeted in his chair, looked at this person, then at that person, tried to break into their talk, opened his mouth and shut it again. They were talking about the fishing industry. Why did no one ask him his opinion? What did they know about the fishing industry?

Lily Briscoe knew all that. Sitting opposite him could she not see, as in an X-ray photograph, the ribs and thigh bones of the young man's desire to impress himself lying dark in the mist of his flesh – that thin mist which convention had laid over his burning desire to break into the conversation? But, she thought, screwing up her Chinese eyes, and remembering how he sneered at women, 'can't paint, can't write', why should I help him to relieve himself?

There is a code of behaviour she knew, whose seventh article (it may be) says that on occasions of this sort it behoves the woman, whatever her own occupation may be, to go to the help of the young man opposite so that he may expose and relieve the thigh bones, the ribs, of his vanity, of his urgent desire to assert himself; as indeed it is their duty, she reflected, in her old-maidenly fairness, to help us, suppose the Tube were to burst into flames. Then, she thought, I should certainly expect Mr Tansley to get me out. But how would it be, she thought, if neither of us did either of these things? So she sat there smiling.

'You're not planning to go to the Lighthouse, are you, Lily?' said Mrs Ramsay. 'Remember poor Mr Langley; he had been round the world dozens of times, but he told me he never suffered as he did when my husband took him there. Are you a good sailor, Mr Tansley?' she asked.

Mr Tansley raised a hammer: swung it high in air; but realising, as it descended, that he could not smite that butterfly with such an instrument as this, said only that he had never been sick in his life. But in that one sentence lay compact, like gunpowder, that his grandfather was a fisherman; his father a chemist; that he had worked his way up entirely himself; that he was proud of it; that he was Charles Tansley – a fact that nobody there seemed to realise; but one of these days every single person would know it. He scowled ahead of him. He could almost pity these mild cultivated people, who would be blown sky high, like bales of wool and barrels of apples, one of these days by the gunpowder that was in him.

'Will you take me, Mr Tansley?' said Lily, quickly, kindly, for, of course, if Mrs Ramsay said to her, as in effect she did, 'I am drowning, my dear, in seas of fire. Unless you apply some balm to the anguish of this hour and say something nice to that young man there, life will run upon the rocks – indeed I hear the grating and the growling at this minute. My nerves are taut as fiddle strings. Another touch and they will snap' – when Mrs Ramsay said all this, as the glance in her eyes said it, of course for the hundred and fiftieth time Lily Briscoe had to renounce the experiment – what happens if one is not nice to that young man there – and be nice.

Judging the turn in her mood correctly – that she was friendly to him now – he was relieved of his egotism, and told her how he had been thrown out of a boat when he was a baby; how his father used to fish him out with a boat-hook; that was how he had learnt to swim. One of his uncles kept the light on some rock or other off the Scottish coast, he said. He had been there with him in a storm. This was said loudly in a pause. They had to listen to him when he said that he had been with his uncle in a lighthouse in a storm. Ah, thought Lily Briscoe, as the conversation took this auspicious turn, and she felt Mrs Ramsay's gratitude (for Mrs Ramsay was free now to talk for a moment herself), ah, she thought, but what haven't I paid to get it for you? She had not been sincere.

She had done the usual trick – been nice. She would never know him. He would never know her. Human relations were all like that, she thought, and the worst (if it had not been for Mr Bankes) were between men and women. Inevitably these were extremely insincere. Then her eye caught the salt cellar, which she had placed there to remind her, and she remembered that next morning she would move the tree further towards the middle, and her spirits rose so high at the thought of painting tomorrow that she laughed out loud at what Mr Tansley was saying. Let him talk all night if he liked it.

'But how long do they leave men on a lighthouse?' she asked. He told her. He was amazingly well informed. And as he was grateful, and as he liked her, and as he was beginning to enjoy himself, so now, Mrs Ramsay thought, she could return to that dream land, that unreal but fascinating place, the Mannings' drawing-room at Marlow twenty years ago; where one moved about without haste or anxiety, for there was no future to worry about. She knew what had happened to them, what to her. It was like reading a good book again, for she knew the end of that story, since it had happened twenty years ago, and life, which shot down even from this dining-room table in cascades, heaven knows where, was sealed up there, and lay, like a lake, placidly between its banks. He said they had built a billiard room – was it possible? Would William go on talking about the Mannings? She wanted him to. But no – for some reason he was no longer in the mood. She tried. He did not respond. She could not force him. She was disappointed.

'The children are disgraceful,' she said, sighing. He said something about punctuality being one of the minor virtues which we do not acquire until later in life.

'If at all,' said Mrs Ramsay merely to fill up space, thinking what an old maid William was becoming. Conscious of his treachery, conscious of her wish to talk about something more intimate, yet out of mood for it at present, he felt come over him the disagreeableness of life, sitting there, waiting. Perhaps the others were saying something interesting? What were they saying?

That the fishing season was bad; that the men were emigrating. They were talking about wages and unemployment. The young man was abusing the government. William

Bankes, thinking what a relief it was to catch on to something of this sort when private life was disagreeable, heard him say something about 'one of the most scandalous acts of the present government.' Lily was listening; Mrs Ramsay was listening; they were all listening. But already bored, Lily felt that something was lacking; Mr Bankes felt that something was lacking. Pulling her shawl round her, Mrs Ramsay felt that something was lacking. All of them bending themselves to listen thought, 'Pray heaven that the inside of my mind may not be exposed,' for each thought, 'The others are feeling this. They are outraged and indignant with the government about the fishermen. Whereas, I feel nothing at all.' But perhaps, thought Mr Bankes, as he looked at Mr Tansley, here is the man. One was always waiting for the man. There was always a chance. At any moment the leader might arise; the man of genius, in politics as in anything else. Probably he will be extremely disagreeable to us old fogies, thought Mr Bankes, doing his best to make allowances, for he knew by some curious physical sensation, as of nerves erect in his spine, that he was jealous, for himself partly, partly more probably for his work, for his point of view, for his science; and therefore he was not entirely open-minded or altogether fair, for Mr Tansley seemed to be saying, You have wasted your lives. You are all of you wrong. Poor old fogies, you're hopelessly behind the times. He seemed to be rather cocksure, this young man; and his manners were bad. But Mr Bankes bade himself observe, he had courage; he had ability; he was extremely well up in the facts. Probably, Mr Bankes thought, as Tansley abused the government, there is a good deal in what he says.

'Tell me now . . .' he said. So they argued about politics, and Lily looked at the leaf on the table-cloth; and Mrs Ramsay, leaving the argument entirely in the hands of the two men, wondered why she was so bored by this talk, and wished, looking at her husband at the other end of the table, that he would say something. One word, she said to herself. For if he said a thing, it would make all the difference. He went to the heart of things. He cared about fishermen and their wages. He could not sleep for thinking of them. It was altogether different when he spoke; one did not feel then, pray heaven you don't see how little I care, because one did care. Then, realising that it was because she admired him so much that she was waiting for him to speak, she felt as if somebody had been praising her husband to her and their marriage, and she glowed all over without realising that it was she herself who had praised him. She looked at him thinking to find this shown in his face; he would be looking magnificent . . . But not in the least! He was screwing his face up, he was scowling and frowning, and flushing with anger. What on earth was it about? she wondered. What could be the matter? Only that poor old Augustus had asked for another plate of soup – that was all. It was unthinkable, it was detestable (so he signalled to her across the table) that Augustus should be beginning his soup over again. He loathed people eating when he had finished. She saw his anger fly like a pack of hounds into his eyes, his brow, and she knew that in a moment something violent would explode, and then – but thank goodness! she saw him clutch himself and clap a brake on the wheel, and the whole of his body seemed to emit sparks but not words. He sat there scowling. He had said nothing, he would have her observe. Let her give him the credit for that! But why after all should poor Augustus not ask for another plate of soup? He had merely touched Ellen's arm and said:

'Ellen, please, another plate of soup,' and then Mr Ramsay scowled like that.

And why not? Mrs Ramsay demanded. Surely they could let Augustus have his soup if he wanted it. He hated people wallowing in food, Mr Ramsay frowned at her. He hated everything dragging on for hours like this. But he had controlled himself, Mr Ramsay would have her observe, disgusting though the sight was. But why show it so plainly, Mrs Ramsay demanded (they looked at each other down the long table sending these questions and answers across, each knowing exactly what the other felt). Everybody could see, Mrs Ramsay thought. There was Rose gazing at her father, there was Roger gazing at his father; both would be off in spasms of laughter in another second, she knew, and so she said promptly (indeed it was time):

'Light the candles,' and they jumped up instantly and went and fumbled at the sideboard.

Why could he never conceal his feelings? Mrs Ramsay wondered, and she wondered if Augustus Carmichael had noticed. Perhaps he had; perhaps he had not. She could not help respecting the composure with which he sat there, drinking his soup. If he wanted soup, he asked for soup. Whether people laughed at him or were angry with him he was the same. He did not like her, she knew that; but partly for that very reason she respected him, and looking at him, drinking soup, very large and calm in the failing light, and monumental, and contemplative, she wondered what he did feel then, and why he was always content and dignified; and she thought how devoted he was to Andrew, and would call him into his room, and, Andrew said, 'show him things'. And there he would lie all day long on the lawn brooding presumably over his poetry, till he reminded one of a cat watching birds, and then he clapped his paws together when he had found the word, and her husband said, 'Poor old Augustus – he's a true poet', which was high praise from her husband.

Now eight candles were stood down the table, and after the first stoop the flames stood upright and drew with them into visibility the long table entire, and in the middle a yellow and purple dish of fruit. What had she done with it, Mrs Ramsay wondered, for Rose's arrangement of the grapes and pears, of the horny pink-lined shell, of the bananas, made her think of a trophy fetched from the bottom of the sea, of

Neptune's banquet, of the bunch that hangs with vine leaves over the shoulder of Bacchus (in some picture), among the leopard skins and the torches lolloping red and gold . . . Thus brought up suddenly into the light it seemed possessed of great size and depth, was like a world in which one could take one's staff and climb up hills, she thought, and go down into valleys, and to her pleasure (for it brought them into sympathy momentarily) she saw that Augustus too feasted his eyes on the same plate of fruit, plunged in, broke off a bloom there, a tassel here, and returned, after feasting, to his hive. That was his way of looking, different from hers. But looking together united them.

Now all the candles were lit, and the faces on both sides of the table were brought nearer by the candle-light, and composed, as they had not been in the twilight, into a party round a table, for the night was now shut off by panes of glass, which, far from giving any accurate view of the outside world, rippled it so strangely that here, inside the room, seemed to be order and dry land; there, outside, a reflection in which things wavered and vanished, waterily.

Some change at once went through them all, as if this had really happened, and they were all conscious of making a party together in a hollow, on an island; had their common cause against that fluidity out there. Mrs Ramsay, who had been uneasy, waiting for Paul and Minta to come in, and unable, she felt, to settle to things, now felt her uneasiness changed to expectation. For now they must come, and Lily Briscoe, trying to analyse the cause of the sudden exhilaration, compared it with that moment on the tennis lawn, when solidity suddenly vanished, and such vast spaces lay between them; and now the same effect was got by the many candles in the sparely furnished room, and the uncurtained windows, and the bright mask-like look of faces seen by candlelight. Some weight was taken off them; anything might happen, she felt. They must come now, Mrs Ramsay thought, looking at the door, and at that instant, Minta Doyle, Paul Rayley, and a maid carrying a great dish in her hands came in together. They were awfully late; they were horribly late, Minta said, as they found their way to different ends of the table.

'I lost my brooch – my grandmother's brooch,' said Minta with a sound of lamentation in her voice, and a suffusion in her large brown eyes, looking down, looking up, as she sat by Mr Ramsay, which roused his chivalry so that he bantered her.

How could she be such a goose, he asked, as to scramble about the rocks in jewels?

She was by way of being terrified of him – he was so fearfully clever, and the first night when she had sat by him, and he talked about George Eliot, she had been really frightened, for she had left the third volume of *Middlemarch* in the train and she never knew what happened in the end; but afterwards she got on perfectly, and made herself out even more ignorant than she was, because he liked telling her she was a fool. And so tonight, directly he laughed at her she was not frightened. Besides, she knew, directly she came into the room, that the miracle had happened; she wore her golden haze. Sometimes she had it; sometimes not. She never knew why it came or why it went, or if she had it until she came into the room and then she knew instantly by the way some man looked at her. Yes, tonight she had it, tremendously; she knew that by the way Mr Ramsay told her not to be a fool. She sat beside him, smiling.

It must have happened then, thought Mrs Ramsay; they are engaged. And for a moment she felt what she had never expected to feel again – jealousy. For he, her husband, felt it too – Minta's glow; he liked these girls, these golden-reddish girls, with something flying, something a little wild and harum-scarum about them, who didn't 'scrape their hair off', weren't, as he said about poor Lily Briscoe, 'skimpy'. There was some quality which she herself had not, some lustre, some richness, which attracted him, amused him, led him to make favourites of girls like Minta. They might cut his hair for him, plait him watch-chains, or interrupt him at his work, hailing him (she heard them), 'Come along, Mr Ramsay; it's our turn to beat them now,' and out he came to play tennis.

But indeed she was not jealous, only, now and then, when she made herself look in her glass a little resentful that she had grown old, perhaps, by her own fault. (The bill for the greenhouse and all the rest of it.) She was grateful to them for laughing at him ('How many pipes have you smoked today, Mr Ramsay?' and so on), till he seemed a young man; a man very attractive to women, not burdened, not weighed down with the greatness of his labours and the sorrows of the world and his fame or his failure, but again as she had first known him, gaunt but gallant; helping her out of a boat, she remembered; with delightful ways, like that (she looked at him, and he looked astonishingly young, teasing Minta). For herself – 'Put it down there,' she said, helping the Swiss girl to place gently before her the huge brown pot in which was the *Bœuf en Daube* – for her own part she liked her boobies. Paul must sit by her. She had kept a place for him. Really, she sometimes thought she liked the boobies best. They did not bother one with their dissertations. How much they missed, after all, these very clever men! How dried up they did become, to be sure. There was something, she thought as he sat down, very charming about Paul. His manners were delightful to her, and his sharp-cut nose and his bright blue eyes. He was so considerate. Would he tell her – now that they were all talking again – what had happened?

'We went back to look for Minta's brooch,' he said, sitting down by her. 'We' – that was enough. She knew from the effort, the rise in his voice to surmount a difficult word that it was the first time he had said 'we'. 'We' did this, 'we' did that. They'll say that all their lives, she thought, and an exquisite scent of olives and oil and juice rose from the great brown dish as Marthe, with a little flourish, took the cover off. The cook had spent three days over that dish. And she must take great care, Mrs Ramsay thought, diving into the soft mass, to choose a specially tender piece for William Bankes. And she peered into the dish, with its shiny walls and its confusion of savoury brown and yellow meats, and its bay leaves and its wine, and thought, This will celebrate the occasion – a curious sense rising in her, at once freakish and tender, of celebrating a festival, as if two emotions were called up in her, one profound – for what could be more serious than the love of man for woman, what more commanding, more impressive, bearing in its bosom the seeds of death; at the same time these lovers, these people entering into illusion glittering-eyed, must be danced round with mockery, decorated with garlands.

'It is a triumph,' said Mr Bankes, laying his knife down for a moment. He had eaten attentively. It was rich; it was tender. It was perfectly cooked. How did she manage these things in the depths of the country? he asked her. She was a wonderful woman. All his love, all his reverence had returned; and she knew it.

'It is a French recipe of my grandmother's,' said Mrs Ramsay, speaking with a ring of great pleasure in her voice. Of course it was French. What passes for cookery in England is an abomination (they agreed). It is putting cabbages in water. It is roasting meat till it is like leather. It is cutting off the delicious skins of vegetables. 'In which', said Mr Bankes, 'all the virtue of the vegetable is contained.' And the waste, said Mrs Ramsay. A whole French family could live on what an English cook throws away. Spurred on by her sense that William's affection had come back to her, and that everything was all right again, and that her suspense was over, and that now she was free both to triumph and to mock, she laughed, she gesticulated, till Lily thought, How childlike, how absurd she was, sitting up there with all her beauty opened again in her, talking about the skins of vegetables. There was something frightening about her. She was irresistible. Always she got her own way in the end, Lily thought. Now she had brought this off – Paul and Minta, one might suppose, were engaged. Mr Bankes was dining here. She put a spell on them all, by wishing, so simply, so directly, and Lily contrasted that abundance with her own poverty of spirit, and supposed that it was partly that belief (for her face was all lit up – without looking young, she looked radiant) in this strange, this terrifying thing, which made Paul Rayley, the centre of it, all of a tremor, yet abstract, absorbed, silent. Mrs Ramsay, Lily felt, as she talked about the skins of vegetables, exalted that, worshipped that; held her hands over it to warm them, to protect it, and yet, having brought it all about, somehow laughed, led her victims, Lily felt, to the altar. It came over her too now – the emotion, the vibration of love. How inconspicuous she felt herself by Paul's side! He, glowing, burning; she, aloof, satirical; he, bound for adventure; she, moored to the shore; he, launched, incautious; she solitary, left out – and, ready to implore a share, if it were disaster, in his disaster, she said shyly:

'When did Minta lose her brooch?'

He smiled the most exquisite smile, veiled by memory, tinged by dreams. He shook his head. 'On the beach,' he said.

'I'm going to find it,' he said, 'I'm getting up early.' This being kept secret from Minta, he lowered his voice, and turned his eyes to where she sat, laughing, beside Mr Ramsay.

Lily wanted to protest violently and outrageously her desire to help him, envisaging how in the dawn on the beach she would be the one to pounce on the brooch half-hidden by some stone, and thus herself be included among the sailors and adventurers. But what did he reply to her offer? She actually said with an emotion that she seldom let appear, 'Let me come with you'; and he laughed. He meant yes or no – either perhaps. But it was not his meaning – it was the odd chuckle he gave, as if he had said, Throw yourself over the cliff if you like, I don't care. He turned on her cheek the heat of love, its horror, its cruelty, its unscrupulosity. It scorched her, and Lily, looking at Minta being charming to Mr Ramsay at the other end of the table, flinched for her exposed to those fangs, and was thankful. For at any rate, she said to herself, catching sight of the salt cellar on the pattern, she need not marry, thank Heaven: she need not undergo that degradation. She was saved from that dilution. She would move the tree rather more to the middle.

Such was the complexity of things. For what happened to her, especially staying with the Ramsays, was to be made to feel violently two opposite things at the same time; that's what you feel, was one; that's what I feel was the other, and then they fought together in her mind, as now. It is so beautiful, so exciting, this love, that I tremble on the verge of it, and offer, quite out of my own habit, to look for a brooch on a beach; also it is the stupidest, the most barbaric of human passions, and turns a nice young man with a profile like a gem (Paul's was exquisite) into a bully with a crowbar (he was swaggering, he was insolent) in the Mile End Road. Yet she said to herself, from the dawn of time odes have been sung to love; wreaths heaped and roses; and if you asked nine people out of ten they would say they wanted nothing but this; while the women, judging from her own experience, would all the time be feeling, This is not what we want; there is nothing more tedious, puerile, and inhumane than love; yet it is also beautiful and necessary. Well then, well then? she asked, somehow expecting the others to go on with the argument, as if in an argument like this one threw one's own little bolt which fell short obviously and left the others to carry it on. So she listened again to what they were saying in case they should throw any light upon the question of love.

'Then,' said Mr Bankes, 'there is that liquid the English call coffee.'

'Oh coffee!' said Mrs Ramsay. But it was much rather a question (she was thoroughly roused, Lily could see, and talked very emphatically) of real butter and clean milk. Speaking with warmth and eloquence she described the iniquity of the English dairy system, and in what state milk was delivered at the door, and was about to prove her charges, for she had gone into the matter, when all round the table, beginning with Andrew in the middle, like a fire leaping from tuft to tuft of furze, her children laughed; her husband laughed; she was laughed at, fire-encircled, and forced to vail her crest, dismount her batteries, and only retaliate by displaying the raillery and ridicule of the table to Mr Bankes as an example of what one suffered if one attacked the prejudices of the British Public.

Purposely, however, for she had it on her mind that Lily, who had helped her with Mr Tansley, was out of things, she exempted her from the rest; said 'Lily anyhow agrees with me,' and so drew her in, a little fluttered, a little startled. (For she was thinking about love.) They were both out of things, Mrs Ramsay had been thinking, both Lily and Charles Tansley. Both suffered from the glow of the other two. He, it was clear, felt himself utterly in the cold; no woman would look at him with Paul Rayley in the room. Poor fellow! Still, he had his dissertation, the influence of somebody upon something: he could take care of himself. With Lily it was different. She faded, under Minta's glow; became more inconspicuous than ever, in her little grey dress with her little puckered face and her little Chinese eyes. Everything about her was so small. Yet, thought Mrs Ramsay, comparing her with Minta, as she claimed her help (for Lily should bear her out she talked no more about her dairies than her husband did about his boots – he would talk by the hour about his boots), of the two Lily at forty will be the better. There was in Lily a thread of something; a flare of something; something of her own which Mrs Ramsay liked very much indeed, but no man would, she feared. Obviously, not, unless it were a much older man, like William Bankes. But then he cared, well, Mrs Ramsay sometimes thought that he cared, since his wife's death, perhaps for her. He was not 'in love' of course; it was one of those unclassified affections of which there are so many. Oh but nonsense, she thought; William must marry Lily. They have so many things in common. Lily is so fond of flowers. They are both cold and aloof and rather self-sufficing. She must arrange for them to take a long walk together.

Foolishly, she had set them opposite each other. That could be remedied tomorrow. If it were fine, they should go for a picnic. Everything seemed possible. Everything seemed right. Just now (but this cannot last, she thought, dissociating herself from the moment while they were all talking about boots) just now she had reached security; she hovered like a hawk suspended; like a flag floated in an element of joy which filled every nerve of her body fully and sweetly, not noisily, solemnly rather, for it arose, she thought, looking at them all eating there, from husband and children and friends; all of which rising in this profound stillness (she was helping William Bankes to one very small piece more and peered into the depths of the earthenware pot) seemed now for no special reason to stay there like a smoke, like a fume rising upwards, holding them safe together. Nothing need be said; nothing could be said. There it was, all round them. It partook, she felt, carefully helping Mr Bankes to a specially tender piece, of eternity; as she had already felt about something different once before that afternoon; there is a coherence in things, a stability; something, she meant, is immune from change, and shines out (she glanced at the window with its ripple of reflected lights) in the face of the flowing, the fleeting, the spectral, like a ruby; so that again tonight she had the feeling she had had once today already, of peace, of rest. Of such moments, she thought, the thing is made that remains for ever after. This would remain.

'Yes,' she assured William Bankes, 'there is plenty for everybody.'

'Andrew,' she said, 'hold your plate lower, or I shall spill it.' (The *Bœuf en Daube* was a perfect triumph.) Here, she felt, putting the spoon down, was the still space that lies about the heart of things, where one could move or rest; could wait now (they were all helped) listening; could then, like a hawk which lapses suddenly from its high station, flaunt and sink on laughter easily, resting her whole weight upon what at the other end of the table her husband was saying about the square root of one thousand two hundred and fifty-three, which happened to be the number on his railway ticket.

What did it all mean? To this day she had no notion. A square root? What was that? Her sons knew. She leant on them; on cubes and square roots; that was what they were talking about now; on Voltaire and Madame de Staël; on the character of Napoleon; on the French system of land tenure; on Lord Rosebery; on Creevey's Memoirs: she let it uphold her and sustain her, this admirable fabric of the masculine intelligence, which ran up and down, crossed this way and that, like iron girders spanning the swaying fabric, upholding the world, so that she could trust herself to it utterly, even shut her eyes, or flicker them for a moment, as a child staring up from its pillow winks at the myriad layers of the leaves of a tree. Then she woke up. It was still being fabricated. William Bankes was praising the Waverley novels.

He read one of them every six months, he said. And why should that make Charles Tansley angry? He rushed in (all, thought Mrs Ramsay, because Prue will not be nice to him) and denounced the Waverley novels when he knew nothing about it, nothing about it whatsoever, Mrs Ramsay thought, observing him rather than listening to what he said. She could see how it was from his manner – he wanted to assert himself, and so it would always be with him till he got his Professorship or married his wife, and so need not be always saying,

'I—I—I.' For that was what his criticism of poor Sir Walter, or perhaps it was Jane Austen, amounted to. 'I—I—I.' He was thinking of himself and the impression he was making, as she could tell by the sound of his voice, and his emphasis and his uneasiness. Success would be good for him. At any rate they were off again. Now she need not listen. It could not last she knew, but at the moment her eyes were so clear that they seemed to go round the table unveiling each of these people, and their thoughts and their feelings, without effort like a light stealing under water so that its ripples and the reeds in it and the minnows balancing themselves, and the sudden silent trout are all lit up hanging, trembling. So she saw them; she heard them; but whatever they said had also this quality, as if what they said was like the movement of a trout when, at the same time, one can see the ripple and the gravel, something to the right, something to the left; and the whole is held together; for whereas in active life she would be netting and separating one thing from another; she would be saying she liked the Waverley novels or had not read them; she would be urging herself forward; now she said nothing. For the moment she hung suspended.

'Ah, but how long do you think it'll last?' said somebody. It was as if she had antennae trembling out from her, which, intercepting certain sentences, forced them upon her attention. This was one of them. She scented danger for her husband. A question like that would lead, almost certainly, to something being said which reminded him of his own failure. How long would he be read – he would think at once. William Bankes (who was entirely free from all such vanity) laughed, and said he attached no importance to changes in fashion. Who could tell what was going to last – in literature or indeed in anything else?

'Let us enjoy what we do enjoy,' he said. His integrity seemed to Mrs Ramsay quite admirable. He never seemed for a moment to think, But how does this affect me? But then if you had the other temperament, which must have praise, which must have encouragement, naturally you began (and she knew that Mr Ramsay was beginning) to be uneasy; to want somebody to say, Oh, but your work will last, Mr Ramsay, or something like that. He showed his uneasiness quite clearly now by saying, with some irritation, that, anyhow, Scott (or was it Shakespeare?) would last him his lifetime. He said it irritably. Everybody, she thought, felt a little uncomfortable, without knowing why. Then Minta Doyle, whose instinct was fine, said bluffly, absurdly, that she did not believe that any one really enjoyed reading Shakespeare. Mr Ramsay said grimly (but his mind was turned away again) that very few people liked it as much as they said they did. But, he added, there is considerable merit in some of the plays nevertheless, and Mrs Ramsay saw that it would be all right for the moment anyhow; he would laugh at Minta, and she, Mrs Ramsay saw, realising his extreme anxiety about himself, would, in her own way, see that he was taken care of, and praise him, somehow or other. But she wished it was not necessary: perhaps it was her fault that it was necessary. Anyhow, she was free now to listen to what Paul Rayley was trying to say about books one had read as a boy. They lasted, he said. He had read some of Tolstoi at school. There was one he always remembered, but he had forgotten the name. Russian names were impossible, said Mrs Ramsay. 'Vronsky,' said Paul. He remembered that because he always thought it such a good name for a villain. 'Vronsky,' said Mrs Ramsay; 'O, *Anna Karenina*,' but that did not take them very far; books were not in their line. No, Charles Tansley would put them both right in a second about books, but it was all so mixed up with, Am I saying the right thing? Am I making a good impression? that, after all, one knew more about him than about Tolstoi, whereas what Paul said was about the thing simply, not himself. Like all stupid people, he had a kind of modesty too, a consideration for what you were feeling, which, once in a way at least, she found attractive. Now he was thinking, not about himself or about Tolstoi, but whether she was cold, whether she felt a draught, whether she would like a pear.

No, she said, she did not want a pear. Indeed she had been keeping guard over the dish of fruit (without realising it) jealously, hoping that nobody would touch it. Her eyes had been going in and out among the curves and shadows of the fruit, among the rich purples of the lowland grapes, then over the horny ridge of the shell, putting a yellow against a purple, a curved shape against a round shape, without knowing why she did it, or why, every time she did it, she felt more and more serene; until, oh, what a pity that they should do it – a hand reached out, took a pear, and spoilt the whole thing. In sympathy she looked at Rose. She looked at Rose sitting between Jasper and Prue. How odd that one's child should do that!

How odd to see them sitting there, in a row, her children, Jasper, Rose, Prue, Andrew, almost silent, but with some joke of their own going on, she guessed, from the twitching at their lips. It was something quite apart from everything else, something they were hoarding up to laugh over in their own room. It was not about their father, she hoped. No, she thought not. What was it, she wondered, sadly rather, for it seemed to her that they would laugh when she was not there. There was all that hoarded behind those rather set, still, mask-like faces, for they did not join in easily; they were like watchers, surveyors, a little raised or set apart from the grown-up people. But when she looked at Prue tonight, she saw that this was not now quite true of her. She was just beginning, just moving, just descending. The faintest light was on her face, as if the glow of Minta opposite, some excitement, some anticipation of happiness was reflected in her, as if the sun of the love of men and women rose over the rim of the table-cloth, and without knowing what it was she bent towards it and greeted it. She kept looking at Minta, shyly, yet curiously, so that Mrs Ramsay looked from one to the other and said, speaking to

Prue in her own mind, You will be as happy as she is one of these days. You will be much happier, she added, because you are my daughter, she meant; her own daughter must be happier than other people's daughters. But dinner was over. It was time to go. They were only playing with things on their plates. She would wait until they had done laughing at some story her husband was telling. He was having a joke with Minta about a bet. Then she would get up.

She liked Charles Tansley, she thought, suddenly; she liked his laugh. She liked him for being so angry with Paul and Minta. She liked his awkwardness. There was a lot in that young man after all. And Lily, she thought, putting her napkin beside her plate, she always has some joke of her own. One need never bother about Lily. She waited. She tucked her napkin under the edge of her plate. Well, were they done now? No. That story had led to another story. Her husband was in great spirits tonight, and wishing, she supposed, to make it all right with old Augustus after that scene about the soup, had drawn him in – they were telling stories about some one they had both known at college. She looked at the window in which the candle flames burnt brighter now that the panes were black, and looking at that outside the voices came to her very strangely, as if they were voices at a service in a cathedral, for she did not listen to the words. The sudden bursts of laughter and then one voice (Minta's) speaking alone, reminded her of men and boys crying out the Latin words of a service in some Roman Catholic cathedral. She waited. Her husband spoke. He was repeating something, and she knew it was poetry from the rhythm and the ring of exaltation and melancholy in his voice:

> Come out and climb the garden path,
> > Luriana Lurilee.
> The China rose is all abloom and buzzing with
> > the yellow bee.

The words (she was looking at the window) sounded as if they were floating like flowers on water out there, cut off from them all, as if no one had said them, but they had come into existence of themselves.

> And all the lives we ever lived and all the lives to be
> Are full of trees and changing leaves.

She did not know what they meant, but, like music, the words seemed to be spoken by her own voice, outside her self, saying quite easily and naturally what had been in her mind the whole evening while she said different things. She knew, without looking round, that every one at the table was listening to the voice saying:

> I wonder if it seems to you
>   Luriana, Lurilee

with the same sort of relief and pleasure that she had, as if this were, at last, the natural thing to say, this were their own voice speaking.

But the voice stopped. She looked round. She made herself get up. Augustus Carmichael had risen and, holding his table napkin so that it looked like a long white robe he stood chanting:

> To see the Kings go riding by
> Over lawn and daisy lea
> With their palm leaves and cedar sheaves,
>   Luriana, Lurilee,

and as she passed him he turned slightly towards her repeating the last words:

> Luriana, Lurilee,

and bowed to her as if he did her homage. Without knowing why, she felt that he liked her better than he had ever done before; and with a feeling of relief and gratitude she returned his bow and passed through the door which he held open for her.

It was necessary now to carry everything a step further. With her foot on the threshold she waited a moment longer in a scene which was vanishing even as she looked, and then, as she moved and took Minta's arm and left the room, it changed, it shaped itself differently; it had become, she knew, giving one last look at it over her shoulder, already the past.

XVIII

As usual, Lily thought. There was always something that had to be done at that precise moment, something that Mrs Ramsay had decided for reasons of her own to do instantly, it might be with every one standing about making jokes, as now, not being able to decide whether they were going into the smoking-room, into the drawing-room, up to the attics. Then one saw Mrs Ramsay in the midst of this hubbub standing there with Minta's arm in hers, bethink her 'Yes, it is time for that now,' and so make off at once with an air of secrecy to do something alone. And directly she went a sort of disintegration set in; they wavered about, went different ways, Mr Bankes took Charles Tansley by the arm and went off to finish on the terrace the discussion they had begun at dinner about politics, thus giving a turn to the whole poise of the evening, making the weight fall in a different direction, as if, Lily thought, seeing them go, and hearing a word or two about the policy of the Labour Party, they had gone up on to the bridge of the ship and were taking their bearings; the change from poetry to politics struck her like that; so Mr Bankes and Charles Tansley went off, while the others stood looking at Mrs Ramsay going upstairs in the lamplight alone. Where, Lily wondered, was she going so quickly?

Not that she did in fact run or hurry; she went indeed rather slowly. She felt rather inclined just for a moment to stand still after all that chatter, and pick out one particular thing; the thing that mattered; to detach it; separate it off; clean it of all the emotions and odds and ends of things, and so hold it before her, and bring it to the tribunal where, ranged about in conclave, sat the judges she had set up to decide these things. Is it good, is it bad, is it right or wrong? Where are we going to? and so on. So she righted herself after the shock of the event, and quite unconsciously and incongruously, used the branches of the elm trees outside to help her to stabilise her position. Her world was changing: they were still. The event had given her a sense of movement. All must be in order. She must get that right and that right, she thought, insensibly approving of the dignity of the trees' stillness, and now again of the superb upward rise (like the beak of a ship up a wave) of the elm branches as the wind raised them. For it was windy (she stood a moment to look out). It was windy, so that the leaves now and then brushed open a star, and the stars themselves seemed to be shaking and darting light and trying to flash out between the edges of the leaves. Yes, that was done then, accomplished; and as with all things done, become solemn. Now one thought of it, cleared of chatter and emotion, it seemed always to have been, only was shown now, and so being shown struck everything into stability. They would, she thought, going on again, however long they lived, come back to this night; this moon; this wind; this house: and to her too. It flattered her, where she was most susceptible of flattery, to think how, wound about in their hearts, however long they lived she would be woven; and this, and this, and this, she thought, going upstairs, laughing, but affectionately, at the sofa on the landing (her mother's) at the rocking-chair (her father's); at the map of the Hebrides. All that would be revived again in the lives of Paul and Minta; 'the Rayleys' – she tried the new name over; and she felt, with her hand on the nursery door, that community of feeling with other people which emotion gives as if the walls of partition had become so thin that practically (the feeling was one of relief and happiness) it was all one stream, and chairs, tables, maps, were hers, were theirs, it did not matter whose, and Paul and Minta would carry it on when she was dead.

She turned the handle, firmly, lest it should squeak, and went in, pursing her lips slightly, as if to remind herself that she must not speak aloud. But directly she came in she saw, with annoyance, that the precaution was not needed. The children were not asleep. It was most annoying. Mildred should be more careful. There was James wide awake and Cam sitting bolt upright, and Mildred out of bed in her bare feet, and it was almost eleven and they were all talking. What was the matter? It was that horrid skull again. She had told Mildred to move it, but Mildred, of course, had forgotten, and now there was Cam wide awake and James wide awake quarrelling when they ought to have been asleep hours ago. What had possessed Edward to send them this horrid skull? She had been so foolish as to let them nail it up there. It was nailed fast, Mildred said, and Cam couldn't go to sleep with it in the room, and James screamed if she touched it.

Then Cam must go to sleep (it had great horns said Cam –) must go to sleep and dream of lovely palaces, said Mrs Ramsay, sitting down on the bed by her side. She could see the horns, Cam said, all over the room. It was true. Wherever they put the light (and James could not sleep without a light) there was always a shadow somewhere.

'But think, Cam, it's only an old pig,' said Mrs Ramsay, 'a nice black pig like the pigs at the farm.' But Cam thought it was a horrid thing, branching at her all over the room.

'Well then,' said Mrs Ramsay, 'we will cover it up,' and they all watched her go to the chest of drawers, and open the little drawers quickly one after another, and not seeing anything that would do, she quickly took her own shawl off and wound it round the skull, round and round and round, and then she came back to Cam and laid her head almost flat on the pillow beside Cam's and said how lovely it looked now; how the fairies would love it; it was like a bird's nest; it was like a beautiful mountain such as she had seen abroad, with valleys and flowers and bells ringing and birds singing and little goats and antelopes . . . She could see the words echoing as she spoke them rhythmically in Cam's mind, and Cam was repeating after her how it was like a mountain, a bird's nest, a garden, and there were little antelopes, and her eyes were opening and shutting, and Mrs Ramsay went on saying still more monotonously, and more rhythmically and more nonsensically, how she must shut her eyes and go to sleep and dream of mountains and valleys and stars falling and parrots and antelopes and gardens, and everything lovely, she said, raising her head very slowly and speaking more and more mechanically, until she sat upright and saw that Cam was asleep.

Now, she whispered, crossing over to his bed, James must go to sleep too, for see, she said, the boar's skull was still there; they had not touched it; they had done just what he wanted; it was there quite unhurt. He made sure that the skull was still there under the shawl. But he wanted to ask her something more. Would they go to the Lighthouse tomorrow?

No, not tomorrow, she said, but soon, she promised him; the next fine day. He was very good. He lay down. She covered him up. But he would never forget, she knew, and she felt angry with Charles Tansley, with her husband, and with herself, for she had raised his hopes. Then feeling for her shawl and remembering that she had wrapped it round the boar's skull, she got up, and pulled the window down another inch or two, and heard the wind, and got a breath of the perfectly indifferent chill night air and murmured good-night to Mildred and left the room and let the tongue of the door slowly lengthen in the lock and went out.

She hoped he would not bang his books on the floor above their heads, she thought, still thinking how annoying Charles Tansley was. For neither of them slept well; they were excitable children, and since he said things like that about the Lighthouse, it seemed to her likely that he would knock a pile of books over, just as they were going to sleep, clumsily sweeping them off the table with his elbow. For she supposed that he had gone upstairs to work. Yet he looked so desolate; yet she would feel relieved when he went; yet she would see that he was better treated tomorrow; yet he was admirable with her husband; yet his manners certainly wanted improving; yet she liked his laugh – thinking this, as she came downstairs, she noticed that she could now see the moon itself through the staircase window – the yellow harvest moon – and turned, and they saw her, standing above them on the stairs.

'That's my mother,' thought Prue. Yes; Minta should look at her; Paul Rayley should look at her. That is the thing itself, she felt, as if there were only one person like that in the world; her mother. And, from having been quite grown up, a moment before, talking with the others, she became a child again, and what they had been doing was a game, and would her mother sanction their game, or condemn it, she wondered. And thinking what a chance it was for Minta and Paul and Lily to see her, and feeling what an extraordinary stroke of fortune it was for her to have her, and how she would never grow up and never leave home, she said, like a child, 'We thought of going down to the beach to watch the waves.'

Instantly, for no reason at all, Mrs Ramsay became like a girl of twenty, full of gaiety. A mood of revelry suddenly took possession of her. Of course they must go; of course they must go, she cried, laughing; and running down the last three or four steps quickly, she began turning from one to the other and laughing and drawing Minta's wrap round her and saying she only wished she could come too, and would they be very late, and had any of them got a watch?

'Yes, Paul has,' said Minta. Paul slipped a beautiful gold watch out of a little wash-leather case to show her. And as he held it in the palm of his hand before her, he felt 'She knows all about it. I need not say anything.' He was saying to her as he showed her the watch, 'I've done it, Mrs Ramsay. I owe it all to you.' And seeing the gold watch lying in his hand, Mrs Ramsay felt, How extraordinarily lucky Minta is! She is marrying a man who has a gold watch in a wash-leather bag!

'How I wish I could come with you!' she cried. But she was withheld by something so strong that she never even thought of asking herself what it was. Of course it was impossible for her to go with them. But she would have liked to go, had it not been for the other thing, and tickled by the absurdity of her thought (how lucky to marry a man with a wash-leather bag for his watch) she went with a smile on her lips into the other room, where her husband sat reading.

XIX

Of course, she said to herself, coming into the room, she had to come here to get something she wanted. First she wanted to sit down in a particular chair under a particular lamp. But she wanted something more, though she did not know, could not think what it was that she wanted. She looked at her husband (taking up her stocking and beginning to knit), and saw that he did not want to be interrupted – that was clear. He was reading something that moved him very much. He was half smiling and then she knew he was controlling his emotion. He was tossing the pages over. He was acting it – perhaps he was thinking himself the person in the book. She wondered what book it was. Oh, it was one of old Sir Walter's, she saw, adjusting the shade of her lamp so that the light fell on her knitting. For Charles Tansley had been saying (she looked up as if she expected to hear the crash of books on the floor above) had been saying that people don't read Scott any more. Then her husband thought, 'That's what they'll say of me'; so he went and got one of those books. And if he came to the conclusion 'That's true' what Charles Tansley said, he would accept it about Scott. (She could see that he was weighing, considering, putting this with that as he read.) But not about himself. He was always uneasy about himself. That troubled her. He would always be worrying about his own books – will they be read, are they good, why aren't they better, what do people think of me? Not liking to think of him so, and wondering if they had guessed at dinner why he suddenly became irritable when they talked about fame and books lasting, wondering if the children were laughing at that, she twitched the stocking out, and all the fine gravings came drawn with steel instruments about her lips and forehead, and she grew still like a tree which has been tossing and quivering and now, when the breeze falls, settles, leaf by leaf, into quiet.

It didn't matter, any of it, she thought. A great man, a great book, fame – who could tell? She knew nothing about it. But it was his way with him, his truthfulness – for instance at dinner she had been thinking quite instinctively, If only he would speak! She had complete trust in him. And dismissing all this, as one passes in diving now a weed, now a straw, now a bubble, she felt again, sinking deeper, as she had felt in the hall when the others were talking, There is something I want – something I have come to get, and she fell deeper and deeper without knowing quite what it was, with her eyes closed. And she waited a little, knitting, wondering, and slowly those words they had said at dinner, 'the China rose is all abloom and buzzing with the honey bee,' began washing from side to side of her mind rhythmically, and as they washed, words, like little shaded lights, one red, one blue, one yellow, lit up in the dark of her mind, and seemed leaving their perches up there to fly across and across, or to cry out and to be echoed; so she turned and felt on the table beside her for a book.

> And all the lives we ever lived
> And all the lives to be,
> Are full of trees and changing leaves,

she murmured, sticking her needles into the stocking. And she opened the book and began reading here and there at random, and as she did so she felt that she was climbing backwards, upwards, shoving her way up under petals that curved over her, so that she only knew this is white, or this is red. She did not know at first what the words meant at all.

> Steer, hither steer your winged pines, all beaten
> Mariners

she read and turned the page, swinging herself, zigzagging this way and that, from one line to another as from one branch to another, from one red and white flower to another, until a little sound roused her – her husband slapping his thighs. Their eyes met for a second; but they did not want to speak to each other. They had nothing to say, but something seemed, nevertheless, to go from him to her. It was the life, it was the power of it, it was the tremendous humour, she knew, that made him slap his thighs. Don't interrupt me, he seemed to be saying, don't say anything; just sit there. And he went on reading. His lips twitched. It filled him. It fortified him. He clean forgot all the little rubs and digs of the evening, and how it bored him unutterably to sit still while people ate and drank interminably, and his being so irritable with his wife and so touchy and minding when they passed his books over as if they didn't exist at all. But now, he felt, it didn't matter a damn who reached Z (if thought ran like an alphabet from A to Z). Somebody would reach it – if not he, then another.

This man's strength and sanity, his feeling for straightforward simple things, these fishermen, the poor old crazed creature in Mucklebackit's cottage made him feel so vigorous, so relieved of something that he felt roused and triumphant and could not choke back his tears. Raising the book a little to hide his face he let them fall and shook his head from side to side and forgot himself completely (but not one or two reflections about morality and French novels and English novels and Scott's hands being tied but his view perhaps being as true as the other view) forgot his own bothers and failures completely in poor Steenie's drowning and Mucklebackit's sorrow (that was Scott at his best) and the astonishing delight and feeling of vigour that it gave him.

Well, let them improve upon that, he thought as he finished the chapter. He felt that he had been arguing with somebody, and had got the better of him. They could not improve upon that, whatever they might say; and his own position became more secure. The lovers were fiddlesticks, he thought, collecting it all in his mind again. That's fiddlesticks, that's first-rate, he thought, putting one thing beside another. But he must read it again. He could not remember the whole shape of the thing. He had to keep his judgement in suspense. So he returned to the other thought – if young men did not care for this, naturally they did not care for him either. One ought not to complain, thought Mr Ramsay, trying to stifle his desire to complain to his wife that young men did not admire him. But he was determined; he would not bother her again. Here he looked at her reading. She looked very peaceful, reading. He liked to think that every one had taken themselves off and that he and she were alone. The whole of life did not consist in going to bed with a woman, he thought, returning to Scott and Balzac, to the English novel and the French novel.

Mrs Ramsay raised her head and like a person in a light sleep seemed to say that if he wanted her to wake she would, she really would, but otherwise, might she go on sleeping, just a little longer, just a little longer? She was climbing up those branches, this way and that, laying hands on one flower and then another.

Nor praise the deep vermilion in the rose,

she read, and so reading she was ascending, she felt, on to the top, on to the summit. How satisfying! How restful! All the odds and ends of the day stuck to this magnet; her mind felt swept, felt clean. And then there it was, suddenly entire shaped in her hands, beautiful and reasonable, clear and complete, the essence sucked out of life and held rounded here – the sonnet.

But she was becoming conscious of her husband looking at her. He was smiling at her, quizzically, as if he were ridiculing her gently for being asleep in broad daylight, but at the same time he was thinking, Go on reading. You don't look sad now, he thought. And he wondered what she was reading, and exaggerated her ignorance, her simplicity, for he liked to think that she was not clever, not book-learned at all. He wondered if she understood what she was reading. Probably not, he thought. She was astonishingly beautiful. Her beauty seemed to him, if that were possible, to increase.

Yet seem'd it winter still, and, you away,
As with your shadow I with these did play,

she finished.

'Well?' she said, echoing his smile dreamily, looking up from her book.

As with your shadow I with these did play,

she murmured putting the book on the table.

What had happened she wondered, as she took up her

knitting, since she had last seen him alone? She remembered dressing, and seeing the moon; Andrew holding his plate too high at dinner; being depressed by something William had said; the birds in the trees; the sofa on the landing; the children being awake; Charles Tansley waking them with his books falling – oh no, that she had invented; and Paul having a wash-leather case for his watch. Which should she tell him about?

'They're engaged,' she said, beginning to knit, 'Paul and Minta.'

'So I guessed,' he said. There was nothing very much to be said about it. Her mind was still going up and down, up and down with the poetry; he was still feeling very vigorous, very forthright, after reading about Steenie's funeral. So they sat silent. Then she became aware that she wanted him to say something.

Anything, anything, she thought, going on with her knitting. Anything will do.

'How nice it would be to marry a man with a wash-leather bag for his watch,' she said, for that was the sort of joke they had together.

He snorted. He felt about this engagement as he always felt about any engagement; the girl is much too good for that young man. Slowly it came into her head, why is it then that one wants people to marry? What was the value, the meaning of things? (Every word they said now would be true.) Do say something, she thought, wishing only to hear his voice. For the shadow, the thing folding them in was beginning, she felt, to close round her again. Say anything, she begged, looking at him, as if for help.

He was silent, swinging the compass on his watch-chain to and fro, and thinking of Scott's novels and Balzac's novels. But through the crepuscular walls of their intimacy, for they were drawing together, involuntarily, coming side by side, quite close, she could feel his mind like a raised hand shadowing her mind; and he was beginning now that her thoughts took a turn he disliked – towards this 'pessimism' as he called it – to fidget, though he said nothing, raising his hand to his forehead, twisting a lock of hair, letting it fall again.

'You won't finish that stocking tonight,' he said, pointing to her stocking. That was what she wanted – the asperity in his voice reproving her. If he says it's wrong to be pessimistic probably it is wrong, she thought; the marriage will turn out all right.

'No,' she said, flattening the stocking out upon her knee, 'I shan't finish it.'

And what then? For she felt that he was still looking at her, but that his look had changed. He wanted something – wanted the thing she always found it so difficult to give him; wanted her to tell him that she loved him. And that, no, she could not do. He found talking so much easier than she did. He could say things – she never could. So naturally it was always he that said the things, and then for some reason he would mind this suddenly, and would reproach her. A heartless woman he called her; she never told him that she loved him. But it was not so – it was not so. It was only that she never could say what she felt. Was there no crumb on his coat? Nothing she could do for him? Getting up she stood at the window with the reddish-brown stocking in her hands, partly to turn away from him, partly because she did not mind looking now, with him watching, at the Lighthouse. For she knew that he had turned his head as she turned; he was watching her. She knew that he was thinking, You are more beautiful than ever. And she felt herself very beautiful. Will you not tell me just for once that you love me? He was thinking that, for he was roused, what with Minta and his book, and its being the end of the day and their having quarrelled about going to the Lighthouse. But she could not do it; she could not say it. Then, knowing that he was watching her, instead of saying anything she turned, holding her stocking, and looked at him. And as she looked at him she began to smile, for though she had not said a word, he knew, of course he knew, that she loved him. He could not deny it. And smiling she looked out of the window and said (thinking to herself, Nothing on earth can equal this happiness) –

'Yes, you were right. It's going to be wet tomorrow.' She had not said it, but he knew it. And she looked at him smiling. For she had triumphed again.

CHAPTER 2

Time Passes

I

'Well, we must wait for the future to show,' said Mr Bankes, coming in from the terrace.

'It's almost too dark to see,' said Andrew, coming up from the beach.

'One can hardly tell which is the sea and which is the land,' said Prue.

'Do we leave that light burning?' said Lily as they took their coats off indoors.

'No,' said Prue, 'not if everyone's in.'

'Andrew,' she called back, 'just put out the light in the hall.'

One by one the lamps were all extinguished, except that Mr Carmichael, who liked to lie awake a little reading Virgil, kept his candle burning rather longer than the rest.

II

So with the lamps all put out, the moon sunk, and a thin rain drumming on the roof a downpouring of immense darkness began. Nothing, it seemed, could survive the flood, the profusion of darkness which, creeping in at keyholes and crevices, stole round window blinds, came into bedrooms, swallowed up here a jug and basin, there a bowl of red and yellow dahlias, there the sharp edges and firm bulk of a chest of drawers. Not only was furniture confounded; there was scarcely anything left of body or mind by which one could say 'This is he' or 'This is she.' Sometimes a hand was raised as if to clutch something or ward off something, or somebody groaned, or somebody laughed aloud as if sharing a joke with nothingness.

Nothing stirred in the drawing-room or in the diningroom or on the staircase. Only through the rusty hinges and swollen sea-moistened woodwork certain airs, detached from the body of the wind (the house was ramshackle after all) crept round corners and ventured indoors. Almost one might imagine them, as they entered the drawing-room, questioning and wondering, toying with the flap of hanging wall-paper, asking, would it hang much longer, when would it fall? Then smoothly brushing the walls, they passed on musingly as if asking the red and yellow roses on the wall-paper whether they would fade, and questioning (gently, for there was time at their disposal) the torn letters in the wastepaper basket, the flowers, the books, all of which were now open to them and asking, Were they allies? Were they enemies? How long would they endure?

So some random light directing them from some uncovered star, or wandering ship, or the Lighthouse even, with its pale footfall upon stair and mat, the little airs mounted the staircase and nosed round bedroom doors. But here surely, they must cease. Whatever else may perish and disappear what lies here is steadfast. Here one might say to those sliding lights, those fumbling airs, that breathe and bend over the bed itself, here you can neither touch nor destroy. Upon which, wearily, ghostlily as if they had feather-light fingers and the light persistency of feathers, they would look, once, on the shut eyes and the loosely clasping fingers, and fold their garments wearily and disappear. And so, nosing, rubbing, they went to the window on the staircase, to the servants' bedrooms, to the boxes in the attics; descending, blanched the apples on the diningroom table, fumbled the petals of roses, tried the picture on the easel, brushed the mat and blew a little sand along the floor. At length, desisting, all ceased together, gathered together, all sighed together; all together gave off an aimless gust of lamentation to which some door in the kitchen replied; swung wide; admitted nothing; and slammed to.

[Here Mr Carmichael, who was reading Virgil, blew out his candle. It was past midnight.]

III

But what after all is one night? A short space, especially when the darkness dims so soon, and so soon a bird sings, a cock crows, or a faint green quickens, like a turning leaf, in the hollow of the wave. Night, however, succeeds to night. The winter holds a pack of them in store and deals them equally, evenly, with indefatigable fingers. They lengthen; they darken. Some of them hold aloft clear planets, plates of brightness. The autumn trees, ravaged as they are, take on the flash of tattered flags kindling in the gloom of cool cathedral caves where gold letters on marble pages describe death in battle and how bones bleach and burn far away in Indian sands. The autumn trees gleam in the yellow moonlight, in the light of harvest moons, the light which mellows the energy of labour, and smooths the stubble, and brings the wave lapping blue to the shore.

It seemed now as if, touched by human penitence and all its toil, divine goodness had parted the curtain and displayed behind it, single, distinct, the hare erect; the wave falling; the boat rocking, which, did we deserve them, should be ours always. But alas, divine goodness, twitching the cord, draws the curtain; it does not please him; he covers his treasures in a drench of hail, and so breaks them, so confuses them that it seems impossible that their calm should ever return or that we should ever compose from their fragments a perfect whole or read in the littered pieces the clear words of truth. For our penitence deserves a glimpse only; our toil respite only.

The nights now are full of wind and destruction; the trees plunge and bend and their leaves fly helter skelter until the lawn is plastered with them and they lie packed in gutters and choke rain pipes and scatter damp paths. Also the sea tosses itself and breaks itself, and should any sleeper fancying that he might find on the beach an answer to his doubts, a sharer of his solitude, throw off his bedclothes and go down by himself to walk on the sand, no image with semblance of serving and divine promptitude comes readily to hand bringing the night to order and making the world reflect the compass of the soul. The hand dwindles in his hand; the voice bellows in his ear. Almost it would appear that it is useless in such confusion to ask the night those questions as to what, and why, and wherefore, which tempt the sleeper from his bed to seek an answer.

[Mr Ramsay stumbling along a passage stretched his arms out one dark morning, but, Mrs Ramsay having died rather suddenly the night before, he stretched his arms out. They remained empty.]

IV

So with the house empty and the doors locked and the mattresses rolled round, those stray airs, advance guards of great armies, blustered in, brushed bare boards, nibbled and fanned, met nothing in bedroom or drawing-room that wholly resisted them but only hangings that flapped, wood that creaked, the bare legs of tables, saucepans and china already furred, tarnished, cracked. What people had shed and left – a pair of shoes, a shooting cap, some faded skirts and coats in wardrobes – those alone kept the human shape and in the emptiness indicated how once they were filled and animated; how once hands were busy with hooks and buttons; how once the looking-glass had held a face; had held a world hollowed out in which a figure turned, a hand flashed, the door opened, in came children rushing and tumbling; and went out again. Now, day after day, light turned, like a flower reflected in water, its clear image on the wall opposite.

Only the shadows of the trees, flourishing in the wind, made obeisance on the wall, and for a moment darkened the pool in which light reflected itself; or birds, flying, made a soft spot flutter slowly across the bedroom floor.

So loveliness reigned and stillness, and together made the shape of loveliness itself, a form from which life had parted; solitary like a pool at evening, far distant, seen from a train window, vanishing so quickly that the pool, pale in the evening, is scarcely robbed of its solitude, though once seen. Loveliness and stillness clasped hands in the bedroom, and among the shrouded jugs and sheeted chairs even the prying of the wind, and the soft nose of the clammy sea airs, rubbing, snuffling, iterating, and reiterating their questions – 'Will you fade? Will you perish?' – scarcely disturbed the peace, the indifference, the air of pure integrity, as if the question they asked scarcely needed that they should answer: we remain.

Nothing it seemed could break that image, corrupt that innocence, or disturb the swaying mantle of silence which, week after week, in the empty room, wove into itself the falling cries of birds, ships hooting, the drone and hum of the fields, a dog's bark, a man's shout, and folded them round the house in silence. Once only a board sprang on the landing; once in the middle of the night with a roar, with a rupture, as after centuries of quiescence, a rock rends itself from the mountain and hurtles crashing into the valley, one fold of the shawl loosened and swung to and fro. Then again peace descended; and the shadow wavered; light bent to its own image in adoration on the bedroom wall; when Mrs McNab, tearing the veil of silence with hands that had stood in the wash-tub, grinding it with boots that had crunched the shingle, came as directed to open all windows, and dust the bedrooms.

V

As she lurched (for she rolled like a ship at sea) and leered (for her eyes fell on nothing directly, but with a sidelong glance that deprecated the scorn and anger of the world – she was witless, she knew it), as she clutched the banisters and hauled herself upstairs and rolled from room to room, she sang. Rubbing the glass of the long looking-glass and leering sideways at her swinging figure a sound issued from her lips – something that had been gay twenty years before on the stage perhaps, had been hummed and danced to, but now, coming from the toothless, bonneted, care-taking woman, was robbed of meaning, was like the voice of witlessness, humour, persistency itself, trodden down but springing up again, so that as she lurched, dusting, wiping, she seemed to say how it was one long sorrow and trouble, how it was getting up and going to bed again, and bringing things out and putting them away again. It was not easy or snug this world she had known for close on seventy years. Bowed down she was with weariness. How long, she asked, creaking and groaning on her knees under the bed, dusting the boards, how long shall it endure? but hobbled to her feet again, pulled herself up, and again with her sidelong leer which slipped and turned aside even from her own face, and her own sorrows, stood and gaped in the glass, aimlessly smiling, and began again the old amble and hobble, taking up mats, putting down china, looking sideways in the glass, as if, after all, she had her consolations, as if indeed there twined about her dirge some incorrigible hope. Visions of joy there must have been at the wash-tub, say with her children (yet two had been base-born and one had deserted her), at the public-house, drinking; turning over scraps in her drawers. Some cleavage of the dark there must have been, some channel in the depths of obscurity through which light enough issued to twist her face grinning in the glass and make her, turning to her job again, mumble out the old music hall song. Meanwhile the mystic, the visionary, walked the beach, stirred a puddle, looked at a stone, and asked themselves 'What am I?' 'What is this?' and suddenly an answer was vouchsafed them (what it was they could not say): so that they were warm in the frost and had comfort in the desert. But Mrs McNab continued to drink and gossip as before.

VI

The spring without a leaf to toss, bare and bright like a virgin fierce in her chastity, scornful in her purity, was laid out on fields wide-eyed and watchful and entirely careless of what was done or thought by the beholders.

[Prue Ramsay, leaning on her father's arm, was given in marriage that May. What, people said, could have been more fitting? And, they added, how beautiful she looked!]

As summer neared, as the evenings lengthened, there came to the wakeful, the hopeful, walking the beach, stirring the pool, imaginations of the strangest kind – of flesh turned to atoms which drove before the wind, of stars flashing in their hearts, of cliff, sea, cloud, and sky brought purposely together to assemble outwardly the scattered parts of the vision within. In those mirrors, the minds of men, in those pools of uneasy water, in which clouds for ever turn and shadows form, dreams persisted, and it was impossible to resist the strange intimation which every gull, flower, tree, man and woman, and the white earth itself seemed to declare (but if questioned at once to withdraw) that good triumphs, happiness prevails, order rules; or to resist the extraordinary stimulus to range hither and thither in search of some absolute good, some crystal of intensity, remote from the known pleasures and familiar virtues, something alien to the processes of domestic life, single, hard, bright, like a diamond in the sand, which would render the possessor secure. Moreover, softened and acquiescent, the spring with her bees humming and gnats dancing threw her cloak about her, veiled her eyes, averted her head, and among passing shadows and flights of small rain seemed to have taken upon her a knowledge of the sorrows of mankind.

[Prue Ramsay died that summer in some illness connected with childbirth, which was indeed a tragedy, people said. They said nobody deserved happiness more.]

And now in the heat of summer the wind sent its spies about the house again. Flies wove a web in the sunny rooms; weeds that had grown close to the glass in the night tapped methodically at the window pane. When darkness fell, the stroke of the Lighthouse, which had laid itself with such authority upon the carpet in the darkness, tracing its pattern, came now in the softer light of spring mixed with moonlight gliding gently as if it laid its caress and lingered stealthily and looked and came lovingly again. But in the very lull of this loving caress, as the long stroke leant upon the bed, the rock was rent asunder; another fold of the shawl loosened; there it hung, and swayed. Through the short summer nights and the long summer days, when the empty rooms seemed to murmur with the echoes of the fields and the hum of flies, the long streamer waved gently, swayed aimlessly; while the sun so striped and barred the rooms and filled them with yellow haze that Mrs McNab, when she broke in and lurched about, dusting, sweeping, looked like a tropical fish oaring its way through sunlanced waters.

But slumber and sleep though it might there came later in the summer ominous sounds like the measured blows of hammers dulled on felt, which, with their repeated shocks still further loosened the shawl and cracked the tea-cups. Now and again some glass tinkled in the cupboard as if a giant voice had shrieked so loud in its agony that tumblers stood inside a cupboard vibrated too. Then again silence fell; and then, night after night, and sometimes in plain mid-day when the roses were bright and light turned on the wall its shape clearly there seemed to drop into this silence this indifference, this integrity, the thud of something falling.

[A shell exploded. Twenty or thirty young men were blown up in France, among them Andrew Ramsay, whose death, mercifully, was instantaneous.]

At that season those who had gone down to pace the beach and ask of the sea and sky what message they reported or what vision they affirmed had to consider among the usual tokens of divine bounty – the sunset on the sea, the pallor of dawn, the moon rising, fishing-boats against the moon, and children pelting each other with handfuls of grass, something out of harmony with this jocundity, this serenity. There was the silent apparition of an ashen-coloured ship for instance, come, gone; there was a purplish stain upon the bland surface of the sea as if something had boiled and bled, invisibly, beneath. This intrusion into a scene calculated to stir the most sublime reflections and lead to the most comfortable conclusions stayed their pacing. It was difficult blandly to overlook them, to abolish their significance in the landscape; to continue, as one walked by the sea, to marvel how beauty outside mirrored beauty within.

Did Nature supplement what man advanced? Did she complete what he began? With equal complacence she saw his misery, condoned his meanness, and acquiesced in his torture. That dream, then, of sharing, completing, finding in solitude on the beach an answer, was but a reflection in a mirror, and the mirror itself was but the surface glassiness which forms in quiescence when the nobler powers sleep beneath? Impatient, despairing yet loth to go (for beauty offers her lures, has her consolations), to pace the beach was impossible; contemplation was unendurable; the mirror was broken.

[Mr Carmichael brought out a volume of poems that spring, which had an unexpected success. The war, people said, had revived their interest in poetry.]

VII

Night after night, summer and winter, the torment of storms, the arrow-like stillness of fine weather, held their court without interference. Listening (had there been any one to listen) from the upper rooms of the empty house only gigantic chaos streaked with lightning could have been heard tumbling and tossing, as the winds and waves disported themselves like the amorphous bulks of leviathans whose brows are pierced by no light of reason, and mounted one on top of another, and lunged and plunged in the darkness or the daylight (for night and day, month and year ran shapelessly together) in idiot games, until it seemed as if the universe were battling and tumbling, in brute confusion and wanton lust aimlessly by itself.

In spring the garden urns, casually filled with windblown plants, were gay as ever. Violets came and daffodils. But the stillness and the brightness of the day were as strange as the chaos and tumult of night, with the trees standing there, and the flowers standing there, looking before them, looking up, yet beholding nothing, eyeless, and so terrible.

VIII

Thinking no harm, for the family would not come, never again, some said, and the house would be sold at Michaelmas perhaps, Mrs McNab stooped and picked a bunch of flowers to take home with her. She laid them on the table while she dusted. She was fond of flowers. It was a pity to let them waste. Suppose the house were sold (she stood arms akimbo in front of the looking-glass) it would want seeing to – it would. There it had stood all these years without a soul in it. The books and things were mouldy, for, what with the war and help being hard to get, the house had not been cleaned as she could have wished. It was beyond one person's strength to get it straight now. She was too old. Her legs pained her. All those books needed to be laid out on the grass in the sun; there was plaster fallen in the hall; the rain-pipe had blocked over the study window and let the water in; the carpet was ruined quite. But people should come themselves; they should have sent somebody down to see. For there were clothes in the cupboards; they had left clothes in all the bedrooms. What was she to do with them? They had the moth in them – Mrs Ramsay's things. Poor lady! She would never want *them* again. She was dead, they said;

years ago, in London. There was the old grey cloak she wore gardening. (Mrs McNab fingered it.) She could see her, as she came up the drive with the washing, stooping over her flowers (the garden was a pitiful sight now, all run to riot, and rabbits scuttling at you out of the beds) – she could see her with one of the children by her in that grey cloak. There were boots and shoes; and a brush and comb left on the dressing-table, for all the world as if she expected to come back tomorrow. (She had died very sudden at the end, they said.) And once they had been coming, but had put off coming, what with the war, and travel being so difficult these days; they had never come all these years; just sent her money; but never wrote, never came, and expected to find things as they had left them, ah dear! Why the dressing-table drawers were full of things (she pulled them open), handkerchiefs, bits of ribbon. Yes, she could see Mrs Ramsay as she came up the drive with the washing.

'Good evening, Mrs McNab,' she would say.

She had a pleasant way with her. The girls all liked her. But dear, many things had changed since then (she shut the drawer); many families had lost their dearest. So she was dead; and Mr Andrew killed; and Miss Prue dead too, they said, with her first baby; but every one had lost some one these years. Prices had gone up shamefully, and didn't come down again neither. She could well remember her in her grey cloak.

'Good evening, Mrs McNab,' she said, and told cook to keep a plate of milk soup for her – quite thought she wanted it, carrying that heavy basket all the way up from town. She could see her now, stooping over her flowers; (and faint and flickering, like a yellow beam or the circle at the end of a telescope, a lady in a grey cloak, stooping over her flowers, went wandering over the bedroom wall, up the dressing-table, across the washstand, as Mrs McNab hobbled and ambled, dusting, straightening).

And cook's name now? Mildred? Marian? – some name like that. Ah, she had forgotten – she did forget things. Fiery, like all red-haired women. Many a laugh they had had. She was always welcome in the kitchen. She made them laugh, she did. Things were better then than now.

She sighed; there was too much work for one woman. She wagged her head this side and that. This had been the nursery. Why, it was all damp in here; the plaster was falling. Whatever did they want to hang a beast's skull there for? gone mouldy too. And rats in all the attics. The rain came in. But they never sent; never came. Some of the locks had gone, so the doors banged. She didn't like to be up here at dusk alone neither. It was too much for one woman, too much, too much. She creaked, she moaned. She banged the door. She turned the key in the lock, and left the house shut up, locked, alone.

IX

The house was left; the house was deserted. It was left like a shell on a sandhill to fill with dry salt grains now that life had left it. The long night seemed to have set in; the trifling airs, nibbling, the clammy breaths, fumbling, seemed to have triumphed. The saucepan had rusted and the mat decayed. Toads had nosed their way in. Idly, aimlessly, the swaying shawl swung to and fro. A thistle thrust itself between the tiles in the larder. The swallows nested in the drawing-room; the floor was strewn with straw; the plaster fell in shovelfuls; rafters were laid bare; rats carried off this and that to gnaw behind the wainscots. Tortoise-shell butterflies burst from the chrysalis and pattered their life out on the windowpane. Poppies sowed themselves among the dahlias; the lawn waved with long grass; giant artichokes towered among roses; a fringed carnation flowered among the cabbages; while the gentle tapping of a weed at the window had become, on winters' nights, a drumming from sturdy trees and thorned briars which made the whole room green in summer.

What power could now prevent the fertility, the insensibility of nature? Mrs McNab's dream of a lady, of a child, of a plate of milk soup? It had wavered over the walls like a spot of sunlight and vanished. She had locked the door; she had gone. It was beyond the strength of one woman, she said. They never sent. They never wrote. There were things up there rotting in the drawers – it was a shame to leave them so, she said. The place was gone to rack and ruin. Only the Lighthouse beam entered the rooms for a moment, sent its sudden stare over bed and wall in the darkness of winter, looked with equanimity at the thistle and the swallow, the rat and the straw. Nothing now withstood them; nothing said no to them. Let the wind blow; let the poppy seed itself and the carnation mate with the cabbage. Let the swallow build in the drawing-room, and the thistle thrust aside the tiles, and the butterfly sun itself on the faded chintz of the arm-chairs. Let the broken glass and the china lie out on the lawn and be tangled over with grass and wild berries.

For now had come that moment, that hesitation when dawn trembles and night pauses, when if a feather alight in the scale it will be weighed down. One feather, and the house, sinking, falling, would have turned and pitched downwards to the depths of darkness. In the ruined room, picnickers would have lit their kettles; lovers sought shelter there, lying on the bare boards; and the shepherd stored his dinner on the bricks, and the tramp slept with his coat round him to ward off the cold. Then the roof would have fallen; briars and hemlocks would have blotted out path, step, and window; would have grown, unequally but lustily over the mound, until some tres-passer, losing his way, could have told only by a red-hot poker among the nettles, or a scrap of china in the hemlock, that here once some one had lived; there had been a house.

If the feather had fallen, if it had tipped the scale down-wards, the whole house would have plunged to the depths to lie upon the sands of oblivion. But there was a force working; something not highly conscious; something that leered, some-thing that lurched; something not inspired to go about its work with dignified ritual or solemn chanting. Mrs McNab groaned; Mrs Bast creaked. They were old; they were stiff; their legs ached. They came with their brooms and pails at last; they got to work. All of a sudden, would Mrs McNab see that the house was ready, one of the young ladies wrote: would she get this done; would she get that done; all in a hurry. They might be coming for the summer; had left everything to the last; expected to find things as they had left them. Slowly and painfully, with broom and pail, mopping, scouring, Mrs McNab, Mrs Bast stayed the corruption and the rot; rescued from the pool of Time that was fast closing over them now a basin, now a cupboard; fetched up from oblivion all the Waverley novels and a tea-set one morning; in the after-noon restored to sun and air a brass fender and a set of steel fire-irons. George, Mrs Bast's son, caught the rats, and cut the grass. They had the builders. Attended with the creaking of hinges and the screeching of bolts, the slamming and banging of damp-swollen woodwork, some rusty laborious birth seemed to be taking place, as the women, stooping, rising, groaning, singing, slapped and slammed, upstairs now, now down in the cellars. Oh, they said, the work!

They drank their tea in the bedroom sometimes, or in the study; breaking off work at mid-day with the smudge on their faces, and their old hands clasped and cramped with the broom handles. Flopped on chairs they contemplated now the magnificent conquest over taps and bath; now the more arduous, more partial triumph over long rows of books, black as ravens once, now white-stained, breeding pale mushrooms and secreting furtive spiders. Once more, as she felt the tea warm in her, the telescope fitted itself to Mrs McNab's eyes, and in a ring of light she saw the old gentleman, lean as a rake, wagging his head, as she came up with the washing, talking to himself, she supposed, on the lawn. He never noticed her. Some said he was dead; some said she was dead. Which was it? Mrs Bast didn't know for certain either. The young gentleman was dead. That she was sure. She had read his name in the papers.

There was the cook now, Mildred, Marian, some such name as that – a red-headed woman, quick-tempered like all her sort, but kind, too, if you knew the way with her. Many a laugh they had had together. She saved a plate of soup for Maggie; a bite of ham, sometimes; whatever was over. They lived well in those days. They had everything they wanted (glibly, jovially, with the tea hot in her, she unwound her ball of memories, sitting in the wicker arm-chair by the nursery fender). There was always plenty doing, people in the house, twenty staying sometimes, and washing up till long past midnight.

Mrs Bast (she had never known them; had lived in Glasgow at that time) wondered, putting her cup down, whatever they hung that beast's skull there for? Shot in foreign parts no doubt.

It might well be, said Mrs McNab, wantoning on with her memories; they had friends in eastern countries; gentlemen staying there, ladies in evening dress; she had seen them once through the dining-room door all sitting at dinner. Twenty she dared say in all their jewellery, and she asked to stay help wash up, might be till after midnight.

Ah, said Mrs Bast, they'd find it changed. She leant out of the window. She watched her son George scything the grass. They might well ask, what had been done to it? seeing how old Kennedy was supposed to have charge of it, and then his leg got so bad after he fell from the cart; and perhaps then no one for a year, or the better part of one; and then Davie Macdonald, and seeds might be sent, but who should say if they were ever planted? They'd find it changed.

She watched her son scything. He was a great one for work – one of those quiet ones. Well they must be getting along with the cupboards, she supposed. They hauled themselves up.

At last, after days of labour within, of cutting and digging without, dusters were flicked from the windows, the windows were shut to, keys were turned all over the house; the front door was banged; it was finished.

And now as if the cleaning and the scrubbing and the scything and the mowing had drowned it there rose that half-heard melody, that intermittent music which the ear half catches but lets fall; a bark, a bleat; irregular, intermittent, yet somehow related; the hum of an insect, the tremor of cut grass, dissevered yet somehow belonging; the jar of a dor beetle, the squeak of a wheel, loud, low, but mysteriously related; which the ear strains to bring together and is always on the verge of harmonising but they are never quite heard, never fully harmonised, and at last, in the evening, one after another the sounds die out, and the harmony falters, and silence falls. With the sunset sharpness was lost, and like mist rising, quiet rose, quiet spread, the wind settled; loosely the world shook itself down to sleep, darkly here without a light to it, save what came green suffused through leaves, or pale on the white flowers by the window.

[Lily Briscoe had her bag carried up to the house late one evening in September. Mr Carmichael came by the same train.]

X

Then indeed peace had come. Messages of peace breathed from the sea to the shore. Never to break its sleep any more, to lull it rather more deeply to rest and whatever the dreamers dreamt holily, dreamt wisely, to confirm – what else was it murmuring – as Lily Briscoe laid her head on the pillow in the clean still room and heard the sea. Through the open window the voice of the beauty of the world came murmuring, too softly to hear exactly what it said – but what mattered if the meaning were plain? – entreating the sleepers (the house was full again; Mrs Beckwith was staying there, also Mr Carmichael), if they would not actually come down to the beach itself at least to lift the blind and look out. They would see then night flowing down in purple; his head crowned; his sceptre jewelled; and how in his eyes a child might look. And if they still faltered (Lily was tired out with travelling and slept almost at once; but Mr Carmichael read a book by candlelight), if they still said no, that it was vapour this splendour of his, and the dew had more power than he, and they preferred sleeping; gently then without complaint, or argument, the voice would sing its song. Gently the waves would break (Lily heard them in her sleep); tenderly the light fell (it seemed to come through her eyelids). And it all looked, Mr Carmichael thought, shutting his book, falling asleep, much as it used to look years ago.

Indeed the voice might resume, as the curtains of dark wrapped themselves over the house, over Mrs Beckwith, Mr Carmichael, and Lily Briscoe so that they lay with several folds of blackness on their eyes, why not accept this, be content with this, acquiesce and resign? The sigh of all the seas breaking in measure round the isles soothed them; the night wrapped them; nothing broke their sleep, until, the birds beginning and the dawn weaving their thin voices in to its whiteness, a cart grinding, a dog somewhere barking, the sun lifted the curtains, broke the veil on their eyes, and Lily Briscoe stirring in her sleep clutched at her blankets as a faller clutches at the turf on the edge of a cliff. Her eyes opened wide. Here she was again, she thought, sitting bolt upright in bed. Awake.

CHAPTER 3

The Lighthouse

I

What does it mean then, what can it all mean? Lily Briscoe asked herself, wondering whether, since she had been left alone, it behoved her to go to the kitchen to fetch another cup of coffee or wait here. What does it mean? – a catchword that was, caught up from some book, fitting her thought loosely, for she could not, this first morning with the Ramsays, contract her feelings, could only make a phrase resound to cover the blankness of her mind until these vapours had shrunk. For really, what did she feel, come back after all these years and Mrs Ramsay dead? Nothing, nothing – nothing that she could express at all.

She had come late last night when it was all mysterious, dark. Now she was awake, at her old place at the breakfast table, but alone. It was very early too, not yet eight. There was this expedition – they were going to the Lighthouse, Mr Ramsay, Cam, and James. They should have gone already – they had to catch the tide or something. And Cam was not ready and James was not ready and Nancy had forgotten to order the sandwiches and Mr Ramsay had lost his temper and banged out of the room.

'What's the use of going now?' he had stormed.

Nancy had vanished. There he was, marching up and down the terrace in a rage. One seemed to hear doors slamming and voices calling all over the house. Now Nancy burst in, and asked, looking round the room, in a queer half dazed, half desperate way, 'What does one send to the Lighthouse?' as if she were forcing herself to do what she despaired of ever being able to do.

What does one send to the Lighthouse indeed! At any other time Lily could have suggested reasonably tea, tobacco, newspapers. But this morning everything seemed so extraordinarily queer that a question like Nancy's – What does one send to the Lighthouse? – opened doors in one's mind that went banging and swinging to and fro and made one keep asking, in a stupefied gape, What does one send? What does one do? Why is one sitting here after all?

Sitting alone (for Nancy went out again) among the clean cups at the long table she felt cut off from other people, and able only to go on watching, asking, wondering. The house, the place, the morning, all seemed strangers to her. She had no attachment here, she felt, no relations with it, anything might happen, and whatever did happen, a step outside, a voice calling ('It's not in the cupboard; it's on the landing,' some one cried), was a question, as if the link that usually bound things together had been cut, and they floated up here, down there, off, anyhow. How aimless it was, how chaotic, how unreal it was, she thought, looking at her empty coffee cup. Mrs Ramsay dead; Andrew killed; Prue dead too – repeat it as she might, it roused no feeling in her. And we all get together in a house like this on a morning like this, she said, looking out of the window – it was a beautiful still day.

Suddenly Mr Ramsay raised his head as he passed and looked straight at her, with his distraught wild gaze which was yet so penetrating, as if he saw you, for one second, for the first time, for ever; and she pretended to drink out of her empty coffee cup so as to escape him – to escape his demand on her, to put aside a moment longer that imperious need. And he shook his head at her, and strode on ('Alone' she heard him say, 'Perished' she heard him say) and like everything else this strange morning the words became symbols, wrote themselves all over the grey-green walls. If only she could put them together, she felt, write them out in some sentence, then she would have got at the truth of things. Old Mr Carmichael came padding softly in, fetched his coffee, took his cup and made off to sit in the sun. The extraordinary unreality was frightening; but it was also exciting. Going to the Lighthouse. But what does one send to the Lighthouse? Perished. Alone. The grey-green light on the wall opposite. The empty places. Such were some of the parts, but how bring them together? she asked. As if any interruption would break the frail shape she was building on the table she turned her back to the window lest Mr Ramsay should see her. She must escape somehow, be alone somewhere. Suddenly she remembered. When she had sat there last ten years ago there had been a little sprig or leaf pattern on the table-cloth, which she had looked at in a moment of revelation. There had been a problem about a foreground of a picture. Move the tree to the middle, she had said. She had never finished that picture. It had been knocking about in her mind all these years. She would paint that picture now. Where were her paints, she wondered? Her paints, yes. She had left them in the hall last night. She would start at once. She got up quickly, before Mr Ramsay turned.

She fetched herself a chair. She pitched her easel with her precise old-maidish movements on the edge of the lawn, not too close to Mr Carmichael, but close enough for his protection. Yes, it must have been precisely here that she had stood ten years ago. There was the wall; the hedge; the tree. The question was of some relation between those masses. She had borne it in her mind all these years. It seemed as if the solution had come to her: she knew now what she wanted to do.

But with Mr Ramsay bearing down on her, she could

do nothing. Every time he approached – he was walking up and down the terrace – ruin approached, chaos approached. She could not paint. She stooped, she turned; she took up this rag; she squeezed that tube. But all she did was to ward him off a moment. He made it impossible for her to do anything. For if she gave him the least chance, if he saw her disengaged a moment, looking his way a moment, he would be on her, saying, as he had said last night, 'You find us much changed.' Last night he had got up and stopped before her, and said that. Dumb and staring though they had all sat, the six children whom they used to call after the Kings and Queens of England – the Red, the Fair, the Wicked, the Ruthless, – she felt how they raged under it. Kind old Mrs Beckwith said something sensible. But it was a house full of unrelated passions – she had felt that all the evening. And on top of this chaos Mr Ramsay got up, pressed her hand, and said: 'You will find us much changed' and none of them had moved or had spoken; but had sat there as if they were forced to let him say it. Only James (certainly the Sullen) scowled at the lamp; and Cam screwed her handkerchief round her finger. Then he reminded them that they were going to the Lighthouse tomorrow. They must be ready, in the hall, on the stroke of half-past seven. Then, with his hand on the door, he stopped; he turned upon them. Did they not want to go? he demanded. Had they dared say No (he had some reason for wanting it) he would have flung himself tragically backwards into the bitter waters of despair. Such a gift he had for gesture. He looked like a king in exile. Doggedly James said yes. Cam stumbled more wretchedly. Yes, oh yes, they'd both be ready, they said. And it struck her, this was tragedy – not palls, dust, and the shroud; but children coerced, their spirits subdued. James was sixteen, Cam seventeen, perhaps. She had looked round for someone who was not there, for Mrs Ramsay, presumably. But there was only kind Mrs Beckwith turning over her sketches under the lamp. Then, being tired, her mind still rising and falling with the sea, the taste and smell that places have after long absence possessing her, the candles wavering in her eyes, she had lost herself and gone under. It was a wonderful night, starlit; the waves sounded as they went upstairs; the moon surprised them, enormous, pale, as they passed the staircase window. She had slept at once.

She set her clean canvas firmly upon the easel, as a barrier, frail, but she hoped sufficiently substantial to ward off Mr Ramsay and his exactingness. She did her best to look, when his back was turned, at her picture; that line there, that mass there. But it was out of the question. Let him be fifty feet away, let him not even speak to you, let him not even see you, he permeated, he prevailed, he imposed himself. He changed everything. She could not see the colour; she could not see the lines; even with his back turned to her, she could only think, But he'll be down on me in a moment, demanding – something she felt she could not give him. She rejected one brush; she chose another. When would those children come? When would they all be off? she fidgeted. That man, she thought, her anger rising in her, never gave; that man took. She, on the other hand, would be forced to give. Mrs Ramsay had given. Giving, giving, giving, she had died – and had left all this. Really, she was angry with Mrs Ramsay. With the brush slightly trembling in her fingers she looked at the hedge, the step, the wall. It was all Mrs Ramsay's doing. She was dead. Here was Lily, at forty-four, wasting her time, unable to do a thing, standing there, playing at painting, playing at the one thing one did not play at, and it was all Mrs Ramsay's fault. She was dead. The step where she used to sit was empty. She was dead.

But why repeat this over and over again? Why be always trying to bring up some feeling she had not got? There was a kind of blasphemy in it. It was all dry: all withered: all spent. They ought not to have asked her; she ought not to have come. One can't waste one's time at forty-four, she thought. She hated playing at painting. A brush, the one dependable thing in a world of strife, ruin, chaos – that one should not play with, knowingly even: she detested it. But he made her. You shan't touch your canvas, he seemed to say, bearing down on her, till you've given me what I want of you. Here he was, close upon her again, greedy, distraught. Well, thought Lily in despair, letting her right hand fall at her side, it would be simpler then to have it over. Surely she could imitate from recollection the glow, the rhapsody, the self-surrender she had seen on so many women's faces (on Mrs Ramsay's, for instance) when on some occasion like this they blazed up – she could remember the look on Mrs Ramsay's face – into a rapture of sympathy, of delight in the reward they had, which, though the reason of it escaped her, evidently conferred on them the most supreme bliss of which human nature was capable. Here he was, stopped by her side. She would give him what she could.

II

She seemed to have shrivelled slightly, he thought. She looked a little skimpy, wispy; but not unattractive. He liked her. There had been some talk of her marrying William Bankes once, but nothing had come of it. His wife had been fond of her. He had been a little out of temper too at breakfast. And then, and then – this was one of those moments when an enormous need urged him, without being conscious what it was, to approach any woman, to force them, he did not care how, his need was so great, to give him what he wanted: sympathy.

Was anybody looking after her? he said. Had she every-thing she wanted?

'Oh, thanks, everything,' said Lily Briscoe nervously. No; she could not do it. She ought to have floated off instantly upon some wave of sympathetic expansion: the pressure on her was tremendous. But she remained stuck. There was an awful pause. They both looked at the sea. Why, thought Mr Ramsay, should she look at the sea when I am here? She hoped it would be calm enough for them to land at the Lighthouse, she said. The Lighthouse! The Lighthouse! What's that got to do with it? he thought impatiently. Instantly, with the force of some primeval gust (for really he could not restrain himself any longer), there issued from him such a groan that any other woman in the whole world would have done something, said something – all except myself, thought Lily, girding at herself bitterly, who am not a woman, but a peevish, ill-tempered, dried-up old maid presumably.

Mr Ramsay sighed to the full. He waited. Was she not going to say anything? Did she not see what he wanted from her? Then he said he had a particular reason for wanting to go to the Lighthouse. His wife used to send the men things. There was a poor boy with a tuberculous hip, the lightkeeper's son. He sighed profoundly. He sighed significantly. All Lily wished was that this enormous flood of grief, this insatiable hunger for sympathy, this demand that she should surrender herself up to him entirely, and even so he had sorrows enough to keep her supplied for ever, should leave her, should be diverted (she kept looking at the house, hoping for an interruption) before it swept her down in its flow.

'Such expeditions,' said Mr Ramsay, scraping the ground with his toe, 'are very painful.' Still Lily said nothing. (She is a stock, she is a stone, he said to himself.) 'They are very exhausting,' he said, looking, with a sickly look that nauseated her (he was acting, she felt, this great man was dramatising himself), at his beautiful hands. It was horrible, it was indecent. Would they never come, she asked, for she could not sustain this enormous weight of sorrow, support these heavy draperies of grief (he had assumed a pose of extreme decrepitude; he even tottered a little as he stood there) a moment longer.

Still she could say nothing; the whole horizon seemed swept bare of objects to talk about; could only feel, amazedly, as Mr Ramsay stood there, how his gaze seemed to fall dolefully over the sunny grass and discolour it, and cast over the rubicund, drowsy, entirely contented figure of Mr Carmichael, reading a French novel on a deck-chair, a veil of crape, as if such an existence, flaunting its prosperity in a world of woe, were enough to provoke the most dismal thoughts of all. Look at him, he seemed to be saying, look at me; and indeed, all the time he was feeling, Think of me, think of me. Ah, could that bulk only be wafted alongside of them, Lily wished; had she only pitched her easel a yard or two closer to him; a man, any man, would staunch this effusion, would stop these lamentations. A woman, she had provoked this horror; a woman, she should have known how to deal with it. It was immensely to her discredit, sexually, to stand there dumb. One said – what did one say? – Oh, Mr Ramsay! Dear Mr Ramsay! That was what that kind old lady who sketched, Mrs Beckwith, would have said instantly, and rightly. But no. They stood there, isolated from the rest of the world. His immense self-pity, his demand for sympathy poured and spread itself in pools at her feet, and all she did, miserable sinner that she was, was to draw her skirts a little closer round her ankles, lest she should get wet. In complete silence she stood there, grasping her paint brush.

Heaven could never be sufficiently praised! She heard sounds in the house. James and Cam must be coming. But Mr Ramsay, as if he knew that his time ran short, exerted upon her solitary figure the immense pressure of his concentrated woe; his age; his frailty; his desolation; when suddenly, tossing his head impatiently, in his annoyance – for, after all, what woman could resist him? – he noticed that his boot-laces were untied. Remarkable boots they were too, Lily thought, looking down at them: sculptured; colossal; like everything that Mr Ramsay wore, from his frayed tie to his half-buttoned waistcoat, his own indisputably. She could see them walking to his room of their own accord, expressive in his absence of pathos, surliness, ill-temper, charm.

'What beautiful boots!' she exclaimed. She was ashamed of herself. To praise his boots when he asked her to solace his soul; when he had shown her his bleeding hands, his lacerated heart, and asked her to pity them, then to say, cheerfully, 'Ah, but what beautiful boots you wear!' deserved, she knew, and she looked up expecting to get it, in one of his sudden roars of ill-temper, complete annihilation.

Instead, Mr Ramsay smiled. His pall, his draperies, his infirmities fell from him. Ah yes, he said, holding his foot up for her to look at, they were first-rate boots. There was only one man in England who could make boots like that. Boots are among the chief curses of mankind, he said. 'Bootmakers make it their business,' he exclaimed, 'to cripple and torture the human foot.' They are also the most obstinate and perverse of mankind. It had taken him the best part of his youth to get boots made as they should be made. He would have her observe (he lifted his right foot and then his left) that she had never seen boots made quite that shape before. They were made of the finest leather in the world, also. Most leather was mere brown paper and cardboard. He looked complacently at his foot, still held in the air. They had reached, she felt, a sunny island where peace dwelt, sanity reigned and the sun for ever shone, the blessed island of good boots. Her heart warmed to him. 'Now let me see if you can tie a knot,' he said. He poohpoohed her feeble system. He showed her his own invention. Once you tied it, it never came undone. Three times he knotted her shoe; three times he unknotted it.

Why, at this completely inappropriate moment, when he was stooping over her shoe, should she be so tormented with sympathy for him that, as she stooped too, the blood rushed to her face, and, thinking of her callousness (she had called him a play-actor) she felt her eyes swell and tingle with tears? Thus occupied he seemed to her a figure of infinite pathos. He tied knots. He bought boots. There was no helping Mr Ramsay on the journey he was going. But now just as she wished to say something, could have said something, perhaps, here they were – Cam and James. They appeared on the terrace. They came, lagging, side by side, a serious, melancholy couple.

But why was it like *that* they came? She could not help feeling annoyed with them; they might have come more cheerfully; they might have given him what, now that they were off, she would not have the chance of giving him. For she felt a sudden emptiness; a frustration. Her feeling had come too late; there it was ready; but he no longer needed it. He had become a very distinguished, elderly man, who had no need of her whatsoever. She felt snubbed. He slung a knapsack round his shoulders. He shared out the parcels – there were a number of them, ill tied, in brown paper. He sent Cam for a cloak. He had all the appearance of a leader making ready for an expedition. Then, wheeling about, he led the way with his firm military tread, in those wonderful boots, carrying brown paper parcels, down the path, his children following him. They looked, she thought, as if fate had devoted them to some stern enterprise, and they went to it, still young enough to be drawn acquiescent in their father's wake, obediently, but with a pallor in their eyes which made her feel that they suffered something beyond their years in silence. So they passed the edge of the lawn, and it seemed to Lily that she watched a procession go, drawn on by some stress of common feeling which made it, faltering and flagging as it was, a little company bound together and strangely impressive to her. Politely, but very distantly, Mr Ramsay raised his hand and saluted her as they passed.

But what a face, she thought, immediately finding the sympathy which she had not been asked to give troubling her for expression. What had made it like that? Thinking, night after night, she supposed – about the reality of kitchen tables, she added, remembering the symbol which in her vagueness as to what Mr Ramsay did think about Andrew had given her. (He had been killed by the splinter of a shell instantly, she bethought her.) The kitchen table was something visionary, austere; something bare, hard, not ornamental. There was no colour to it; it was all edges and angles; it was uncompromisingly plain. But Mr Ramsay kept always his eyes fixed upon it, never allowed himself to be distracted or deluded, until his face became worn too and ascetic and partook of this unornamented beauty which so deeply impressed her. Then, she recalled (standing where he had left her, holding her brush), worries had fretted it – not so nobly. He must have had his doubts about that table, she supposed; whether the table was a real table; whether it was worth the time he gave to it; whether he was able after all to find it. He had had doubts, she felt, or he would have asked less of people. That was what they talked about late at night sometimes, she suspected; and then next day Mrs Ramsay looked tired, and Lily flew into a rage with him over some absurd little thing. But now he had nobody to talk to about that table, or his boots, or his knots; and he was like a lion seeking whom he could devour, and his face had that touch of desperation, of exaggeration in it which alarmed her, and made her pull her skirts about her. And then, she recalled, there was that sudden revivication, that sudden flare (when she praised his boots), that sudden recovery of vitality and interest in ordinary human things, which too passed and changed (for he was always changing, and hid nothing) into that other final phase which was new to her and had, she owned, made herself ashamed of her own irritability, when it seemed as if he had shed worries and ambitions, and the hope of sympathy and the desire for praise, had entered some other region, was drawn on, as if by curiosity, in dumb colloquy, whether with himself or another, at the head of that little procession out of one's range. An extraordinary face! The gate banged.

III

So they're gone, she thought, sighing with relief and disappointment. Her sympathy seemed to fly back in her face, like a bramble sprung. She felt curiously divided, as if one part of her were drawn out there – it was a still day, hazy; the Lighthouse looked this morning at an immense distance; the other had fixed itself doggedly, solidly, here on the lawn. She saw her canvas as if it had floated up and placed itself white and uncompromising directly before her. It seemed to rebuke her with its cold stare for all this hurry and agitation; this folly and waste of emotion; it drastically recalled her and spread through her mind first a peace, as her disorderly sensations (he had gone and she had been so sorry for him and she had said nothing) trooped off the field; and then, emptiness. She looked blankly at the canvas, with its uncompromising white stare; from the canvas to the garden. There was something (she stood screwing up her little Chinese eyes in her small puckered face) something she remembered in the relations of those lines cutting across, slicing down, and in the mass of the hedge with its green cave of blues and browns, which had stayed in her mind; which had tied a knot in her mind so that at odds and ends of time, involuntarily, as she walked along the Brompton Road, as she brushed her hair, she found herself painting that picture, passing her eye over it, and untying the knot in imagination. But there was all the difference in the world between this planning airily away from the canvas, and actually taking her brush and making the first mark.

She had taken the wrong brush in her agitation at Mr Ramsay's presence, and her easel, rammed into the earth so nervously, was at the wrong angle. And now that she had put that right, and in so doing had subdued the impertinences and irrelevances that plucked her attention and made her remember how she was such and such a person, had such and such relations to people, she took her hand and raised her brush. For a moment it stayed trembling in a painful but exciting ecstasy in the air. Where to begin? – that was the question; at what point to make the first mark? One line placed on the canvas committed her to innumerable risks, to frequent and irrevocable decisions. All that in idea seemed simple became in practice immediately complex; as the waves shape themselves symmetrically from the cliff top, but to the swimmer among them are divided by steep gulfs, and foaming crests. Still the risk must be run; the mark made.

With a curious physical sensation, as if she were urged forward and at the same time must hold herself back, she made her first quick decisive stroke. The brush descended. It flickered brown over the white canvas; it left a running mark. A second time she did it – a third time. And so pausing and so flickering, she attained a dancing rhythmical movement, as if the pauses were one part of the rhythm and the strokes another, and all were related; and so, lightly and swiftly pausing, striking, she scored her canvas with brown running nervous lines which had no sooner settled there than they enclosed (she felt it looming out at her) a space. Down in the hollow of one wave she saw the next wave towering higher and higher above her. For what could be more formidable than that space? Here she was again, she thought, stepping back to look at it, drawn out of gossip, out of living, out of community with people into the presence of this formidable ancient enemy of hers – this other thing, this truth, this reality, which suddenly laid hands on her, emerged stark at the back of appearances and commanded her attention. She was half unwilling, half reluctant. Why always be drawn out and haled away? Why not left in peace, to talk to Mr Carmichael on the lawn? It was an exacting form of intercourse anyhow. Other worshipful objects were content with worship; men, women, God, all let one kneel prostrate; but this form, were it only the shape of a white lamp-shade looming on a wicker table, roused one to perpetual combat, challenged one to a fight in which one was bound to be worsted. Always (it was in her nature, or in her sex, she did not know which) before she exchanged the fluidity of life for the concentration of painting she had a few moments of nakedness when she seemed like an unborn soul, a soul reft of body, hesitating on some windy pinnacle and exposed without protection to all the blasts of doubt. Why then did she do it? She looked at the canvas, lightly scored with running lines. It would be hung in the servants' bedrooms. It would be rolled up and stuffed under a sofa. What was the good of doing it then, and she heard some voice saying she couldn't paint, saying she couldn't create, as if she were caught up in one of those habitual currents which after a certain time experience forms in the mind, so that one repeats words without being aware any longer who originally spoke them.

Can't paint, can't write, she murmured monotonously, anxiously considering what her plan of attack should be. For the mass loomed before her; it protruded; she felt it pressing on her eyeballs. Then, as if some juice necessary for the lubrication of her faculties were spontaneously squirted, she began precariously dipping among the blues and ambers, moving her brush hither and thither, but it was now heavier and went slower, as if it had fallen in with some rhythm which was dictated to her (she kept looking at the hedge, at the canvas) by what she saw, so that while her hand quivered with life, this rhythm was strong enough to bear her along with it on its current. Certainly she was losing consciousness of outer things. And as she lost consciousness of outer things, and her name and her personality and her appearance, and whether Mr Carmichael was there or not, her mind kept throwing up from its depths, scenes, and names, and sayings, and memories and ideas, like a fountain spurting over that glaring, hideously difficult white space, while she modelled it with greens and blues.

Charles Tansley used to say that, she remembered, women can't paint, can't write. Coming up behind her he had stood close beside her, a thing she hated, as she painted here on this very spot. 'Shag tobacco', he said, 'fivepence an ounce', parading his poverty, his principles. (But the war had drawn the sting of her femininity. Poor devils, one thought, poor devils of both sexes, getting into such messes.) He was always carrying a book about under his arm – a purple book. He 'worked'. He sat, she remembered, working in a blaze of sun. At dinner he would sit right in the middle of the view. And then, she reflected, there was that scene on the beach. One must remember that. It was a windy morning. They had all gone to the beach. Mrs Ramsay sat and wrote letters by a rock. She wrote and wrote. 'Oh,' she said, looking up at last at something floating in the sea, 'is it a lobster pot? Is it an upturned boat?' She was so short-sighted that she could not see, and then Charles Tansley became as nice as he could possibly be. He began playing ducks and drakes. They chose little flat black stones and sent them skipping over the waves. Every now and then Mrs Ramsay looked up over her spectacles and laughed at them. What they said she could not remember, but only she and Charles throwing stones and getting on very well all of a sudden and Mrs Ramsay watching them. She was highly conscious of that. Mrs Ramsay, she thought, stepping back and screwing up her eyes. (It must have altered the design a good deal when she was sitting on the step with James. There must have been a shadow.) Mrs Ramsay. When she thought of herself and Charles throwing ducks and drakes and of the whole scene on the beach, it seemed to depend somehow upon Mrs Ramsay sitting under the rock, with a pad on her knee, writing letters. (She wrote innumerable letters, and sometimes the wind took them and she and Charles just saved a page from the sea.) But what a power was in the human soul! she thought. That woman sitting there, writing under the rock resolved everything into simplicity; made these angers, irritations fall off like old rags; she brought together this and that and then this, and so made out of that miserable silliness and spite (she and Charles squabbling, sparring, had been silly and spiteful) something

– this scene on the beach for example, this moment of friendship and liking – which survived, after all these years, complete, so that she dipped into it to re-fashion her memory of him, and it stayed in the mind almost like a work of art.

'Like a work of art,' she repeated, looking from her canvas to the drawing-room steps and back again. She must rest for a moment. And, resting, looking from one to the other vaguely, the old question which traversed the sky of the soul perpetually, the vast, the general question which was apt to particularise itself at such moments as these, when she released faculties that had been on the strain, stood over her, paused over her, darkened over her. What is the meaning of life? That was all – a simple question; one that tended to close in on one with years. The great revelation had never come. The great revelation perhaps never did come. Instead there were little daily miracles, illuminations, matches struck unexpectedly in the dark; here was one. This, that, and the other; herself and Charles Tansley and the breaking wave; Mrs Ramsay bringing them together; Mrs Ramsay saying 'Life stand still here'; Mrs Ramsay making of the moment something permanent (as in another sphere Lily herself tried to make of the moment something permanent) – this was of the nature of a revelation. In the midst of chaos there was shape; this eternal passing and flowing (she looked at the clouds going and the leaves shaking) was struck into stability. Life stand still here, Mrs Ramsay said. 'Mrs Ramsay! Mrs Ramsay!' she repeated. She owed this revelation to her.

All was silence. Nobody seemed yet to be stirring in the house. She looked at it there sleeping in the early sunlight with its windows green and blue with the reflected leaves. The faint thought she was thinking of Mrs Ramsay seemed in consonance with this quiet house; this smoke; this fine early morning air. Faint and unreal, it was amazingly pure and exciting. She hoped nobody would open the window or come out of the house, but that she might be left alone to go on thinking, to go on painting. She turned to her canvas. But impelled by some curiosity, driven by the discomfort of the sympathy which she held undischarged, she walked a pace or so to the end of the lawn to see whether, down there on the beach, she could see that little company setting sail. Down there among the little boats which floated, some with their sails furled, some slowly, for it was very calm, moving away, there was one rather apart from the others. The sail was even now being hoisted. She decided that there in that very distant and entirely silent little boat Mr Ramsay was sitting with Cam and James. Now they had got the sail up; now after a little flagging and hesitation the sails filled and, shrouded in profound silence, she watched the boat take its way with deliberation past the other boats out to sea.

IV

The sails flapped over their heads. The water chuckled and slapped the sides of the boat, which drowsed motionless in the sun. Now and then the sails rippled with a little breeze in them, but the ripple ran over them and ceased. The boat made no motion at all. Mr Ramsay sat in the middle of the boat. He would be impatient in a moment, James thought, and Cam thought, looking at their father, who sat in the middle of the boat between them (James steered; Cam sat alone in the bow) with his legs tightly curled. He hated hanging about. Sure enough, after fidgeting a second or two, he said something sharp to Macalister's boy, who got out his oars and began to row. But their father, they knew, would never be content until they were flying along. He would keep looking for a breeze, fidgeting, saying things under his breath, which Macalister and Macalister's boy would overhear, and they would both be made horribly uncomfortable. He had made them come. He had forced them to come. In their anger they hoped that the breeze would never rise, that he might be thwarted in every possible way, since he had forced them to come against their wills.

All the way down to the beach they had lagged behind together, though he bade them 'Walk up, walk up', without speaking. Their heads were bent down, their heads were pressed down by some remorseless gale. Speak to him they could not. They must come; they must follow. They must walk behind him carrying brown paper parcels. But they vowed, in silence, as they walked, to stand by each other and carry out the great compact – to resist tyranny to the death. So there they would sit, one at one end of the boat, one at the other, in silence. They would say nothing, only look at him now and then where he sat with his legs twisted, frowning and fidgeting, and pishing and pshawing and muttering things to himself, and waiting impatiently for a breeze. And they hoped it would be calm. They hoped he would be thwarted. They hoped the whole expedition would fail, and they would have to put back, with their parcels, to the beach.

But now, when Macalister's boy had rowed a little way out, the sails slowly swung round, the boat quickened itself, flattened itself, and shot off. Instantly, as if some great strain had been relieved, Mr Ramsay uncurled his legs, took out his tobacco pouch, handed it with a little grunt to Macalister, and felt, they knew, for all they suffered, perfectly content. Now they would sail on for hours like this, and Mr Ramsay would ask old Macalister a question – about the great storm last winter probably – and old Macalister would answer it, and they would puff their pipes together, and Macalister would take a tarry rope in his fingers, tying or untying some knot, and the boy would fish, and never say a word to any one. James would be forced to keep his eye all the time on the sail. For if he forgot, then the sail puckered, and shivered, and the boat slackened, and Mr Ramsay would say sharply, 'Look out! Look out!' and old Macalister would turn slowly on his seat. So they heard Mr Ramsay asking some question about the great storm at Christmas. 'She comes driving round the point,' old Macalister said, describing the great storm last

Christmas, when ten ships had been driven into the bay for shelter, and he had seen 'one there, one there, one there' (he pointed slowly round the bay. Mr Ramsay followed him, turning his head). He had seen three men clinging to the mast. Then she was gone. 'And at last we shoved her off,' he went on (but in their anger and their silence they only caught a word here and there, sitting at opposite ends of the boat, united by their compact to fight tyranny to the death). At last they had shoved her off, they had launched the lifeboat, and they had got her out past the point – Macalister told the story; and though they only caught a word here and there, they were conscious all the time of their father – how he leant forward, how he brought his voice into tune with Macalister's voice; how, puffing at his pipe, and looking there and there where Macalister pointed, he relished the thought of the storm and the dark night and the fishermen striving there. He liked that men should labour and sweat on the windy beach at night, pitting muscle and brain against the waves and the wind; he liked men to work like that, and women to keep house, and sit beside sleeping children indoors, while men were drowned, out there in a storm. So James could tell, so Cam could tell (they looked at him, they looked at each other), from his toss and his vigilance and the ring in his voice, and the little tinge of Scottish accent which came into his voice, making him seem like a peasant himself, as he questioned Macalister about the eleven ships that had been driven into the bay in a storm. Three had sunk.

He looked proudly where Macalister pointed; and Cam thought, feeling proud of him without knowing quite why, had he been there he would have launched the lifeboat, he would have reached the wreck, Cam thought. He was so brave, he was so adventurous, Cam thought. But she remembered. There was the compact; to resist tyranny to the death. Their grievance weighed them down. They had been forced; they had been bidden. He had borne them down once more with his gloom and his authority, making them do his bidding, on this fine morning, come, because he wished it, carrying these parcels, to the Lighthouse; take part in those rites he went through for his own pleasure in memory of dead people, which they hated, so that they lagged after him, and all the pleasure of the day was spoilt.

Yes, the breeze was freshening. The boat was leaning, the water was sliced sharply and fell away in green cascades, in bubbles, in cataracts. Cam looked down into the foam, into the sea with all its treasure in it, and its speed hypnotised her, and the tie between her and James sagged a little. It slackened a little. She began to think, How fast it goes. Where are we going? and the movement hypnotised her, while James, with his eye fixed on the sail and on the horizon, steered grimly. But he began to think as he steered that he might escape; he might be quit of it all. They might land somewhere; and be free then. Both of them, looking at each other for a moment, had a sense of escape and exaltation, what with the speed and the change. But the breeze bred in Mr Ramsay too the same excitement, and, as old Macalister turned to fling his line overboard, he cried aloud, 'We perished', and then again, 'each alone'. And then with his usual spasm of repentance or shyness, pulled himself up, and waved his hand towards the shore.

'See the little house,' he said pointing, wishing Cam to look. She raised herself reluctantly and looked. But which was it? She could no longer make out, there on the hillside, which was their house. All looked distant and peaceful and strange. The shore seemed refined, far away, unreal. Already the little distance they had sailed had put them far from it and given it the changed look, the composed look, of something receding in which one has no longer any part. Which was their house? She could not see it.

'But I beneath a rougher sea,' Mr Ramsay murmured. He had found the house and so seeing it, he had also seen himself there; he had seen himself walking on the terrace, alone. He was walking up and down between the urns; and he seemed to himself very old, and bowed. Sitting in the boat he bowed, he crouched himself, acting instantly his part – the part of a desolate man, widowed, bereft; and so called up before him in hosts people sympathising with him; staged for himself as he sat in the boat, a little drama; which required of him decrepitude and exhaustion and sorrow (he raised his hands and looked at the thinness of them, to confirm his dream) and then there was given him in abundance women's sympathy, and he imagined how they would soothe him and sympathise with him, and so getting in his dream some reflection of the exquisite pleasure women's sympathy was to him, he sighed and said gently and mournfully:

> But I beneath a rougher sea
> Was whelmed in deeper gulfs than he,

so that the mournful words were heard quite clearly by them all. Cam half started on her seat. It shocked her – it outraged her. The movement roused her father; and he shuddered, and broke off, exclaiming: 'Look! Look!' so urgently that James also turned his head to look over his shoulder at the island. They all looked. They looked at the island.

But Cam could see nothing. She was thinking how all those paths and the lawn, thick and knotted with the lives they had lived there, were gone: were rubbed out; were past; were unreal, and now this was real; the boat and the sail with its patch; Macalister with his earrings; the noise of the waves – all this was real. Thinking this, she was murmuring to herself 'We perished, each alone', for her father's words broke and broke again in her mind, when her father, seeing her gazing so vaguely, began to tease her. Didn't she know the points of the compass? he asked. Didn't she know the North from the South? Did she really think they lived right out there? And he pointed again, and showed her where their house was, there, by those trees. He wished she would try to be more accurate, he said: 'Tell me – which is East, which is West?' he said, half laughing at her, half scolding her, for he could not understand the state of mind of any one, not absolutely imbecile, who did not know the points of the compass. Yet she did not know. And seeing her gazing, with her vague, now rather frightened, eyes fixed where no house was Mr Ramsay forgot his dream; how he walked up and down between the urns on the terrace; how the arms were stretched out to him. He thought, women are always like that; the vagueness of their minds is hopeless; it was a thing he had never been able to understand; but so it was. It had been so with her – his wife. They could not keep anything clearly fixed in their minds. But he had been wrong to be angry with her; moreover, did he not rather like this vagueness in women? It was part of their extraordinary charm. I will make her smile at me, he thought. She looks frightened. She was so silent. He clutched his fingers, and determined that his voice and his face and all the quick expressive gestures which had been at his command making people pity him and praise him all these years should subdue themselves. He would make her smile at him. He would find some simple easy thing to say to her. But what? For, wrapped up in his work as he was, he forgot the sort of thing one said. There was a puppy. They had a puppy. Who was looking after the puppy today? he asked. Yes, thought James pitilessly, seeing his sister's head against the sail, now she will give way. I shall be left to fight the tyrant alone. The compact would be left to him to carry out. Cam would never resist tyranny to the death, he thought grimly, watching her face, sad, sulky, yielding. And as sometimes happens when a cloud falls on a green hillside and gravity descends and there among all the surrounding hills is gloom and sorrow, and it seems as if the hills themselves must ponder the fate of the clouded, the darkened, either in pity, or maliciously rejoicing in her dismay: so Cam now felt herself overcast, as she sat there among calm, resolute people and wondered how to answer her father about the puppy; how to resist his entreaty – forgive me, care for me; while James the lawgiver, with the tablets of eternal wisdom laid open on his knee (his hand on the tiller had become symbolical to her), said, Resist him. Fight him. He said so rightly; justly. For they must fight tyranny to the death, she thought. Of all human qualities she reverenced justice most. Her brother was most god-like, her father most suppliant. And to which did she yield, she thought, sitting between them, gazing at the shore whose points were all unknown to her, and thinking how the lawn and the terrace and the house were smoothed away now and peace dwelt there.

'Jasper,' she said sullenly. He'd look after the puppy.

And what was she going to call him? her father persisted. He had had a dog when he was a little boy, called Frisk. She'll give way, James thought, as he watched a look come upon her face, a look he remembered. They look down, he thought, at their knitting or something. Then suddenly they look up. There was a flash of blue, he remembered, and then somebody sitting with him laughed, surrendered, and he was very angry. It must have been his mother, he thought, sitting on a low chair, with his father standing over her. He began to search among the infinite series of impressions which time had laid down, leaf upon leaf, fold upon fold softly, incessantly upon his brain; among scents, sounds; voices, harsh, hollow, sweet; and lights passing, and brooms tapping; and the wash and hush of the sea, how a man had marched up and down and stopped dead, upright, over them. Meanwhile, he noticed, Cam dabbled her fingers in the water, and stared at the shore and said nothing. No, she won't give way, he thought; she's different, he thought. Well, if Cam would not answer him, he would not bother her, Mr Ramsay decided, feeling in his pocket for a book. But she would answer him; she wished, passionately, to move some obstacle that lay upon her tongue and to say, Oh yes, Frisk. I'll call him Frisk. She wanted even to say, Was that the dog that found its way over the moor alone? But try as she might, she could think of nothing to say like that, fierce and loyal to the compact, yet passing on to her father, unsuspected by James, a private token of the love she felt for him. For she thought, dabbling her hand (and now Macalister's boy had caught a mackerel, and it lay kicking on the floor, with blood on its gills) for she thought, looking at James who kept his eyes dispassionately on the sail, or glanced now and then for a second at the horizon, you're not exposed to it, to this pressure and division of feeling, this extraordinary temptation. Her father was feeling in his pockets; in another second, he would have found his book. For no one attracted her more; his hands were beautiful to her and his feet, and his voice, and his words, and his haste, and his temper, and his oddity, and his passion, and his saying straight out before every one, we perish, each alone, and his remoteness. (He had opened his book.) But what remained intolerable, she thought, sitting upright, and watching Macalister's boy tug the hook out of the gills of another fish, was that crass blindness and tyranny of his which had poisoned her childhood and raised bitter storms, so that even now she woke in the night trembling with rage and remembered some command of his; some insolence: 'Do this', 'Do that'; his dominance: his 'Submit to me'.

So she said nothing, but looked doggedly and sadly at the shore, wrapped in its mantle of peace; as if the people there had fallen asleep, she thought; were free like smoke, were free to come and go like ghosts. They have no suffering there, she thought.

V

Yes, that is their boat, Lily Briscoe decided, standing on the edge of the lawn. It was the boat with greyish-brown sails, which she saw now flatten itself upon the water and shoot off across the bay. There he sits, she thought, and the children are quite silent still. And she could not reach him either. The sympathy she had not given him weighed her down. It made it difficult for her to paint.

She had always found him difficult. She had never been able to praise him to his face, she remembered. And that reduced their relationship to something neutral, without that element of sex in it which made his manner to Minta so gallant, almost gay. He would pick a flower for her, lend her his books. But could he believe that Minta read them? She dragged them about the garden, sticking in leaves to mark the place.

'D'you remember, Mr Carmichael?' she was inclined to ask, looking at the old man. But he had pulled his hat half over his forehead; he was asleep, or he was dreaming, or he was lying there catching words, she supposed.

'D'you remember?' she felt inclined to ask him as she passed him, thinking again of Mrs Ramsay on the beach; the cask bobbing up and down; and the pages flying. Why, after all these years had that survived, ringed round, lit up, visible to the last detail, with all before it blank and all after it blank, for miles and miles?

'Is it a boat? Is it a cork?' she would say, Lily repeated, turning back, reluctantly again, to her canvas. Heaven be praised for it, the problem of space remained, she thought, taking up her brush again. It glared at her. The whole mass of the picture was poised upon that weight. Beautiful and bright it should be on the surface, feathery and evanescent, one colour melting into another like the colours on a butterfly's wing; but beneath the fabric must be clamped together with bolts of iron. It was to be a thing you could ruffle with your breath; and a thing you could not dislodge with a team of horses. And she began to lay on a red, a grey, and she began to model her way into the hollow there. At the same time, she seemed to be sitting beside Mrs Ramsay on the beach.

'Is it a boat? Is it a cask?' Mrs Ramsay said. And she began hunting round for her spectacles. And she sat, having found them, silent, looking out to sea. And Lily, painting steadily, felt as if a door had opened, and one went in and stood gazing silently about in a high cathedral-like place, very dark, very solemn. Shouts came from a world far away. Steamers vanished in stalks of smoke on the horizon. Charles threw stones and sent them skipping.

Mrs Ramsay sat silent. She was glad, Lily thought, to rest in silence, uncommunicative; to rest in the extreme obscurity of human relationships. Who knows what we are, what we feel? Who knows even at the moment of intimacy, This is knowledge? Aren't things spoilt then, Mrs Ramsay may have asked (it seemed to have happened so often, this silence by her side) by saying them? Aren't we more expressive thus? The moment at least seemed extraordinarily fertile. She rammed a little hole in the sand and covered it up, by way of burying in it the perfection of the moment. It was like a drop of silver in which one dipped and illumined the darkness of the past.

Lily stepped back to get her canvas – so – into perspective. It was an odd road to be walking, this of painting. Out and out one went, further and further, until at last one seemed to be on a narrow plank, perfectly alone, over the sea. And as she dipped into the blue paint, she dipped too into the past there. Now Mrs Ramsay got up, she remembered. It was time to go back to the house – time for luncheon. And they all walked up from the beach together, she walking behind with William Bankes, and there was Minta in front of them with a hole in her stocking. How that little round hole of pink heel seemed to flaunt itself before them! How William Bankes deplored it, without, so far as she could remember, saying anything about it! It meant to him the annihilation of womanhood, and dirt and disorder, and servants leaving and beds not made at midday – all the things he most abhorred. He had a way of shuddering and spreading his fingers out as if to cover an unsightly object, which he did now – holding his hand in front of him. And Minta walked on ahead, and presumably Paul met her and she went off with Paul in the garden.

The Rayleys, thought Lily Briscoe, squeezing her tube of green paint. She collected her impressions of the Rayleys. Their lives appeared to her in a series of scenes; one, on the staircase at dawn. Paul had come in and gone to bed early; Minta was late. There was Minta, wreathed, tinted, garish on the stairs about three o'clock in the morning. Paul came out in his pyjamas carrying a poker in case of burglars. Minta was eating a sandwich, standing half-way up by a window, in the cadaverous early morning light, and the carpet had a hole in it. But what did they say? Lily asked herself, as if by looking she could hear them. Something violent. Minta went on eating her sandwich, annoyingly, while he spoke. He spoke indignant, jealous words, abusing her, in a mutter so as not to wake the children, the two little boys. He was withered, drawn; she flamboyant, careless. For things had worked loose after the first year or so; the marriage had turned out rather badly.

And this, Lily thought, taking the green paint on her brush, this making up scenes about them, is what we call 'knowing' people, 'thinking' of them, 'being fond' of them! Not a word of it was true; she had made it up; but it was what she knew them by all the same. She went on tunnelling her way into her picture, into the past.

Another time, Paul said he 'played chess in coffee-houses'. She had built up a whole structure of imagination on that saying too. She remembered how, as he said it, she thought how he rang up the servant, and she said 'Mrs Rayley's out, sir', and he decided that he would not come home either. She saw him sitting in the corner of some lugubrious place where the smoke attached itself to the red plush seats, and the waitresses got to know you, playing chess with a little man who was in the tea trade and lived at Surbiton, but that was all Paul knew about him. And then Minta was out when he came home and then there was that scene on the stairs, when he got the poker in case of burglars (no doubt to frighten her too) and spoke so bitterly, saying she had ruined his life. At any rate when she went down to see them at a cottage near Rickmansworth, things were horribly strained. Paul took her down the garden to look at the Belgian hares which he bred, and Minta followed them, singing, and put her bare arm on his shoulder, lest he should tell her anything.

Minta was bored by hares, Lily thought. But Minta never gave herself away. She never said things like that about playing chess in coffee-houses. She was far too conscious, far too wary. But to go on with their story – they had got through the dangerous stage by now. She had been staying with them last summer some time and the car broke down and Minta had to hand him his tools. He sat on the road mending the car, and it was the way she gave him the tools – business-like, straightforward, friendly – that proved it was all right now. They were 'in love' no longer; no, he had taken up with another woman, a serious woman, with her hair in a plait and a case in her hand (Minta had described her gratefully, almost admiringly), who went to meetings and shared Paul's views (they had got more and more pronounced) about the taxation of land values and a capital levy. Far from breaking up the marriage, that alliance had righted it. They were excellent friends, obviously, as he sat on the road and she handed him his tools.

So that was the story of the Rayleys, Lily smiled. She imagined herself telling it to Mrs Ramsay, who would be full of curiosity to know what had become of the Rayleys. She would feel a little triumphant, telling Mrs Ramsay that the marriage had not been a success.

But the dead, thought Lily, encountering some obstacle in her design which made her pause and ponder, stepping back a foot or so, Oh the dead! she murmured, one pitied them, one brushed them aside, one had even a little contempt for them. They are at our mercy. Mrs Ramsay has faded and gone, she thought. We can over-ride her wishes, improve away her limited, old-fashioned ideas. She recedes further and further from us. Mockingly she seemed to see her there at the end of the corridor of years saying, of all incongruous things, 'Marry, marry!' (sitting very upright early in the morning with the birds beginning to cheep in the garden outside). And one would have to say to her, It has all gone against your wishes. They're happy like that; I'm happy like this. Life has changed completely. At that all her being, even her beauty, became for a moment, dusty and out of date. For a moment Lily, standing there, with the sun hot on her back, summing up the Rayleys, triumphed over Mrs Ramsay, who would never know how Paul went to coffee-houses and had a mistress; how he sat on the ground and Minta handed him his tools; how she stood here painting, had never married, not even William Bankes.

Mrs Ramsay had planned it. Perhaps, had she lived, she would have compelled it. Already that summer he was 'the kindest of men'. He was 'the first scientist of his age, my husband says'. He was also 'poor William – it makes me so unhappy, when I go to see him, to find nothing nice in his house – no one to arrange the flowers'. So they were sent for walks together, and she was told, with that faint touch of irony that made Mrs Ramsay slip through one's fingers, that she had a scientific mind; she liked flowers; she was so exact. What was this mania of hers for marriage? Lily wondered, stepping to and fro from her easel.

(Suddenly, as suddenly as a star slides in the sky, a reddish light seemed to burn in her mind, covering Paul Rayley, issuing from him. It rose like a fire sent up in token of some celebration by savages on a distant beach. She heard the roar and the crackle. The whole sea for miles round ran red and gold.

Some winy smell mixed with it and intoxicated her, for she felt again her own headlong desire to throw herself off the cliff and be drowned looking for a pearl brooch on a beach. And the roar and the crackle repelled her with fear and disgust, as if while she saw its splendour and power she saw too how it fed on the treasure of the house, greedily, disgustingly, and she loathed it. But for a sight, for a glory it surpassed everything in her experience, and burnt year after year like a signal fire on a desert island at the edge of the sea, and one had only to say 'in love' and instantly, as happened now, up rose Paul's fire again. And it sank and she said to herself, laughing, 'The Rayleys'; how Paul went to coffee-houses and played chess.)

She had only escaped by the skin of her teeth though, she thought. She had been looking at the table-cloth, and it had flashed upon her that she would move the tree to the middle, and need never marry anybody, and she had felt an enormous exultation. She had felt, now she could stand up to Mrs Ramsay – a tribute to the astonishing power that Mrs Ramsay had over one. Do this, she said, and one did it. Even her shadow at the window with James was full of authority. She remembered how William Bankes had been shocked by her neglect of the significance of mother and son. Did she not admire their beauty? he said. But William, she remembered, had listened to her with his wise child's eyes when she explained how it was not irreverence: how a light there needed a shadow there and so on. She did not intend to disparage a subject which, they agreed, Raphael had treated divinely. She was not cynical. Quite the contrary. Thanks to his scientific mind he understood – a proof of disinterested intelligence which had pleased her and comforted her enormously. One could talk of painting then seriously to a man. Indeed, his friendship had been one of the pleasures of her life. She loved William Bankes.

They went to Hampton Court and he always left her, like the perfect gentleman he was, plenty of time to wash her hands, while he strolled by the river. That was typical of their relationship. Many things were left unsaid. Then they strolled through the courtyards, and admired, summer after summer, the proportions and the flowers, and he would tell her things, about perspective, about architecture, as they walked, and he would stop to look at a tree, or the view over the lake, and admire a child (it was his great grief – he had no daughter) in the vague aloof way that was natural to a man who spent so much time in laboratories that the world when he came out seemed to dazzle him, so that he walked slowly, lifted his hand to screen his eyes and paused, with his head thrown back, merely to breathe the air. Then he would tell her how his housekeeper was on her holiday; he must buy a new carpet for the staircase. Perhaps she would go with him to buy a new carpet for the staircase. And once something led him to talk about the Ramsays and he had said how when he first saw her she had been wearing a grey hat; she was not more than nineteen or twenty. She was astonishingly beautiful. There he stood looking down the avenue at Hampton Court, as if he could see her there among the fountains.

She looked now at the drawing-room step. She saw, through William's eyes, the shape of a woman, peaceful and silent, with downcast eyes. She sat musing, pondering (she was in grey that day, Lily thought). Her eyes were bent. She would never lift them. Yes, thought Lily, looking intently, I must have seen her look like that, but not in grey; nor so still, nor so young, nor so peaceful. The figure came readily enough. She was astonishingly beautiful, William said. But beauty was not everything. Beauty had this penalty – it came too readily, came too completely. It stilled life – froze it. One forgot the little agitations; the flush, the pallor, some queer distortion, some light or shadow, which made the face unrecognisable for a moment and yet added a quality one saw for ever after. It was simpler to smooth that all out under the cover of beauty. But what was the look she had, Lily wondered, when she clapped her deer-stalker's hat on her head, or ran across the grass, or scolded Kennedy, the gardener? Who could tell her? Who could help her?

Against her will she had come to the surface, and found herself half out of the picture, looking, a little dazedly, as if at unreal things, at Mr Carmichael. He lay on his chair with his hands clasped above his paunch not reading, or sleeping, but basking like a creature gorged with existence. His book had fallen on to the grass.

She wanted to go straight up to him and say, 'Mr Carmichael!' Then he would look up benevolently as always, from his smoky vague green eyes. But one only woke people if one knew what one wanted to say to them. And she wanted to say not one thing, but everything. Little words that broke up the thought and dismembered it said nothing. 'About life, about death; about Mrs Ramsay' – no, she thought, one could say nothing to nobody. The urgency of the moment always missed its mark. Words fluttered sideways and struck the object inches too low. Then one gave it up; then the idea sunk back again; then one became like most middle-aged people, cautious, furtive, with wrinkles between the eyes and a look of perpetual apprehension. For how could one express in words these emotions of the body? express that emptiness there? (She was looking at the drawing-room steps; they looked extraordinarily empty.) It was one's body feeling, not one's mind. The physical sensations that went with the bare look of the steps had become suddenly extremely unpleasant. To want and not to have, sent all up her body a hardness, a hollowness, a strain. And then to want and not to have – to want and want – how that wrung the heart, and wrung it again and again! Oh Mrs Ramsay! she called out silently, to that essence which sat by the boat, that abstract one made of her, that woman in grey, as if to abuse her for having gone, and then having gone, come back again. It had seemed so safe, thinking of her. Ghost, air, nothingness, a thing you could play with easily and safely at any time of day or night, she had been that, and then suddenly she put her hand out and wrung the heart thus. Suddenly, the empty drawing-room steps, the frill of the chair inside, the puppy tumbling on the terrace, the whole wave and whisper of the garden became like curves and arabesques flourishing round a centre of complete emptiness.

'What does it mean? How do you explain it all?' she wanted to say, turning to Mr Carmichael again. For the whole world seemed to have dissolved in this early morning hour into a pool of thought, a deep basin of reality, and one could almost fancy that had Mr Carmichael spoken, a little tear would have rent the surface of the pool. And then? Something would emerge. A hand would be shoved up, a blade would be flashed. It was nonsense of course.

A curious notion came to her that he did after all hear the things she could not say. He was an inscrutable old man, with the yellow stain on his beard, and his poetry, and his puzzles, sailing serenely through a world which satisfied all his wants, so that she thought he had only to put down his hand where he lay on the lawn to fish up anything he wanted. She looked at her picture. That would have been his answer, presumably – how 'you' and 'I' and 'she' pass and vanish; nothing stays; all changes; but not words, not paint. Yet it would be hung in the attics, she thought; it would be rolled up and flung under a sofa; yet even so, even of a picture like that, it was true. One might say, even of this scrawl, not of that actual picture, perhaps, but of what it attempted, that it 'remained for ever', she was going to say, or, for the words spoken sounded even to herself, too boastful, to hint, wordlessly; when, looking at the picture, she was surprised to find that she could not see it. Her eyes were full of a hot liquid (she did not think of tears at first) which, without disturbing the firmness of her lips, made the air thick, rolled down her cheeks. She had perfect control of herself – Oh yes! – in every other way. Was she crying then for Mrs Ramsay, without being aware of any unhappiness? She addressed old Mr Carmichael again. What was it then? What did it mean? Could things thrust their hands up and grip one; could the blade cut; the fist grasp? Was there no safety? No learning by heart of the ways of the world? No guide, no shelter, but all was miracle, and leaping from the pinnacle of a tower into the air? Could it be, even for elderly people, that this was life? – startling, unexpected, unknown? For one moment she felt that if they both got up, here, now on the lawn, and demanded an explanation, why was it so short, why was it so inexplicable, said it with violence, as two fully equipped human beings from whom nothing should be hid might speak, then, beauty would roll itself up; the space would fill; those empty flourishes would form into shape; if they shouted loud enough Mrs Ramsay would return. 'Mrs Ramsay!' she said aloud, 'Mrs Ramsay!' The tears ran down her face.

VI

[Macalister's boy took one of the fish and cut a square out of its side to bait his hook with. The mutilated body (it was alive still) was thrown back into the sea.]

VII

'Mrs Ramsay!' Lily cried, 'Mrs Ramsay!' But nothing happened. The pain increased. That anguish could reduce one to such a pitch of imbecility, she thought! Anyhow the old man had not heard her. He remained benignant, calm – if one chose to think it, sublime. Heaven be praised, no one had heard her cry that ignominious cry, stop pain, stop! She had not obviously taken leave of her senses. No one had seen her step off her strip of board into the waters of annihilation. She remained a skimpy old maid, holding a paint-brush on the lawn.

And now slowly the pain of the want, and the bitter anger (to be called back, just as she thought she would never feel sorrow for Mrs Ramsay again. Had she missed her among the coffee cups at breakfast? not in the least) lessened; and of their anguish left, as antidote, a relief that was balm in itself, and also, but more mysteriously, a sense of some one there, of Mrs Ramsay, relieved for a moment of the weight that the world had put on her, staying lightly by her side and then (for this was Mrs Ramsay in all her beauty) raising to her forehead a wreath of white flowers with which she went. Lily squeezed her tubes again. She attacked that problem of the hedge. It was strange how clearly she saw her, stepping with her usual quickness across fields among whose folds, purplish and soft, among whose flowers, hyacinths or lilies, she vanished. It was some trick of the painter's eye. For days after she had heard of her death she had seen her thus, putting her wreath to her forehead and going unquestioningly with her companion, a shadow, across the fields. The sight, the phrase, had its power to console. Wherever she happened to be, painting, here, in the country or in London, the vision would come to her, and her eyes, half closing, sought something to base her vision on. She looked down the railway carriage, the omnibus; took a line from shoulder or cheek; looked at the windows opposite; at Piccadilly, lamp-strung in the evening. All had been part of the fields of death. But always something – it might be a face, a voice, a paper boy crying *Standard, News* – thrust through, snubbed her, waked her, required and got in the end an effort of attention, so that the vision must be perpetually remade. Now again, moved as she was by some instinctive need of distance and blue, she looked at the bay beneath her, making hillocks of the blue bars of the waves, and stony fields of the purpler spaces. Again she was roused as usual by something incongruous. There was a brown spot in the middle of the bay. It was a boat. Yes, she realised that after a second. But whose boat? Mr Ramsay's boat, she replied. Mr Ramsay; the man who had marched past her, with his hand raised, aloof, at the head of a procession, in his beautiful boots, asking her for sympathy, which she had refused. The boat was now half way across the bay.

So fine was the morning except for a streak of wind here and there that the sea and sky looked all one fabric, as if sails were stuck high up in the sky, or the clouds had dropped down into the sea. A steamer far out at sea had drawn in the air a great scroll of smoke which stayed there curving and circling decoratively, as if the air were a fine gauze which held things and kept them softly in its mesh, only gently swaying them this way and that. And as happens sometimes when the weather is very fine, the cliffs looked as if they were conscious of the ships, and the ships looked as if they were conscious of the cliffs, as if they signalled to each other some secret message of their own. For sometimes quite close to the shore, the Lighthouse looked this morning in the haze an enormous distance away.

'Where are they now?' Lily thought, looking out to sea. Where was he, that very old man who had gone past her silently, holding a brown paper parcel under his arm? The boat was in the middle of the bay.

VIII

They don't feel a thing there, Cam thought, looking at the shore, which, rising and falling, became steadily more distant and more peaceful. Her hand cut a trail in the sea, as her mind made the green swirls and streaks into patterns and, numbed and shrouded, wandered in imagination in that underworld of waters where the pearls stuck in clusters to white sprays, where in the green light a change came over one's entire mind and one's body shone half transparent enveloped in a green cloak.

Then the eddy slackened round her hand. The rush of the water ceased; the world became full of little creaking and squeaking sounds. One heard the waves breaking and flapping against the side of the boat as if they were anchored in harbour.

Everything became very close to one. For the sail, upon which James had his eyes fixed until it had become to him like a person whom he knew, sagged entirely; there they came to a stop, flapping about waiting for a breeze, in the hot sun, miles from shore, miles from the Lighthouse. Everything in the whole world seemed to stand still. The Lighthouse became immovable, and the line of the distant shore became fixed. The sun grew hotter and everybody seemed to come very close together and to feel each other's presence, which they had almost forgotten. Macalister's fishing line went plumb down into the sea. But Mr Ramsay went on reading with his legs curled under him.

He was reading a little shiny book with covers mottled like a plover's egg. Now and again, as they hung about in that horrid calm, he turned a page. And James felt that each page was turned with a peculiar gesture aimed at him: now assertively, now commandingly; now with the intention of making people pity him; and all the time, as his father read and turned one after another of those little pages, James kept dreading the moment when he would look up and speak sharply to him about something or other. Why were they lagging about here? he would demand, or something quite unreasonable like that. And if he does, James thought, then I shall take a knife and strike him to the heart.

He had always kept this old symbol of taking a knife and striking his father to the heart. Only now, as he grew older, and sat staring at his father in an impotent rage, it was not him, that old man reading, whom he wanted to kill, but it was the thing that descended on him – without his knowing it perhaps: that fierce sudden black-winged harpy, with its talons and its beak all cold and hard, that struck and struck at you (he could feel the beak on his bare legs, where it had struck when he was a child) and then made off, and there he was again, an old man, very sad, reading his book. That he would kill, that he would strike to the heart. Whatever he did – (and he might do anything, he felt, looking at the Lighthouse and the distant shore) whether he was in a business, in a bank, a barrister, a man at the head of some enterprise, that he would fight, that he would track down and stamp out – tyranny, despotism, he called it – making people do what they did not want to do, cutting off their right to speak. How could any of them say, But I won't, when he said, Come to the Lighthouse. Do this. Fetch me that. The black wings spread, and the hard beak tore. And then next moment, there he sat reading his book; and he might look up – one never knew quite reasonably. He might talk to the Macalisters. He might be pressing a sovereign into some frozen old woman's hand in the street, James thought; he might be shouting out at some fisherman's sports; he might be waving his arms in the air with excitement. Or he might sit at the head of the table dead silent from one end of dinner to the other. Yes, thought James, while the boat slapped and dawdled there in the hot sun; there was a waste of snow and rock very lonely and austere; and there he had come to feel, quite often lately, when his father said something which surprised the others, were two pairs of footprints only; his own and his father's. They alone knew each other. What then was this terror, this hatred? Turning back among the many leaves which the past had folded in him, peering into the heart of that forest where light and shade so chequer each other that all shape is distorted, and one blunders, now with the sun in one's eyes, now with a dark shadow, he sought an image to cool and detach and round off his feeling in a concrete shape. Suppose then that as a child sitting helpless in a perambulator, or on someone's knee, he had seen a waggon crush ignorantly and innocently, someone's foot? Suppose he had seen the foot first, in the grass, smooth, and whole; then the wheel; and the same foot, purple, crushed. But the wheel was innocent. So now, when his father came striding down the passage knocking them up early in the morning to go to the Lighthouse down it came over his foot, over Cam's foot, over anybody's foot. One sat and watched it.

But whose foot was he thinking of, and in what garden did all this happen? For one had settings for these scenes; trees that grew there; flowers; a certain light; a few figures. Everything tended to set itself in a garden where there was none of this gloom and none of this throwing of hands about; people spoke in an ordinary tone of voice. They went in and out all day long. There was an old woman gossiping in the kitchen; and the blinds were sucked in and out by the breeze; all was blowing, all was growing; and over all those plates and bowls and tall brandishing red and yellow flowers a very thin yellow veil would be drawn, like a vine leaf, at night. Things became stiller and darker at night. But the leaf-like veil was so fine that lights lifted it, voices crinkled it; he could see through it a figure stooping, hear, coming close, going away, some dress rustling, some chain tinkling.

It was in this world that the wheel went over the person's foot. Something, he remembered, stayed and darkened over him; would not move; something flourished up in the air, something arid and sharp descended even there, like a blade, a scimitar, smiting through the leaves and flowers even of that happy world and making them shrivel and fall.

'It will rain,' he remembered his father saying. 'You won't be able to go to the Lighthouse.'

The Lighthouse was then a silvery, misty-looking tower with a yellow eye that opened suddenly and softly in the evening. Now—

James looked at the Lighthouse. He could see the white-washed rocks; the tower, stark and straight; he could see that it was barred with black and white; he could see windows in it; he could even see washing spread on the rocks to dry. So that was the Lighthouse, was it?

No, the other was also the Lighthouse. For nothing was simply one thing. The other was the Lighthouse too. It was sometimes hardly to be seen across the bay. In the evening one looked up and saw the eye opening and shutting and the light seemed to reach them in that airy sunny garden where they sat.

But he pulled himself up. Whenever he said 'they' or 'a person', and then began hearing the rustle of some one coming, the tinkle of some one going, he became extremely sensitive to the presence of whoever might be in the room. It was his father now. The strain became acute. For in one moment if there was no breeze, his father would slap the covers of his book together, and say: 'What's happening now? What are we dawdling about here for, eh?' as, once before he had brought his blade down among them on the terrace and she had gone stiff all over, and if there had been an axe handy, a knife, or anything with a sharp point he would have seized it and struck his father through the heart. His mother had gone stiff all over, and then, her arm slackening, so that he felt she listened to him no longer, she had risen somehow and gone away and left him there, impotent, ridiculous, sitting on the floor grasping a pair of scissors.

Not a breath of wind blew. The water chuckled and gurgled in the bottom of the boat where three or four mackerel beat their tails up and down in a pool of water not deep enough to cover them. At any moment Mr Ramsay (James scarcely dared look at him) might rouse himself, shut his book, and say something sharp; but for the moment he was reading, so that James stealthily, as if he were stealing downstairs on bare feet, afraid of waking a watch-dog by a creaking board, went on thinking what was she like, where did she go that day? He began following her from room to room and at last they came to a room where in a blue light, as if the reflection came from many china dishes, she talked to somebody; he listened to her talking. She talked to a servant, saying simply whatever came into her head. 'We shall need a big dish tonight. Where is it – the blue dish?' She alone spoke the truth; to her alone could he speak it. That was the source of her everlasting attraction for him, perhaps; she was a person to whom one could say what came into one's head. But all the time he thought of her, he was conscious of his father following his thought, shadowing it, making it shiver and falter.

At last he ceased to think; there he sat with his hand on the tiller in the sun, staring at the Lighthouse, powerless to move, powerless to flick off these grains of misery which settled on his mind one after another. A rope seemed to bind him there, and his father had knotted it and he could only escape by taking a knife and plunging it . . . But at that moment the sail swung slowly round, filled slowly out, the boat seemed to shake herself, and then to move off half conscious in her sleep, and then she woke and shot through the waves. The relief was extraordinary. They all seemed to fall away from each other again and to be at their ease and the fishing-lines slanted taut across the side of the boat. But his father did not rouse himself. He only raised his right hand mysteriously high in the air, and let it fall upon his knee again as if he were conducting some secret symphony.

IX

[The sea without a stain on it, thought Lily Briscoe, still standing and looking out over the bay. The sea is stretched like silk across the bay. Distance had an extraordinary power; they had been swallowed up in it, she felt, they were gone for ever, they had become part of the nature of things. It was so calm; it was so quiet. The steamer itself had vanished, but the great scroll of smoke still hung in the air and drooped like a flag mournfully in valediction.]

X

It was like that then, the island, thought Cam, once more drawing her fingers through the waves. She had never seen it from out at sea before. It lay like that on the sea, did it, with a dent in the middle and two sharp crags, and the sea swept in there, and spread away for miles and miles on either side of the island. It was very small; shaped something like a leaf stood on end. So we took a little boat, she thought, beginning to tell herself a story of adventure about escaping from a sinking ship. But with the sea streaming through her fingers, a spray of seaweed vanishing behind them, she did not want to tell herself seriously a story; it was the sense of adventure and escape that she wanted, for she was thinking, as the boat sailed on, how her father's anger about the points of the compass, James's obstinacy about the compact, and her own anguish, all had slipped, all had passed, all had streamed away. What then came next? Where were they going? From her hand, ice cold, held deep in the sea, there spurted up a fountain of joy at the change, at the escape, at the adventure (that she should be alive, that she should be there). And the drops falling from this sudden and unthinking fountain of joy fell here and there on the dark, the slumbrous shapes in her mind; shapes of a world not realised but turning in their darkness, catching here and there, a spark of light; Greece, Rome, Constantinople. Small as it was, and shaped something like a leaf stood on end with the gold sprinkled waters flowing in and about it, it had, she supposed, a place in the universe – even that little island? The old gentlemen in the study she thought could have told her. Sometimes she strayed in from the garden purposely to catch them at it. There they were (it might be Mr Carmichael or Mr Bankes, very old, very stiff) sitting opposite each other in their low arm-chairs. They were crackling in front of them the pages of *The Times*, when she came in from the garden, all in a muddle, about something some one had said about Christ; a mammoth had been dug up in a London street; what was the great Napoleon like? Then they took all this with their clean hands (they wore grey coloured clothes; they smelt of heather) and they brushed the scraps together, turning the paper, crossing their knees, and said something now and then very brief. In a kind of trance she would take a book from the shelf and stand there, watching her father write, so equally, so neatly from one side of the page to another, with a little cough now and then, or something said briefly to the other old gentleman opposite. And she thought, standing there with her book open, here one could let whatever one thought expand like a leaf in water; and if it did well here, among the old gentlemen smoking and *The Times* crackling, then it was right. And watching her father as he wrote in his study, she thought (now sitting in the boat) he was most lovable, he was most wise; he was not vain nor a tyrant. Indeed, if he saw she was there, reading a book, he would ask her, as gently as any one could, Was there nothing he could give her?

Lest this should be wrong, she looked at him reading the little book with the shiny cover mottled like a plover's egg. No; it was right. Look at him now, she wanted to say aloud to James. (But James had his eye on the sail.) He is a sarcastic brute, James would say. He brings the talk round to himself and his books, James would say. He is intolerably egotistical. Worst of all, he is a tyrant. But look! she said, looking at him. Look at him now. She looked at him reading the little book with his legs curled; the little book whose yellowish pages she knew, without knowing what was written on them. It was small; it was closely printed; on the fly-leaf, she knew, he had written that he had spent fifteen francs on dinner; the wine had been so much; he had given so much to the waiter; all was added up neatly at the bottom of the page. But what might be written in the book which had rounded its edges off in his pocket, she did not know. What he thought they none of them knew. But he was absorbed in it, so that when he looked up, as he did now for an instant, it was not to see anything; it was to pin down some thought more exactly. That done, his mind flew back again and he plunged into his reading. He read, she thought, as if he were guiding something, or wheedling a large flock of sheep, or pushing his way up and up a single narrow path; and sometimes he went fast and straight, and broke his way through the thicket, and sometimes it seemed a branch struck at him, a bramble blinded him, but he was not going to let himself be beaten by that; on he went, tossing over page after page. And she went on telling herself a story about escaping from a sinking ship, for she was safe, while he sat there; safe, as she felt herself when she crept in from the garden, and took a book down, and the old gentleman, lowering the paper suddenly, said something very brief over the top of it about the character of Napoleon.

She gazed back over the sea, at the island. But the leaf was losing its sharpness. It was very small; it was very distant. The sea was more important now than the shore. Waves were all round them, tossing and sinking, with a log wallowing down one wave; a gull riding on another. About here, she thought, dabbling her fingers in the water, a ship had sunk, and she murmured, dreamily, half asleep, how we perished, each alone.

XI

So much depends then, thought Lily Briscoe, looking at the sea which had scarcely a stain on it, which was so soft that the sails and the clouds seemed set in its blue, so much depends, she thought, upon distance: whether people are near us or far from us; for her feeling for Mr Ramsay changed as he sailed further and further across the bay. It seemed to be elongated, stretched out; he seemed to become more and more remote. He and his children seemed to be swallowed up in that blue, that distance; but here, on the lawn, close at hand, Mr Carmichael suddenly grunted. She laughed. He clawed his book up from the grass. He settled into his chair again puffing and blowing like some sea monster. That was different altogether, because he was so near. And now again all was quiet. They must be out of bed by this time, she supposed, looking at the house, but nothing appeared there. But then, she remembered, they had always made off directly a meal was over, on business of their own. It was all in keeping with this silence, this emptiness, and the unreality of the early morning hour. It was a way things had sometimes, she thought, lingering for a moment and looking at the long glittering windows and the plume of blue smoke: they became unreal. So coming back from a journey, or after an illness, before habits had spun themselves across the surface, one felt that same unreality, which was so startling; felt something emerge. Life was most vivid then. One could be at one's ease. Mercifully one need not say, very briskly, crossing the lawn to greet old Mrs Beckwith, who would be coming out to find a corner to sit in, 'Oh good-morning, Mrs Beckwith! What a lovely day! Are you going to be so bold as to sit in the sun? Jasper's hidden the chairs. Do let me find you one!' and all the rest of the usual chatter. One need not speak at all. One glided, one shook one's sails (there was a good deal of movement in the bay, boats were starting off) between things, beyond things. Empty it was not, but full to the brim. She seemed to be standing up to the lips in some substance, to move and float and sink in it, yes, for these waters were unfathomably deep. Into them had spilled so many lives. The Ramsays'; the children's; and all sorts of waifs and strays of things besides. A washerwoman with her basket; a rook; a red-hot poker; the purples and grey-greens of flowers: some common feeling which held the whole together.

It was some such feeling of completeness perhaps which, ten years ago, standing almost where she stood now, had made her say that she must be in love with the place. Love had a thousand shapes. There might be lovers whose gift it was to choose out the elements of things and place them together and so, giving them a wholeness not theirs in life, make of some scene, or meeting of people (all now gone and separate), one of those globed compacted things over which thought lingers, and love plays.

Her eyes rested on the brown speck of Mr Ramsay's sailing boat. They would be at the Lighthouse by lunch time she supposed. But the wind had freshened, and, as the sky changed slightly and the sea changed slightly and the boats altered their positions, the view, which a moment before had seemed miraculously fixed, was now unsatisfactory. The wind had blown the trail of smoke about; there was something displeasing about the placing of the ships.

The disproportion there seemed to upset some harmony in her own mind. She felt an obscure distress. It was confirmed when she turned to her picture. She had been wasting her morning. For whatever reason she could not achieve that razor edge of balance between two opposite forces; Mr Ramsay and the picture; which was necessary. There was something perhaps wrong with the design? Was it, she wondered, that the line of the wall wanted breaking, was it that the mass of the trees was too heavy? She smiled ironically; for had she not thought, when she began, that she had solved her problem?

What was the problem then? She must try to get hold of something that evaded her. It evaded her when she thought of Mrs Ramsay; it evaded her now when she thought of her picture. Phrases came. Visions came. Beautiful pictures. Beautiful phrases. But what she wished to get hold of was that very jar on the nerves, the thing itself before it has been made anything. Get that and start afresh; get that and start afresh; she said desperately, pitching herself firmly again before her easel. It was a miserable machine, an inefficient machine, she thought, the human apparatus for painting or for feeling; it always broke down at the critical moment; heroically, one must force it on. She stared, frowning. There was the hedge, sure enough. But one got nothing by soliciting urgently. One got only a glare in the eye from looking at the line of the wall, or from thinking – she wore a grey hat. She was astonishingly beautiful. Let it come, she thought, if it will come. For there are moments when one can neither think nor feel. And if one can neither think nor feel, she thought, where is one?

Here on the grass, on the ground, she thought, sitting down, and examining with her brush a little colony of plantains. For the lawn was very rough. Here sitting on the world, she thought, for she could not shake herself free from the sense that everything this morning was happening for the first time, perhaps for the last time, as a traveller, even though he is half asleep, knows, looking out of the train window, that he must look now, for he will never see that town, or that mule-cart, or that woman at work in the fields, again. The lawn was the world; they were up here together, on this exalted station, she thought, looking at old Mr Carmichael, who seemed (though they had not said a word all this time) to share her thoughts. And she would never see him again perhaps. He was growing old. Also, she remembered, smiling at the slipper that dangled from his foot, he was growing famous. People said that his poetry was 'so beautiful.' They went and published things he had written forty years ago. There was a famous man now called Carmichael, she smiled, thinking how many shapes one person might wear, how he was that in the newspapers, but here the same as he had always been. He looked the same – greyer, rather. Yes, he looked the same, but somebody had said, she recalled, that when he had heard of Andrew Ramsay's death (he was killed in a second by a shell; he should have been a great mathematician) Mr Carmichael had 'lost all interest in life'. What did it mean – that? she wondered. Had he marched through Trafalgar Square grasping a big stick? Had he turned pages over and over, without reading them, sitting in his room in St John's Wood alone? She did not know what he had done, when he heard that Andrew was killed, but she felt it in him all the same. They only mumbled at each other on staircases; they looked up at the sky and said it will be fine or it won't be fine. But this was one way of knowing people, she thought: to know the outline, not the detail, to sit in one's garden and look at the slopes of a hill running purple down into the distant heather. She knew him in that way. She knew that he had changed somehow. She had never read a line of his poetry. She thought that she knew how it went though, slowly and sonorously. It was seasoned and mellow. It was about the desert and the camel. It was about the palm tree and the sunset. It was extremely impersonal; it said something about death; it said very little about love. There was an aloofness about him. He wanted very little of other people. Had he not always lurched rather awkwardly past the drawing-room window with some newspaper under his arm, trying to avoid Mrs Ramsay whom for some reason he did not much like? On that account, of course, she would always try to make him stop. He would bow to her. He would halt unwillingly and bow profoundly. Annoyed that he did not want anything of her, Mrs Ramsay would ask him (Lily could hear her) wouldn't he like a coat, a rug, a newspaper? No, he wanted nothing. (Here he bowed.) There was some quality in her which he did not much like. It was perhaps her masterfulness, her positiveness, something matter-of-fact in her. She was so direct.

(A noise drew her attention to the drawing-room window – the squeak of a hinge. The light breeze was toying with the window.)

There must have been people who disliked her very much, Lily thought (Yes; she realised that the drawing-room step was empty, but it had no effect on her whatever. She did not want Mrs Ramsay now). – People who thought her too sure, too drastic. Also her beauty offended people probably. How monotonous, they would say, and the same always! They preferred another type – the dark, the vivacious. Then she was weak with her husband. She let him make those scenes. Then she was reserved. Nobody knew exactly what had happened to her. And (to go back to Mr Carmichael and his dislike) one could not imagine Mrs Ramsay standing painting, lying reading, a whole morning on the lawn. It was unthinkable. Without saying a word, the only token of her errand a basket on her arm, she went off to the town, to the poor, to sit in some stuffy little bedroom. Often and often Lily had seen her go silently in the midst of some game, some discussion, with her basket on her arm, very upright. She had noted her return. She had thought, half laughing (she was so methodical with the tea cups) half moved (her beauty took one's breath away), eyes that are closing in pain have looked on you. You have been with them there.

And then Mrs Ramsay would be annoyed because somebody was late, or the butter not fresh, or the teapot chipped. And all the time she was saying that the butter was not fresh one would be thinking of Greek temples, and how beauty had been with them there. She never talked of it – she went, punctually, directly. It was her instinct to go, an instinct like the swallows for the south, the artichokes for the sun, turning her infallibly to the human race, making her nest in its heart. And this, like all instincts, was a little distressing to people who did not share it; to Mr Carmichael perhaps, to herself certainly. Some notion was in both of them about the ineffectiveness of action, the supremacy of thought. Her going was a reproach to them, gave a different twist to the world, so that they were led to protest, seeing their own prepossessions disappear, and clutch at them vanishing. Charles Tansley did that too: it was part of the reason why one disliked him. He upset the proportions of one's world. And what had happened to him, she wondered, idly stirring the plantains with her brush. He had got his fellowship. He had married; he lived at Golders Green.

She had gone one day into a Hall and heard him speaking

during the war. He was denouncing something: he was condemning somebody. He was preaching brotherly love. And all she felt was how could he love his kind who did not know one picture from another, who had stood behind her smoking shag ('fivepence an ounce, Miss Briscoe') and making it his business to tell her women can't write, women can't paint, not so much that he believed it, as that for some odd reason he wished it? There he was, lean and red and raucous, preaching love from a platform (there were ants crawling about among the plantains which she disturbed with her brush – red, energetic ants, rather like Charles Tansley). She had looked at him ironically from her seat in the half-empty hall, pumping love into that chilly space, and suddenly, there was the old cask or whatever it was bobbing up and down among the waves and Mrs Ramsay looking for her spectacle case among the pebbles. 'Oh dear! What a nuisance! Lost again. Don't bother, Mr Tansley. I lose thousands every summer,' at which he pressed his chin back against his collar, as if afraid to sanction such exaggeration, but could stand it in her whom he liked, and smiled very charmingly. He must have confided in her on one of those long expeditions when people got separated and walked back alone. He was educating his little sister, Mrs Ramsay had told her. It was immensely to his credit. Her own idea of him was grotesque, Lily knew well, stirring the plantains with her brush. Half one's notions of other people were, after all, grotesque. They served private purposes of one's own. He did for her instead of a whipping-boy. She found herself flagellating his lean flanks when she was out of temper. If she wanted to be serious about him she had to help herself to Mrs Ramsay's sayings, to look at him through her eyes.

She raised a little mountain for the ants to climb over. She reduced them to a frenzy of indecision by this interference in their cosmogony. Some ran this way, others that.

One wanted fifty pairs of eyes to see with, she reflected.

Fifty pairs of eyes were not enough to get round that one woman with, she thought. Among them, must be one that was stone blind to her beauty. One wanted most some secret sense, fine as air, with which to steal through keyholes and surround her where she sat knitting, talking, sitting silent in the window alone; which took to itself and treasured up like the air which held the smoke of the steamer, her thoughts, her imaginations, her desires. What did the hedge mean to her, what did the garden mean to her, what did it mean to her when a wave broke? (Lily looked up, as she had seen Mrs Ramsay look up; she too heard a wave falling on the beach.) And then what stirred and trembled in her mind when the children cried, 'How's that? How's that? Cricketing?' She would stop knitting for a second. She would look intent. Then she would lapse again, and suddenly Mr Ramsay stopped dead in his pacing in front of her, and some curious shock passed through her and seemed to rock her in profound agitation on its breast when stopping there he stood over her, and looked down at her. Lily could see him.

He stretched out his hand and raised her from her chair. It seemed somehow as if he had done it before; as if he had once bent in the same way and raised her from a boat which, lying a few inches off some island, had required that the ladies should thus be helped on shore by the gentlemen. An old-fashioned scene that was, which required, very nearly, crinolines and peg-top trousers. Letting herself be helped by him, Mrs Ramsay had thought (Lily supposed) the time has come now; Yes, she would say it now. Yes, she would marry him. And she stepped slowly, quietly on shore. Probably she said one word only, letting her hand rest still in his. I will marry you, she might have said, with her hand in his; but no more. Time after time the same thrill had passed between them – obviously it had, Lily thought, smoothing a way for her ants. She was not inventing; she was only trying to smooth out something she had been given years ago folded up;

something she had seen. For in the rough and tumble of daily life, with all those children about, all those visitors, one had constantly a sense of repetition – of one thing falling where another had fallen, and so setting up an echo which chimed in the air and made it full of vibrations.

But it would be a mistake, she thought, thinking how they walked off together, she in her green shawl, he with his tie flying, arm in arm, past the greenhouse, to simplify their relationship. It was no monotony of bliss – she with her impulses and quicknesses; he with his shudders and glooms. Oh no. The bedroom door would slam violently early in the morning. He would whizz his plate through the window. Then all through the house there would be a sense of doors slamming and blinds fluttering as if a gusty wind were blowing and people scudded about trying in a hasty way to fasten hatches and make things shipshape. She had met Paul Rayley like that one day on the stairs. They had laughed and laughed, like a couple of children, all because Mr Ramsay, finding an earwig in his milk at breakfast had sent the whole thing flying through the air on to the terrace outside. 'An earwig,' Prue murmured, awestruck, 'in his milk.' Other people might find centipedes. But he had built round him such a fence of sanctity, and occupied the space with such a demeanour of majesty that an earwig in his milk was a monster.

But it tired Mrs Ramsay, it cowed her a little – the plates whizzing and the doors slamming. And there would fall between them sometimes long rigid silences, when, in a state of mind which annoyed Lily in her, half plaintive, half resentful, she seemed unable to surmount the tempest calmly, or to laugh as they laughed, but in her weariness perhaps concealed something. She brooded and sat silent. After a time he would hang stealthily about the places where she was – roaming under the window where she sat writing letters or talking, for she would take care to be busy when he passed, and evade him, and pretend not to see him. Then he would turn smooth as silk, affable, urbane, and try to win her so. Still she would hold off, and now she would assert for a brief season some of those prides and airs the due of her beauty which she was generally utterly without; would turn her head; would look so, over her shoulder, always with some Minta, Paul, or William Bankes at her side. At length, standing outside the group the very figure of a famished wolfhound (Lily got up off the grass and stood looking at the steps, at the window, where she had seen him), he would say her name, once only, for all the world like a wolf barking in the snow, but still she held back; and he would say it once more, and this time something in the tone would rouse her, and she would go to him, leaving them all of a sudden, and they would walk off together among the pear trees, the cabbages, and the raspberry beds. They would have it out together. But with what attitudes and with what words? Such a dignity was theirs in this relationship that, turning away, she and Paul and Minta would hide their curiosity and their discomfort, and begin picking flowers, throwing balls, chattering, until it was time for dinner, and there they were, he at one end of the table, she at the other, as usual.

'Why don't some of you take up botany? . . . With all those legs and arms why doesn't one of you . . .?' So they would talk as usual, laughing, among the children. All would be as usual, save only for some quiver, as of a blade in the air, which came and went between them as if the usual sight of the children sitting round their soup plates had freshened itself in their eyes after that hour among the pears and the cabbages. Especially, Lily thought, Mrs Ramsay would glance at Prue. She sat in the middle between brothers and sisters, always so occupied, it seemed, seeing that nothing went wrong that she scarcely spoke herself. How Prue must have blamed herself for that earwig in the milk! How white she had gone when Mr Ramsay threw his plate through the window! How she drooped under those long silences between them! Anyhow, her mother now would seem to be making it up to her; assuring her that everything was well; promising her that one of these days that same happiness would be hers. She had enjoyed it for less than a year, however.

She had let the flowers fall from her basket, Lily thought, screwing up her eyes and standing back as if to look at her picture, which she was not touching, however, with all her faculties in a trance, frozen over superficially but moving underneath with extreme speed.

She let her flowers fall from her basket, scattered and tumbled them on to the grass and, reluctantly and hesitatingly, but without question or complaint – had she not the faculty of obedience to perfection? – went too. Down fields, across valleys, white, flower-strewn – that was how she would have painted it. The hills were austere. It was rocky; it was steep. The waves sounded hoarse on the stones beneath. They went, the three of them together, Mrs Ramsay walking rather fast in front, as if she expected to meet some one round the corner.

Suddenly the window at which she was looking was whitened by some light stuff behind it. At last then somebody had come into the drawing-room; somebody was sitting in the chair. For Heaven's sake, she prayed, let them sit still there and not come floundering out to talk to her. Mercifully, whoever it was stayed still inside; had settled by some stroke of luck so as to throw an odd-shaped triangular shadow over the step. It altered the composition of the picture a little. It was interesting. It might be useful. Her mood was coming back to her. One must keep on looking without for a second relaxing the intensity of emotion, the determination not to be put off, not to be bamboozled. One must hold the scene – so – in a vice and let nothing come in and spoil it. One wanted, she thought, dipping her brush deliberately, to be on a level with ordinary experience, to feel simply that's a chair, that's a table, and yet at the same time, It's a miracle, it's an ecstasy. The problem might be solved after all. Ah, but what had happened? Some wave of white went over the window pane. The air must have stirred some flounce in the room. Her heart leapt at her and seized her and tortured her.

'Mrs Ramsay! Mrs Ramsay!' she cried, feeling the old horror come back – to want and want and not to have. Could she inflict that still? And then, quietly, as if she refrained, that too became part of ordinary experience, was on a level with the chair, with the table. Mrs Ramsay – it was part of her perfect goodness to Lily – sat there quite simply, in the chair, flicked her needles to and fro, knitted her reddish-brown stocking, cast her shadow on the step. There she sat.

And as if she had something she must share, yet could hardly leave her easel, so full her mind was of what she was thinking, of what she was seeing, Lily went past Mr Carmichael holding her brush to the edge of the lawn. Where was that boat now? Mr Ramsay? She wanted him.

XII

Mr Ramsay had almost done reading. One hand hovered over the page as if to be in readiness to turn it the very instant he had finished it. He sat there bareheaded with the wind blowing his hair about, extraordinarily exposed to everything. He looked very old. He looked, James thought, getting his head now against the Lighthouse, now against the waste of waters running away into the open, like some old stone lying on the sand; he looked as if he had become physically what was always at the back of both of their minds – that loneliness which was for both of them the truth about things.

He was reading very quickly, as if he were eager to get to the end. Indeed they were very close to the Lighthouse now. There it loomed up, stark and straight, glaring white and black, and one could see the waves breaking in white splinters like smashed glass upon the rocks. One could see lines and creases in the rocks. One could see the windows clearly; a dab of white on one of them, and a little tuft of green on the rock. A man had come out and looked at them through a glass and gone in again. So it was like that, James thought, the Lighthouse one had seen across the bay all these years; it was a stark tower on a bare rock. It satisfied him. It confirmed some obscure feeling of his about his own character. The old ladies, he thought, thinking of the garden at home, went dragging their chairs about on the lawn. Old Mrs Beckwith, for example, was always saying how nice it was and how sweet it was and how they ought to be so proud and they ought to be so happy, but as a matter of fact James thought, looking at the Lighthouse stood there on its rock, it's like that. He looked at his father reading fiercely with his legs curled tight. They shared that knowledge. 'We are driving before a gale – we must sink,' he began saying to himself, half aloud exactly as his father said it.

Nobody seemed to have spoken for an age. Cam was tired of looking at the sea. Little bits of black cork had floated past; the fish were dead in the bottom of the boat. Still her father read, and James looked at him and she looked at him, and they vowed that they would fight tyranny to the death, and he went on reading quite unconscious of what they thought. It was thus that he escaped, she thought. Yes, with his great forehead and his great nose, holding his little mottled book firmly in front of him, he escaped. You might try to lay hands on him, but then like a bird, he spread his wings, he floated off to settle out of your reach somewhere far away on some desolate stump. She gazed at the immense expanse of the sea. The island had grown so small that it scarcely looked like a leaf any longer. It looked like the top of a rock which some big wave would cover. Yet in its frailty were all those paths, those terraces, those bedrooms – all those innumerable things. But as, just before sleep, things simplify themselves so that only one of all the myriad details has power to assert itself, so, she felt, looking drowsily at the island, all those paths and terraces and bedrooms were fading and disappearing, and nothing was left but a pale blue censer swinging rhythmically this way and that across her mind. It was a hanging garden; it was a valley, full of birds, and flowers, and antelopes . . . She was falling asleep.

'Come now,' said Mr Ramsay, suddenly shutting his book.

Come where? To what extraordinary adventure? She woke with a start. To land somewhere, to climb somewhere? Where was he leading them? For after his immense silence the words startled them. But it was absurd. He was hungry, he said. It was time for lunch. Besides, look, he said. There's the Lighthouse. 'We're almost there.'

'He's doing very well,' said Macalister, praising James. 'He's keeping her very steady.'

But his father never praised him, James thought grimly.

Mr Ramsay opened the parcel and shared out the sandwiches among them. Now he was happy, eating bread and cheese with these fishermen. He would have liked to live in a cottage and lounge about in the harbour spitting with the other old men, James thought, watching him slice his cheese into thin yellow sheets with his penknife.

This is right, this is it, Cam kept feeling, as she peeled her hard-boiled egg. Now she felt as she did in the study when the old men were reading *The Times*. Now I can go on thinking whatever I like, and I shan't fall over a precipice or be drowned, for there he is, keeping his eye on me, she thought.

At the same time they were sailing so fast along by the rocks that it was very exciting – it seemed as if they were doing two things at once; they were eating their lunch here in the sun and they were also making for safety in a great storm after a shipwreck. Would the water last? Would the provisions last? she asked herself, telling herself a story but knowing at the same time what was the truth.

They would soon be out of it, Mr Ramsay was saying to

old Macalister; but their children would see some strange things. Macalister said he was seventy-five last March; Mr Ramsay was seventy-one. Macalister said he had never seen a doctor; he had never lost a tooth. And that's the way I'd like my children to live – Cam was sure that her father was thinking that, for he stopped her throwing a sandwich into the sea and told her, as if he were thinking of the fishermen and how they live, that if she did not want it she should put it back in the parcel. She should not waste it. He said it so wisely, as if he knew so well all the things that happened in the world, that she put it back at once, and then he gave her, from his own parcel, a gingerbread nut, as if he were a great Spanish gentleman, she thought, handing a flower to a lady at a window (so courteous his manner was). But he was shabby, and simple, eating bread and cheese; and yet he was leading them on a great expedition where, for all she knew, they would be drowned.

'That was where she sunk,' said Macalister's boy suddenly.

'Three men were drowned where we are now,' said the old man. He had seen them clinging to the mast himself. And Mr Ramsay taking a look at the spot was about, James and Cam were afraid, to burst out:

But I beneath a rougher sea,

and if he did, they could not bear it; they would shriek aloud; they could not endure another explosion of the passion that boiled in him; but to their surprise all he said was 'Ah' as if he thought to himself, But why make a fuss about that? Naturally men are drowned in a storm, but it is a perfectly straightforward affair, and the depths of the sea (he sprinkled the crumbs from his sandwich paper over them) are only water after all. Then having lighted his pipe he took out his watch. He looked at it attentively; he made, perhaps, some mathematical calculation. At last he said, triumphantly:

'Well done!' James had steered them like a born sailor.

There! Cam thought, addressing herself silently to James. You've got it at last. For she knew that this was what James had been wanting, and she knew that now he had got it he was so pleased that he would not look at her or at his father or at any one. There he sat with his hand on the tiller sitting bolt upright, looking rather sulky and frowning slightly. He was so pleased that he was not going to let anybody take away a grain of his pleasure. His father had praised him. They must think that he was perfectly indifferent. But you've got it now, Cam thought.

They had tacked, and they were sailing swiftly, buoyantly on long rocking waves which handed them on from one to another with an extraordinary lilt and exhilaration beside the reef. On the left a row of rocks showed brown through the water which thinned and became greener and on one, a higher rock, a wave incessantly broke and spurted a little column of drops which fell down in a shower. One could hear the slap of the water and the patter of falling drops and a kind of hushing and hissing sound from the waves rolling and gambolling and slapping the rocks as if they were wild creatures who were perfectly free and tossed and tumbled and sported like this for ever.

Now they could see two men on the Lighthouse, watching them and making ready to meet them.

Mr Ramsay buttoned his coat, and turned up his trousers. He took the large, badly packed, brown paper parcel which Nancy had got ready and sat with it on his knee. Thus in complete readiness to land he sat looking back at the island. With his long-sighted eyes perhaps he could see the dwindled leaf-like shape standing on end on a plate of gold quite clearly. What could he see? Cam wondered. It was all a blur to her. What was he thinking now? she wondered. What was it he sought, so fixedly, so intently, so silently? They watched him, both of them, sitting bareheaded with his parcel on his knee staring and staring at the frail blue shape which seemed like the vapour of something that had burnt itself away. What do you want? they both wanted to ask. They both wanted to say, Ask us anything and we will give it you. But he did not ask them anything. He sat and looked at the island and he might be thinking, We perished, each alone, or he might be thinking, I have reached it. I have found it, but he said nothing.

Then he put on his hat.

'Bring those parcels,' he said, nodding his head at the things Nancy had done up for them to take to the Lighthouse. 'The parcels for the Lighthouse men,' he said. He rose and stood in the bow of the boat, very straight and tall, for all the world, James thought, as if he were saying, 'There is no God,' and Cam thought, as if he were leaping into space, and they both rose to follow him as he sprang, lightly like a young man, holding his parcel, on to the rock.

XIII

'He must have reached it,' said Lily Briscoe aloud, feeling suddenly completely tired out. For the Lighthouse had become almost invisible, had melted away into a blue haze, and the effort of looking at it and the effort of thinking of him landing there, which both seemed to be one and the same effort, had stretched her body and mind to the utmost. Ah, but she was relieved. What-ever she had wanted to give him, when he left her that morning, she had given him at last.

'He has landed,' she said aloud. 'It is finished.' Then, surging up, puffing slightly, old Mr Carmichael stood beside her, looking like an old pagan god, shaggy, with weeds in his hair and the trident (it was only a French novel) in his hand. He stood by her on the edge of the lawn, swaying a little in his bulk, and said, shading his eyes with his hand: 'They will have landed,' and she felt that she had been right. They had not needed to speak. They had been thinking the same things and he had answered her without her asking him anything. He stood there spreading his hands over all the weakness and suffering of mankind; she thought he was surveying, tolerantly, compassionately, their final destiny. Now he has crowned the occasion, she thought, when his hand slowly fell, as if she had seen him let fall from his great height a wreath of violets and asphodels which, fluttering slowly, lay at length upon the earth.

Quickly, as if she were recalled by something over there, she turned to her canvas. There it was – her picture. Yes, with all its greens and blues, its lines running up and across, its attempt at something. It would be hung in the attics, she thought; it would be destroyed. But what did that matter? she asked herself, taking up her brush again. She looked at the steps; they were empty; she looked at her canvas; it was blurred. With a sudden intensity, as if she saw it clear for a second, she drew a line there, in the centre. It was done; it was finished. Yes, she thought, laying down her brush in extreme fatigue, I have had my vision.

CLASSIC LITERATURE: WORDS AND PHRASES
adapted from the Collins English Dictionary

Accoucheur NOUN a male midwife or doctor ❏ *I think my sister must have had some general idea that I was a young offender whom an Accoucheur Policemen had taken up (on my birthday) and delivered over to her* (*Great Expectations* by Charles Dickens)

addled ADJ confused and unable to think properly ❏ *But she counted and counted till she got that addled* (*The Adventures of Huckleberry Finn* by Mark Twain)

admiration NOUN amazement or wonder ❏ *lifting up his hands and eyes by way of admiration* (*Gulliver's Travels* by Jonathan Swift)

afeard ADJ afeard means afraid ❏ *shake it–and don't be afeard* (*The Adventures of Huckleberry Finn* by Mark Twain)

affected VERB affected means to assume the appearance of ❏ *Hadst thou affected sweet divinity* (*Doctor Faustus 5.2* by Christopher Marlowe)

aground ADV when a boat runs aground, it touches the ground in a shallow part of the water and gets stuck ❏ *what kep' you?–boat get aground?* (*The Adventures of Huckleberry Finn* by Mark Twain)

ague NOUN a fever in which the patient has alternate hot and cold shivering fits ❏ *his exposure to the wet and cold had brought on fever and ague* (*Oliver Twist* by Charles Dickens)

alchemy ADJ false or worthless ❏ *all wealth alchemy* (*The Sun Rising* by John Donne)

all alike PHRASE the same all the time ❏ *Love, all alike* (*The Sun Rising* by John Donne)

alow and aloft PHRASE alow means in the lower part or bottom, and aloft means on the top, so alow and aloft means on the top and in the bottom or throughout ❏ *Someone's turned the chest out alow and aloft* (*Treasure Island* by Robert Louis Stevenson)

ambuscade NOUN ambuscade is not a proper word. Tom means an ambush, which is when a group of people attack their enemies, after hiding and waiting for them ❏ *and so we would lie in ambuscade, as he called it* (*The Adventures of Huckleberry Finn* by Mark Twain)

amiable ADJ likeable or pleasant ❏ *Such amiable qualities must speak for themselves* (*Pride and Prejudice* by Jane Austen)

amulet NOUN an amulet is a charm thought to drive away evil spirits. ❏ *uttered phrases at once occult and familiar, like the amulet worn on the heart* (*Silas Marner* by George Eliot)

amusement NOUN here amusement means a strange and disturbing puzzle ❏ *this was an amusement the other way* (*Robinson Crusoe* by Daniel Defoe)

ancient NOUN an ancient was the flag displayed on a ship to show which country it belongs to. It is also called the ensign ❏ *her ancient and pendants out* (*Robinson Crusoe* by Daniel Defoe)

antic ADJ here antic means horrible or grotesque ❏ *armed and dressed after a very antic manner* (*Gulliver's Travels* by Jonathan Swift)

antics NOUN antics is an old word meaning clowns, or people who do silly things to make other people laugh ❏ *And point like antics at his triple crown* (*Doctor Faustus 3.2* by Christopher Marlowe)

appanage NOUN an appanage is a living allowance ❑ *As if loveliness were not the special prerogative of woman – her legitimate appanage and heritage!* (*Jane Eyre* by Charlotte Brontë)

appended VERB appended means attached or added to ❑ *and these words appended* (*Treasure Island* by Robert Louis Stevenson)

approver NOUN an approver is someone who gives evidence against someone he used to work with ❑ *Mr Noah Claypole: receiving a free pardon from the Crown in consequence of being admitted approver against Fagin* (*Oliver Twist* by Charles Dickens)

areas NOUN the areas is the space, below street level, in front of the basement of a house ❑ *The Dodger had a vicious propensity, too, of pulling the caps from the heads of small boys and tossing them down areas* (*Oliver Twist* by Charles Dickens)

argument NOUN theme or important idea or subject which runs through a piece of writing ❑ *Thrice needful to the argument which now* (*The Prelude* by William Wordsworth)

artificially ADV artfully or cleverly ❑ *and he with a sharp flint sharpened very artificially* (*Gulliver's Travels* by Jonathan Swift)

artist NOUN here artist means a skilled workman ❑ *This man was a most ingenious artist* (*Gulliver's Travels* by Jonathan Swift)

assizes NOUN assizes were regular court sessions which a visiting judge was in charge of ❑ *you shall hang at the next assizes* (*Treasure Island* by Robert Louis Stevenson)

attraction NOUN gravitation, or Newton's theory of gravitation ❑ *he predicted the same fate to attraction* (*Gulliver's Travels* by Jonathan Swift)

aver VERB to aver is to claim something strongly ❑ *for Jem Rodney, the mole catcher, averred that one evening as he was returning homeward* (*Silas Marner* by George Eliot)

baby NOUN here baby means doll, which is a child's toy that looks like a small person ❑ *and skilful dressing her baby* (*Gulliver's Travels* by Jonathan Swift)

bagatelle NOUN bagatelle is a game rather like billiards and pool ❑ *Breakfast had been ordered at a pleasant little tavern, a mile or so away upon the rising ground beyond the green; and there was a bagatelle board in the room, in case we should desire to unbend our minds after the solemnity.* (*Great Expectations* by Charles Dickens)

bah EXCLAM Bah is an exclamation of frustration or anger ❑ *'Bah,' said Scrooge.* (*A Christmas Carol* by Charles Dickens)

bairn NOUN a northern word for child ❑ *Who has taught you those fine words, my bairn?* (*Wuthering Heights* by Emily Brontë)

bait VERB to bait means to stop on a journey to take refreshment ❑ *So, when they stopped to bait the horse, and ate and drank and enjoyed themselves, I could touch nothing that they touched, but kept my fast unbroken.* (*David Copperfield* by Charles Dickens)

balustrade NOUN a balustrade is a row of vertical columns that form railings ❑ *but I mean to say you might have got a hearse up that staircase, and taken it broadwise, with the splinter-bar towards the wall, and the door towards the balustrades: and done it easy* (*A Christmas Carol* by Charles Dickens)

bandbox NOUN a large lightweight box for carrying bonnets or hats ❑ *I am glad I bought my bonnet, if it is only for the fun of having another bandbox* (*Pride and Prejudice* by Jane Austen)

barren NOUN a barren here is a stretch or expanse of barren land ❑ *a line of upright stones, continued the* *length of the barren* (*Wuthering Heights* by Emily Brontë)

basin NOUN a basin was a cup without a handle ❑ *who is drinking his tea out of a basin* (*Wuthering Heights* by Emily Brontë)

battalia NOUN the order of battle ❑ *till I saw part of his army in battalia* (*Gulliver's Travels* by Jonathan Swift)

battery NOUN a Battery is a fort or a place where guns are positioned ❑ *You bring the lot to me, at that old Battery over yonder* (*Great Expectations* by Charles Dickens)

battledore and shuttlecock NOUN The game battledore and shuttlecock was an early version of the game now known as badminton. The aim of the early game was simply to keep the shuttlecock from hitting the ground. ❑ *Battledore and shuttlecock's a wery good game vhen you an't the shuttlecock and two lawyers the battledores, in which case it gets too excitin' to be pleasant* (*Pickwick Papers* by Charles Dickens)

beadle NOUN a beadle was a local official who had power over the poor ❑ *But these impertinences were speedily checked by the evidence of the surgeon, and the testimony of the beadle* (*Oliver Twist* by Charles Dickens)

bearings NOUN the bearings of a place are the measurements or directions that are used to find or locate it ❑ *the bearings of the island* (*Treasure Island* by Robert Louis Stevenson)

beaufet NOUN a beaufet was a sideboard ❑ *and sweet-cake from the beaufet* (*Emma* by Jane Austen)

beck NOUN a beck is a small stream ❑ *a beck which follows the bend of the glen* (*Wuthering Heights* by Emily Brontë)

bedight VERB decorated ❑ *and bedight with Christmas holly stuck into the top.* (*A Christmas Carol* by Charles Dickens)

Bedlam NOUN Bedlam was a lunatic

asylum in London which had statues carved by Caius Gabriel Cibber at its entrance ❑ *Bedlam, and those carved maniacs at the gates* (*The Prelude* by William Wordsworth)

beeves NOUN oxen or castrated bulls which are animals used for pulling vehicles or carrying things ❑ *to deliver in every morning six beeves* (*Gulliver's Travels* by Jonathan Swift)

begot VERB created or caused ❑ *Begot in thee* (*On His Mistress* by John Donne)

behoof NOUN behoof means benefit ❑ *'Yes, young man,' said he, releasing the handle of the article in question, retiring a step or two from my table, and speaking for the behoof of the landlord and waiter at the door* (*Great Expectations* by Charles Dickens)

berth NOUN a berth is a bed on a boat ❑ *this is the berth for me* (*Treasure Island* by Robert Louis Stevenson)

bevers NOUN a bever was a snack, or small portion of food, eaten between main meals ❑ *that buys me thirty meals a day and ten bevers* (*Doctor Faustus 2.1* by Christopher Marlowe)

bilge water NOUN the bilge is the widest part of a ship's bottom, and the bilge water is the dirty water that collects there ❑ *no gush of bilge-water had turned it to fetid puddle* (*Jane Eyre* by Charlotte Brontë)

bills NOUN bills is an old term meaning prescription. A prescription is the piece of paper on which your doctor writes an order for medicine and which you give to a chemist to get the medicine ❑ *Are not thy bills hung up as monuments* (*Doctor Faustus 1.1* by Christopher Marlowe)

black cap NOUN a judge wore a black cap when he was about to sentence a prisoner to death ❑ *The judge assumed the black cap, and the* *prisoner still stood with the same air and gesture.* (*Oliver Twist* by Charles Dickens)

boot-jack NOUN a wooden device to help take boots off ❏ *The speaker appeared to throw a boot-jack, or some such article, at the person he addressed* (*Oliver Twist* by Charles Dickens)

booty NOUN booty means treasure or prizes ❏ *would be inclined to give up their booty in payment of the dead man's debts* (*Treasure Island* by Robert Louis Stevenson)

Bow Street runner PHRASE Bow Street runners were the first British police force, set up by the author Henry Fielding in the eighteenth century ❏ *as would have convinced a judge or a Bow Street runner* (*Treasure Island* by Robert Louis Stevenson)

brawn NOUN brawn is a dish of meat which is set in jelly ❏ *Heaped up upon the floor, to form a kind of throne, were turkeys, geese, game, poultry, brawn, great joints of meat, sucking-pigs* (*A Christmas Carol* by Charles Dickens)

bray VERB when a donkey brays, it makes a loud, harsh sound ❏ *and she doesn't bray like a jackass* (*The Adventures of Huckleberry Finn* by Mark Twain)

break VERB in order to train a horse you first have to break it ❏ *'If a high-mettled creature like this,' said he, 'can't be broken by fair means, she will never be good for anything'* (*Black Beauty* by Anna Sewell)

bullyragging VERB bullyragging is an old word which means bullying. To bullyrag someone is to threaten or force someone to do something they don't want to do ❏ *and a lot of loafers bullyragging him for sport* (*The Adventures of Huckleberry Finn* by Mark Twain)

but PREP except for (this) ❏ *but this, all pleasures fancies be* (*The Good-Morrow* by John Donne)

by hand PHRASE by hand was a common expression of the time meaning that baby had been fed either using a spoon or a bottle rather than by breast-feeding ❏ *My sister, Mrs Joe Gargery, was more than twenty years older than I, and had established a great reputation with herself . . . because she had bought me up 'by hand'* (*Great Expectations* by Charles Dickens)

bye-spots NOUN bye-spots are lonely places ❏ *and bye-spots of tales rich with indigenous produce* (*The Prelude* by William Wordsworth)

calico NOUN calico is plain white fabric made from cotton ❏ *There was two old dirty calico dresses* (*The Adventures of Huckleberry Finn* by Mark Twain)

camp-fever NOUN camp-fever was another word for the disease typhus ❏ *during a severe camp-fever* (*Emma* by Jane Austen)

cant NOUN cant is insincere or empty talk ❏ *'Man,' said the Ghost, 'if man you be in heart, not adamant, forbear that wicked cant until you have discovered What the surplus is, and Where it is.'* (*A Christmas Carol* by Charles Dickens)

canty ADJ canty means lively, full of life ❏ *My mother lived til eighty, a canty dame to the last* (*Wuthering Heights* by Emily Brontë)

canvas VERB to canvas is to discuss ❏ *We think so very differently on this point Mr Knightley, that there can be no use in canvassing it* (*Emma* by Jane Austen)

capital ADJ capital means excellent or extremely good ❏ *for it's capital, so shady, light, and big* (*Little Women* by Louisa May Alcott)

capstan NOUN a capstan is a device used on a ship to lift sails and anchors ❏ *capstans going, ships going out to sea, and unintelligible sea creatures roaring curses over the bulwarks at respondent lightermen*

case-bottle NOUN a square bottle designed to fit with others into a case ❑ *The spirit being set before him in a huge case-bottle, which had originally come out of some ship's locker* (*The Old Curiosity Shop* by Charles Dickens)

casement NOUN casement is a word meaning window. The teacher in *Nicholas Nickleby* misspells window showing what a bad teacher he is ❑ *W-i-n, win, d-e-r, der, winder, a casement.* (*Nicholas Nickleby* by Charles Dickens)

cataleptic ADJ a cataleptic fit is one in which the victim goes into a trancelike state and remains still for a long time ❑ *It was at this point in their history that Silas's cataleptic fit occurred during the prayer-meeting* (*Silas Marner* by George Eliot)

cauldron NOUN a cauldron is a large cooking pot made of metal ❑ *stirring a large cauldron which seemed to be full of soup* (*Alice's Adventures in Wonderland* by Lewis Carroll)

cephalic ADJ cephalic means to do with the head ❑ *with ink composed of a cephalic tincture* (*Gulliver's Travels* by Jonathan Swift)

chaise and four NOUN a closed four-wheel carriage pulled by four horses ❑ *he came down on Monday in a chaise and four to see the place* (*Pride and Prejudice* by Jane Austen)

chamberlain NOUN the main servant in a household ❑ *In those times a bed was always to be got there at any hour of the night, and the chamberlain, letting me in at his ready wicket, lighted the candle next in order on his shelf* (*Great Expectations* by Charles Dickens)

characters NOUN distinguishing marks ❑ *Impressed upon all forms the characters* (*The Prelude* by William Wordsworth)

chary ADJ cautious ❑ *I should have been chary of discussing my guardian too freely even with her* (*Great Expectations* by Charles Dickens)

cherishes VERB here cherishes means cheers or brightens ❑ *some philosophic song of Truth that cherishes our daily life* (*The Prelude* by William Wordsworth)

chickens' meat PHRASE chickens' meat is an old term which means chickens' feed or food ❑ *I had shook a bag of chickens' meat out in that place* (*Robinson Crusoe* by Daniel Defoe)

chimeras NOUN a chimera is an unrealistic idea or a wish which is unlikely to be fulfilled ❑ *with many other wild impossible chimeras* (*Gulliver's Travels* by Jonathan Swift)

chines NOUN chine is a cut of meat that includes part or all of the backbone of the animal ❑ *and they found hams and chines uncut* (*Silas Marner* by George Eliot)

chits NOUN chits is a slang word which means girls ❑ *I hate affected, niminy-piminy chits!* (*Little Women* by Louisa May Alcott)

chopped VERB chopped means come suddenly or accidentally ❑ *if I had chopped upon them* (*Robinson Crusoe* by Daniel Defoe)

chute NOUN a narrow channel ❑ *One morning about day-break, I found a canoe and crossed over a chute to the main shore* (*The Adventures of Huckleberry Finn* by Mark Twain)

circumspection NOUN careful observation of events and circumstances; caution ❑ *I honour your circumspection* (*Pride and Prejudice* by Jane Austen)

clambered VERB clambered means to climb somewhere with difficulty, usually using your hands and your feet ❑ *he clambered up and down stairs* (*Treasure Island* by Robert Louis Stevenson)

clime NOUN climate ❑ *no season knows nor clime* (*The Sun Rising* by John Donne)

clinched VERB clenched ❑ *the tops whereof I could but just reach with my fist clinched* (*Gulliver's Travels* by Jonathan Swift)

close chair NOUN a close chair is a sedan chair, which is an covered chair which has room for one person. The sedan chair is carried on two poles by two men, one in front and one behind ❑ *persuaded even the Empress herself to let me hold her in her close chair* (*Gulliver's Travels* by Jonathan Swift)

clown NOUN clown here means peasant or person who lives off the land ❑ *In ancient days by emperor and clown* (*Ode on a Nightingale* by John Keats)

coalheaver NOUN a coalheaver loaded coal onto ships using a spade ❑ *Good, strong, wholesome medicine, as was given with great success to two Irish labourers and a coalheaver* (*Oliver Twist* by Charles Dickens)

coal-whippers NOUN men who worked at docks using machines to load coal onto ships ❑ *here, were colliers by the score and score, with the coal-whippers plunging off stages on deck* (*Great Expectations* by Charles Dickens)

cobweb NOUN a cobweb is the net which a spider makes for catching insects ❑ *the walls and ceilings were all hung round with cobwebs* (*Gulliver's Travels* by Jonathan Swift)

coddling VERB coddling means to treat someone too kindly or protect them too much ❑ *and I've been coddling the fellow as if I'd been his grandmother* (*Little Women* by Louisa May Alcott)

coil NOUN coil means noise or fuss or disturbance ❑ *What a coil is there?* (*Doctor Faustus 4.7* by Christopher Marlowe)

collared VERB to collar something is a slang term which means to capture. In this sentence, it means he stole it [the money] ❑ *he collared it* (*The Adventures of Huckleberry Finn* by Mark Twain)

colling VERB colling is an old word which means to embrace and kiss ❑ *and no clasping and colling at all* (*Tess of the D'Urbervilles* by Thomas Hardy)

colloquies NOUN colloquy is a formal conversation or dialogue ❑ *Such colloquies have occupied many a pair of pale-faced weavers* (*Silas Marner* by George Eliot)

comfit NOUN sugar-covered pieces of fruit or nut eaten as sweets ❑ *and pulled out a box of comfits* (*Alice's Adventures in Wonderland* by Lewis Carroll)

coming out VERB when a girl came out in society it meant she was of marriageable age. In order to 'come out' girls were expecting to attend balls and other parties during a season ❑ *The younger girls formed hopes of coming out a year or two sooner than they might otherwise have done* (*Pride and Prejudice* by Jane Austen)

commit VERB commit means arrest or stop ❑ *Commit the rascals* (*Doctor Faustus 4.7* by Christopher Marlowe)

commodious ADJ commodious means convenient ❑ *the most commodious and effectual ways* (*Gulliver's Travels* by Jonathan Swift)

commons NOUN commons is an old term meaning food shared with others ❑ *his pauper assistants ranged themselves behind him; the gruel was served out; and a long grace was said over the short commons.* (*Oliver Twist* by Charles Dickens)

complacency NOUN here complacency means a desire to please others. Today complacency means feeling pleased with oneself without good reason. ❑ *Twas thy power that raised the first complacency in me* (*The Prelude* by William Wordsworth)

complaisance NOUN complaisance was eagerness to please ❑ *we cannot wonder at his complaisance* (*Pride and Prejudice* by Jane Austen)

complaisant ADJ complaisant means polite ❑ *extremely cheerful and complaisant to their guest* (*Gulliver's Travels* by Jonathan Swift)

conning VERB conning means learning by heart ❑ *Or conning more* (*The Prelude* by William Wordsworth)

consequent NOUN consequence ❑ *as avarice is the necessary consequent of old age* (*Gulliver's Travels* by Jonathan Swift)

consorts NOUN concerts ❑ *The King, who delighted in music, had frequent consorts at Court* (*Gulliver's Travels* by Jonathan Swift)

conversible ADJ conversible meant easy to talk to, companionable ❑ *He can be a conversible companion* (*Pride and Prejudice* by Jane Austen)

copper NOUN a copper is a large pot that can be heated directly over a fire ❑ *He gazed in stupefied astonishment on the small rebel for some seconds, and then clung for support to the copper* (*Oliver Twist* by Charles Dickens)

copper-stick NOUN a copper-stick is the long piece of wood used to stir washing in the copper (or boiler) which was usually the biggest cooking pot in the house ❑ *It was Christmas Eve, and I had to stir the pudding for next day, with a copper-stick, from seven to eight by the Dutch clock* (*Great Expectations* by Charles Dickens)

counting-house NOUN a counting-house is a place where accountants work ❑ *Once upon a time—of all the good days in the year, on Christmas Eve—old Scrooge sat busy in his counting-house* (*A Christmas Carol* by Charles Dickens)

courtier NOUN a courtier is someone who attends the king or queen—a member of the court ❑ *next the ten courtiers;* (*Alice's Adventures in Wonderland* by Lewis Carroll)

covies NOUN covies were flocks of partridges ❑ *and will save all of the best covies for you* (*Pride and Prejudice* by Jane Austen)

cowed VERB cowed means frightened or intimidated ❑ *it cowed me more than the pain* (*Treasure Island* by Robert Louis Stevenson)

cozened VERB cozened means tricked or deceived ❑ *Do you remember, sir, how you cozened me* (*Doctor Faustus 4.7* by Christopher Marlowe)

cravats NOUN a cravat is a folded cloth that a man wears wrapped around his neck as a decorative item of clothing ❑ *we'd 'a' slept in our cravats tonight* (*The Adventures of Huckleberry Finn* by Mark Twain)

crock and dirt PHRASE crock and dirt is an old expression meaning soot and dirt ❑ *and the mare catching cold at the door, and the boy grimed with crock and dirt* (*Great Expectations* by Charles Dickens)

crockery NOUN here crockery means pottery ❑ *By one of the parrots was a cat made of crockery* (*The Adventures of Huckleberry Finn* by Mark Twain)

crooked sixpence PHRASE it was considered unlucky to have a bent sixpence ❑ *You've got the beauty, you see, and I've got the luck, so you must keep me by you for your crooked sixpence* (*Silas Marner* by George Eliot)

croquet NOUN croquet is a traditional English summer game in which players try to hit wooden balls through hoops ❑ *and once she remembered trying to box her own ears for having cheated herself in a game of croquet* (*Alice's Adventures in Wonderland* by Lewis Carroll)

cross PREP across ❑ *The two great streets, which run cross and divide it into four quarters* (*Gulliver's Travels* by Jonathan Swift)

culpable ADJ if you are culpable for something it means you are to blame ❑ *deep are the sorrows that spring from false ideas for which no man is culpable. (Silas Marner by George Eliot)*

cultured ADJ cultivated ❑ *Nor less when spring had warmed the cultured Vale (The Prelude by William Wordsworth)*

cupidity NOUN cupidity is greed ❑ *These people hated me with the hatred of cupidity and disappoint-ment. (Great Expectations by Charles Dickens)*

curricle NOUN an open two-wheeled carriage with one seat for the driver and space for a single passenger ❑ *and they saw a lady and a gentleman in a curricle (Pride and Prejudice by Jane Austen)*

cynosure NOUN a cynosure is something that strongly attracts attention or admiration ❑ *Then I thought of Eliza and Georgiana; I beheld one the cynosure of a ballroom, the other the inmate of a convent cell (Jane Eyre by Charlotte Brontë)*

dalliance NOUN someone's dalliance with something is a brief involve-ment with it ❑ *nor sporting in the dalliance of love (Doctor Faustus Chorus by Christopher Marlowe)*

darkling ADV darkling is an archaic way of saying in the dark ❑ *Darkling I listen (Ode on a Nightingale by John Keats)*

delf-case NOUN a sideboard for holding dishes and crockery ❑ *at the pewter dishes and delf-case (Wuthering Heights by Emily Brontë)*

determined ■ VERB here determined means ended ❑ *and be out of vogue when that was determined (Gulliver's Travels by Jonathan Swift)* ■ VERB determined can mean to have been learned or found espe-cially by investigation or experience ❑ *All the sensitive feelings it wounded so cruelly, all the shame and misery it kept alive within my breast, became more poignant as I*

thought of this; and I determined that the life was unendurable (David Copperfield by Charles Dickens)

Deuce NOUN a slang term for the Devil ❑ *Ah, I dare say I did. Deuce take me, he added suddenly, I know I did. I find I am not quite unscrewed yet. (Great Expectations by Charles Dickens)*

diabolical ADJ diabolical means devilish or evil ❑ *and with a thou-sand diabolical expressions (Treasure Island by Robert Louis Stevenson)*

direction NOUN here direction means address ❑ *Elizabeth was not surprised at it, as Jane had written the direction remarkably ill (Pride and Prejudice by Jane Austen)*

discover VERB to màke known or announce ❑ *the Emperor would discover the secret while I was out of his power (Gulliver's Travels by Jonathan Swift)*

dissemble VERB hide or conceal ❑ *Dissemble nothing (On His Mistress by John Donne)*

dissolve VERB dissolve here means to release from life, to die ❑ *Fade far away, dissolve, and quite forget (Ode on a Nightingale by John Keats)*

distrain VERB to distrain is to seize the property of someone who is in debt in compensation for the money owed ❑ *for he's threatening to distrain for it (Silas Marner by George Eliot)*

Divan NOUN a Divan was originally a Turkish council of state—the name was transferred to the couches they sat on and is used to mean this in English ❑ *Mr Brass applauded this picture very much, and the bed being soft and comfortable, Mr Quilp determined to use it, both as a sleeping place by night and as a kind of Divan by day. (The Old Curiosity Shop by Charles Dickens)*

divorcement NOUN separation ❑ *By all pains which want and divorcement* *hath* (*On His Mistress* by John Donne)

dog in the manger, PHRASE this phrase describes someone who prevents you from enjoying something that they themselves have no need for ❏ *You are a dog in the manger, Cathy, and desire no one to be loved but yourself* (*Wuthering Heights* by Emily Brontë)

dolorifuge NOUN dolorifuge is a word which Thomas Hardy invented. It means pain-killer or comfort ❏ *as a species of dolorifuge* (*Tess of the D'Urbervilles* by Thomas Hardy)

dome NOUN building ❏ *that river and that mouldering dome* (*The Prelude* by William Wordsworth)

domestic NOUN here domestic means a person's management of the house ❏ *to give some account of my domestic* (*Gulliver's Travels* by Jonathan Swift)

dunce NOUN a dunce is another word for idiot ❏ *Do you take me for a dunce? Go on?* (*Alice's Adventures in Wonderland* by Lewis Carroll)

Ecod EXCLAM a slang exclamation meaning 'oh God!' ❏ *'Ecod,' replied Wemmick, shaking his head, 'that's not my trade.'* (*Great Expectations* by Charles Dickens)

egg-hot NOUN an egg-hot (see also 'flip' and 'negus') was a hot drink made from beer and eggs, sweetened with nutmeg ❏ *She fainted when she saw me return, and made a little jug of egg-hot afterwards to console us while we talked it over.* (*David Copperfield* by Charles Dickens)

encores NOUN an encore is a short extra performance at the end of a longer one, which the entertainer gives because the audience has enthusiastically asked for it ❏ *we want a little something to answer encores with, anyway* (*The Adventures of Huckleberry Finn* by Mark Twain)

equipage NOUN an elegant and impressive carriage ❏ *and besides, the equipage did not answer to any of*

their neighbours (*Pride and Prejudice* by Jane Austen)

exordium NOUN an exordium is the opening part of a speech ❏ *'Now, Handel,' as if it were the grave beginning of a portentous business exordium, he had suddenly given up that tone* (*Great Expectations* by Charles Dickens)

expect VERB here expect means to wait for ❏ *to expect his farther commands* (*Gulliver's Travels* by Jonathan Swift)

familiars NOUN familiars means spirits or devils who come to someone when they are called ❏ *I'll turn all the lice about thee into familiars* (*Doctor Faustus 1.4* by Christopher Marlowe)

fantods NOUN a fantod is a person who fidgets or can't stop moving nervously ❏ *It most give me the fantods* (*The Adventures of Huckleberry Finn* by Mark Twain)

farthing NOUN a farthing is an old unit of British currency which was worth a quarter of a penny ❏ *Not a farthing less. A great many back-payments are included in it, I assure you.* (*A Christmas Carol* by Charles Dickens)

farthingale NOUN a hoop worn under a skirt to extend it ❏ *A bell with an old voice – which I dare say in its time had often said to the house, Here is the green farthingale* (*Great Expectations* by Charles Dickens)

favours NOUN here favours is an old word which means ribbons ❏ *A group of humble mourners entered the gate: wearing white favours* (*Oliver Twist* by Charles Dickens)

feigned VERB pretend or pretending ❏ *not my feigned page* (*On His Mistress* by John Donne)

fence ■ NOUN a fence is someone who receives and sells stolen goods ❏ *What are you up to? Ill-treating the boys, you covetous, avaricious, in-sa-ti-a-ble old fence?* (*Oliver Twist* by

Charles Dickens) ■ NOUN defence or protection ❏ *but honesty hath no fence against superior cunning* (*Gulliver's Travels* by Jonathan Swift)

fess ADJ fess is an old word which means pleased or proud ❏ *You'll be fess enough, my poppet* (*Tess of the D'Urbervilles* by Thomas Hardy)

fettered ADJ fettered means bound in chains or chained ❏ *'You are fettered,' said Scrooge, trembling. 'Tell me why?'* (*A Christmas Carol* by Charles Dickens)

fidges VERB fidges means fidgets, which is to keep moving your hands slightly because you are nervous or excited ❏ *Look, Jim, how my fingers fidges* (*Treasure Island* by Robert Louis Stevenson)

finger-post NOUN a finger-post is a sign-post showing the direction to different places ❏ *'The gallows,' continued Fagin, 'the gallows, my dear, is an ugly finger-post, which points out a very short and sharp turning that has stopped many a bold fellow's career on the broad highway.'* (*Oliver Twist* by Charles Dickens)

fire-irons NOUN fire-irons are tools kept by the side of the fire to either cook with or look after the fire ❏ *the fire-irons came first* (*Alice's Adventures in Wonderland* by Lewis Carroll)

fire-plug NOUN a fire-plug is another word for a fire hydrant ❏ *The pony looked with great attention into a fire-plug, which was near him, and appeared to be quite absorbed in contemplating it* (*The Old Curiosity Shop* by Charles Dickens)

flank NOUN flank is the side of an animal ❏ *And all her silken flanks with garlands dressed* (*Ode on a Grecian Urn* by John Keats)

flip NOUN a flip is a drink made from warmed ale, sugar, spice and beaten egg ❏ *The events of the day, in combination with the twins, if not with the flip, had made Mrs Micawber hysterical, and she shed tears as she replied* (*David Copperfield* by Charles Dickens)

flit VERB flit means to move quickly ❏ *and if he had meant to flit to Thrushcross Grange* (*Wuthering Heights* by Emily Brontë)

floorcloth NOUN a floorcloth was a hard-wearing piece of canvas used instead of carpet ❏ *This avenging phantom was ordered to be on duty at eight on Tuesday morning in the hall (it was two feet square, as charged for floorcloth)* (*Great Expectations* by Charles Dickens)

fly-driver NOUN a fly-driver is a carriage drawn by a single horse ❏ *The fly-drivers, among whom I inquired next, were equally jocose and equally disrespectful* (*David Copperfield* by Charles Dickens)

fob NOUN a small pocket in which a watch is kept ❏ *'Certain,' replied the man, drawing a gold watch from his fob* (*Oliver Twist* by Charles Dickens)

folly NOUN folly means foolishness or stupidity ❏ *the folly of beginning a work* (*Robinson Crusoe* by Daniel Defoe)

fond ADJ fond means foolish ❏ *Fond worldling* (*Doctor Faustus 5.2* by Christopher Marlowe)

fondness NOUN silly or foolish affection ❏ *They have no fondness for their colts or foals* (*Gulliver's Travels* by Jonathan Swift)

for his fancy PHRASE for his fancy means for his liking or as he wanted ❏ *and as I did not obey quick enough for his fancy* (*Treasure Island* by Robert Louis Stevenson)

forlorn ADJ lost or very upset ❏ *you are from that day forlorn* (*Gulliver's Travels* by Jonathan Swift)

foster-sister NOUN a foster-sister was someone brought up by the same nurse or in the same household ❏ *I had been his foster-sister* (*Wuthering Heights* by Emily Brontë)

fox-fire NOUN fox-fire is a weak glow that is given off by decaying, rotten wood ❏ *what we must have was a lot of them rotten chunks that's called fox-fire* (*The Adventures of Huckleberry Finn* by Mark Twain)

frozen sea PHRASE the Arctic Ocean ❏ *into the frozen sea* (*Gulliver's Travels* by Jonathan Swift)

gainsay VERB to gainsay something is to say it isn't true or to deny it ❏ *'So she had,' cried Scrooge. 'You're right. I'll not gainsay it, Spirit. God forbid!'* (*A Christmas Carol* by Charles Dickens)

gaiters NOUN gaiters were leggings made of a cloth or piece of leather which covered the leg from the knee to the ankle ❏ *Mr Knightley was hard at work upon the lower buttons of his thick leather gaiters* (*Emma* by Jane Austen)

galluses NOUN galluses is an old spelling of gallows, and here means suspenders. Suspenders are straps worn over someone's shoulders and fastened to their trousers to prevent the trousers falling down ❏ *and home-knit galluses* (*The Adventures of Huckleberry Finn* by Mark Twain)

galoot NOUN a sailor but also a clumsy person ❏ *and maybe a galoot on it chopping* (*The Adventures of Huckleberry Finn* by Mark Twain)

gayest ADJ gayest means the most lively and bright or merry ❏ *Beth played her gayest march* (*Little Women* by Louisa May Alcott)

gem NOUN here gem means jewellery ❏ *the mountain shook off turf and flower, had only heath for raiment and crag for gem* (*Jane Eyre* by Charlotte Brontë)

giddy ADJ giddy means dizzy ❏ *and I wish you wouldn't keep appearing and vanishing so suddenly; you make one quite giddy.* (*Alice's Adventures in Wonderland* by Lewis Carroll)

gig NOUN a light two-wheeled carriage ❏ *when a gig drove up to the garden gate: out of which there jumped a fat gentleman* (*Oliver Twist* by Charles Dickens)

gladsome ADJ gladsome is an old word meaning glad or happy ❏ *Nobody ever stopped him in the street to say, with gladsome looks* (*A Christmas Carol* by Charles Dickens)

glen NOUN a glen is a small valley; the word is used commonly in Scotland ❏ *a beck which follows the bend of the glen* (*Wuthering Heights* by Emily Brontë)

gravelled VERB gravelled is an old term which means to baffle or defeat someone ❏ *Gravelled the pastors of the German Church* (*Doctor Faustus 1.1* by Christopher Marlowe)

grinder NOUN a grinder was a private tutor ❏ *but that when he had had the happiness of marrying Mrs Pocket very early in his life, he had impaired his prospects and taken up the calling of a Grinder* (*Great Expectations* by Charles Dickens)

gruel NOUN gruel is a thin, watery cornmeal or oatmeal soup ❏ *and the little saucepan of gruel (Scrooge had a cold in his head) upon the hob.* (*A Christmas Carol* by Charles Dickens)

guinea, half a NOUN half a guinea was ten shillings and sixpence ❏ *but lay out half a guinea at Ford's* (*Emma* by Jane Austen)

gull VERB gull is an old term which means to fool or deceive someone ❏ *Hush, I'll gull him supernaturally* (*Doctor Faustus 3.4* by Christopher Marlowe)

gunnel NOUN the gunnel, or gunwale, is the upper edge of a boat's side ❏ *But he put his foot on the gunnel and rocked her* (*The Adventures of Huckleberry Finn* by Mark Twain)

gunwale NOUN the side of a ship ❏ *He dipped his hand in the water over the boat's gunwale* (*Great Expectations* by Charles Dickens)

Gytrash NOUN a Gytrash is an omen of misfortune to the superstitious, usually taking the form of a hound ❑ *I remembered certain of Bessie's tales, wherein figured a North-of-England spirit, called a 'Gytrash'* (*Jane Eyre* by Charlotte Brontë)

hackney-cabriolet NOUN a two-wheeled carriage with four seats for hire and pulled by a horse ❑ *A hackney-cabriolet was in waiting; with the same vehemence which she had exhibited in addressing Oliver, the girl pulled him in with her, and drew the curtains close.* (*Oliver Twist* by Charles Dickens)

hackney-coach NOUN a four-wheeled horse-drawn vehicle for hire ❑ *The twilight was beginning to close in, when Mr Brownlow alighted from a hackney-coach at his own door, and knocked softly.* (*Oliver Twist* by Charles Dickens)

haggler NOUN a haggler is someone who travels from place to place selling small goods and items ❑ *when I be plain Jack Durbeyfield, the haggler* (*Tess of the D'Urbervilles* by Thomas Hardy)

halter NOUN a halter is a rope or strap used to lead an animal or to tie it up ❑ *I had of course long been used to a halter and a headstall* (*Black Beauty* by Anna Sewell)

hamlet NOUN a hamlet is a small village or a group of houses in the country-side ❑ *down from the hamlet* (*Treasure Island* by Robert Louis Stevenson)

hand-barrow NOUN a hand-barrow is a device for carrying heavy objects. It is like a wheelbarrow except that it has handles, rather than wheels, for moving the barrow ❑ *his sea chest following behind him in a hand-barrow* (*Treasure Island* by Robert Louis Stevenson)

handspike NOUN a handspike was a stick which was used as a lever ❑ *a bit of stick like a handspike* (*Treasure Island* by Robert Louis Stevenson)

haply ADV haply means by chance or perhaps ❑ *And haply the Queen-Moon is on her throne* (*Ode on a Nightingale* by John Keats)

harem NOUN the harem was the part of the house where the women lived ❑ *mostly they hang round the harem* (*The Adventures of Huckleberry Finn* by Mark Twain)

hautboys NOUN hautboys are oboes ❑ *sausages and puddings resembling flutes and hautboys* (*Gulliver's Travels* by Jonathan Swift)

hawker NOUN a hawker is someone who sells goods to people as he travels rather than from a fixed place like a shop ❑ *to buy some stockings from a hawker* (*Treasure Island* by Robert Louis Stevenson)

hawser NOUN a hawser is a rope used to tie up or tow a ship or boat ❑ *Again among the tiers of shipping, in and out, avoiding rusty chain-cables, frayed hempen hawsers* (*Great Expectations* by Charles Dickens)

headstall NOUN the headstall is the part of the bridle or halter that goes around a horse's head ❑ *I had of course long been used to a halter and a headstall* (*Black Beauty* by Anna Sewell)

hearken VERB hearken means to listen ❑ *though we sometimes stopped to lay hold of each other and hearken* (*Treasure Island* by Robert Louis Stevenson)

heartless ADJ here heartless means without heart or dejected ❑ *I am not heartless* (*The Prelude* by William Wordsworth)

hebdomadal ADJ hebdomadal means weekly ❑ *It was the hebdomadal treat to which we all looked forward from Sabbath to Sabbath* (*Jane Eyre* by Charlotte Brontë)

highwaymen NOUN highwaymen were people who stopped travellers and robbed them ❑ *We are high-waymen* (*The Adventures of Huckleberry Finn* by Mark Twain)

hinds NOUN hinds means farm hands, or people who work on a farm ❑ *He called his hinds about him* (*Gulliver's Travels* by Jonathan Swift)

histrionic ADJ if you refer to someone's behaviour as histrionic, you are being critical of it because it is dramatic and exaggerated ❑ *But the histrionic muse is the darling* (*The Adventures of Huckleberry Finn* by Mark Twain)

hogs NOUN hogs is another word for pigs ❑ *Tom called the hogs 'ingots'* (*The Adventures of Huckleberry Finn* by Mark Twain)

horrors NOUN the horrors are a fit, called delirium tremens, which is caused by drinking too much alcohol ❑ *I'll have the horrors* (*Treasure Island* by Robert Louis Stevenson)

huffy ADJ huffy means to be obviously annoyed or offended about something ❑ *They will feel that more than angry speeches or huffy actions* (*Little Women* by Louisa May Alcott)

hulks NOUN hulks were prison-ships ❑ *The miserable companion of thieves and ruffians, the fallen outcast of low haunts, the associate of the scourings of the jails and hulks* (*Oliver Twist* by Charles Dickens)

humbug NOUN humbug means nonsense or rubbish ❑ *'Bah,' said Scrooge. 'Humbug!'* (*A Christmas Carol* by Charles Dickens)

humours NOUN it was believed that there were four fluids in the body called humours which decided the temperament of a person depending on how much of each fluid was present ❑ *other peccant humours* (*Gulliver's Travels* by Jonathan Swift)

husbandry NOUN husbandry is farming animals ❑ *bad husbandry were plentifully anointing their wheels* (*Silas Marner* by George Eliot)

huswife NOUN a huswife was a small sewing kit ❑ *but I had put my huswife on it* (*Emma* by Jane Austen)

ideal ADJ ideal in this context means imaginary ❑ *I discovered the yell was not ideal* (*Wuthering Heights* by Emily Brontë)

If our two PHRASE if both our ❑ *If our two loves be one* (*The Good-Morrow* by John Donne)

ignis-fatuus NOUN ignis-fatuus is the light given out by burning marsh gases, which lead careless travellers into danger ❑ *it is madness in all women to let a secret love kindle within them, which, if unreturned and unknown, must devour the life that feeds it; and, if discovered and responded to, must lead ignis-fatuus-like, into miry wilds whence there is no extrication.* (*Jane Eyre* by Charlotte Brontë)

imaginations NOUN here imaginations means schemes or plans ❑ *soon drove out those imaginations* (*Gulliver's Travels* by Jonathan Swift)

impressible ADJ impressible means open or impressionable ❑ *for Marner had one of those impressible, self-doubting natures* (*Silas Marner* by George Eliot)

in good intelligence PHRASE friendly with each other ❑ *that these two persons were in good intelligence with each other* (*Gulliver's Travels* by Jonathan Swift)

inanity NOUN inanity is silliness or dull stupidity ❑ *Do we not wile away moments of inanity* (*Silas Marner* by George Eliot)

incivility NOUN incivility means rudeness or impoliteness ❑ *if it's only for a piece of incivility like tonight's* (*Treasure Island* by Robert Louis Stevenson)

indigenae NOUN indigenae means natives or people from that area ❑ *an exotic that the surly indigenae will not recognise for kin* (*Wuthering Heights* by Emily Brontë)

indocible ADJ unteachable ❑ *so they were the most restive and indocible* (*Gulliver's Travels* by Jonathan Swift)

ingenuity NOUN inventiveness ❑ *entreated me to give him something as an encouragement to ingenuity* (*Gulliver's Travels* by Jonathan Swift)

ingots NOUN an ingot is a lump of a valuable metal like gold, usually shaped like a brick ❑ *Tom called the hogs 'ingots'* (*The Adventures of Huckleberry Finn* by Mark Twain)

inkstand NOUN an inkstand is a pot which was put on a desk to contain either ink or pencils and pens ❑ *throwing an inkstand at the Lizard as she spoke* (*Alice's Adventures in Wonderland* by Lewis Carroll)

inordinate ADJ without order. Today inordinate means 'excessive'. ❑ *Though yet untutored and inordinate* (*The Prelude* by William Wordsworth)

intellectuals NOUN here intellectuals means the minds (of the workmen) ❑ *those instructions they give being too refined for the intellectuals of their workmen* (*Gulliver's Travels* by Jonathan Swift)

interview NOUN meeting ❑ *By our first strange and fatal interview* (*On His Mistress* by John Donne)

jacks NOUN jacks are rods for turning a spit over a fire ❑ *It was a small bit of pork suspended from the kettle hanger by a string passed through a large door key, in a way known to primitive housekeepers unpossessed of jacks* (*Silas Marner* by George Eliot)

jews-harp NOUN a jews-harp is a small, metal, musical instrument that is played by the mouth ❑ *A jews-harp's plenty good enough for a rat* (*The Adventures of Huckleberry Finn* by Mark Twain)

jorum NOUN a large bowl ❑ *while Miss Skiffins brewed such a jorum of tea, that the pig in the back premises became strongly excited* (*Great Expectations* by Charles Dickens)

jostled VERB jostled means bumped or pushed by someone or some people

❑ *being jostled himself into the kennel* (*Gulliver's Travels* by Jonathan Swift)

keepsake NOUN a keepsake is a gift which reminds someone of an event or of the person who gave it to them. ❑ *books and ornaments they had in their boudoirs at home: keepsakes that different relations had presented to them* (*Jane Eyre* by Charlotte Brontë)

kenned VERB kenned means knew ❑ *though little kenned the lamplighter that he had any company but Christmas!* (*A Christmas Carol* by Charles Dickens)

kennel NOUN kennel means gutter, which is the edge of a road next to the pavement, where rain water collects and flows away ❑ *being jostled himself into the kennel* (*Gulliver's Travels* by Jonathan Swift)

knock-knee ADJ knock-knee means slanted, at an angle. ❑ *LOT 1 was marked in whitewashed knock-knee letters on the brewhouse* (*Great Expectations* by Charles Dickens)

ladylike ADJ to be ladylike is to behave in a polite, dignified and graceful way ❑ *No, winking isn't ladylike* (*Little Women* by Louisa May Alcott)

lapse NOUN flow ❑ *Stealing with silent lapse to join the brook* (*The Prelude* by William Wordsworth)

larry NOUN larry is an old word which means commotion or noisy celebration ❑ *That was all a part of the larry!* (*Tess of the D'Urbervilles* by Thomas Hardy)

laths NOUN laths are strips of wood ❑ *The panels shrunk, the windows cracked; fragments of plaster fell out of the ceiling, and the naked laths were shown instead* (*A Christmas Carol* by Charles Dickens)

leer NOUN a leer is an unpleasant smile ❑ *with a kind of leer* (*Treasure Island* by Robert Louis Stevenson)

lenitives NOUN these are different kinds of drugs or medicines: lenitives and palliatives were pain relievers; aperitives were laxatives; abstersives caused vomiting; corrosives destroyed human tissue; restringents caused constipation; cephalalgics stopped headaches; icterics were used as medicine for jaundice; apophlegmatics were cough medicine, and acoustics were cures for the loss of hearing ❑ *lenitives, aperitives, abstersives, corrosives, restringents, palliatives, laxatives, cephalalgics, icterics, apophlegmatics, acoustics* (*Gulliver's Travels* by Jonathan Swift)

lest CONJ in case. If you do something lest something (usually) unpleasant happens you do it to try to prevent it happening ❑ *She went in without knocking, and hurried upstairs, in great fear lest she should meet the real Mary Ann* (*Alice's Adventures in Wonderland* by Lewis Carroll)

levee NOUN a levee is an old term for a meeting held in the morning, shortly after the person holding the meeting has got out of bed ❑ *I used to attend the King's levee once or twice a week* (*Gulliver's Travels* by Jonathan Swift)

life-preserver NOUN a club which had lead inside it to make it heavier and therefore more dangerous ❑ *and with no more suspicious articles displayed to view than two or three heavy bludgeons which stood in a corner, and a 'life-preserver' that hung over the chimney-piece.* (*Oliver Twist* by Charles Dickens)

lighterman NOUN a lighterman is another word for sailor ❑ *in and out, hammers going in ship-builders' yards, saws going at timber, clashing engines going at things unknown, pumps going in leaky ships, capstans going, ships going out to sea, and unintelligible sea creatures roaring curses over the bulwarks at respondent lightermen* (*Great Expectations* by Charles Dickens)

livery NOUN servants often wore a uniform known as a livery ❑ *suddenly a footman in livery came running out of the wood* (*Alice's Adventures in Wonderland* by Lewis Carroll)

livid ADJ livid means pale or ash coloured. Livid also means very angry ❑ *a dirty, livid white* (*Treasure Island* by Robert Louis Stevenson)

lottery-tickets NOUN a popular card game ❑ *and Mrs Philips protested that they would have a nice comfortable noisy game of lottery tickets* (*Pride and Prejudice* by Jane Austen)

lower and upper world PHRASE the earth and the heavens are the lower and upper worlds ❑ *the changes in the lower and upper world* (*Gulliver's Travels* by Jonathan Swift)

lustres NOUN lustres are chandeliers. A chandelier is a large, decorative frame which holds light bulbs or candles and hangs from the ceiling ❑ *the lustres, lights, the carving and the guilding* (*The Prelude* by William Wordsworth)

lynched VERB killed without a criminal trial by a crowd of people ❑ *He'll never know how nigh he come to getting lynched* (*The Adventures of Huckleberry Finn* by Mark Twain)

malingering VERB if someone is malingering they are pretending to be ill to avoid working ❑ *And you stand there malingering* (*Treasure Island* by Robert Louis Stevenson)

managing PHRASE treating with consideration ❑ *to think the honour of my own kind not worth managing* (*Gulliver's Travels* by Jonathan Swift)

manhood PHRASE manhood means human nature ❑ *concerning the nature of manhood* (*Gulliver's Travels* by Jonathan Swift)

man-trap NOUN a man-trap is a set of steel jaws that snap shut when trodden on and trap a person's leg

'Don't go to him,' I called out of the window, 'he's an assassin! A man-trap!' (*Oliver Twist* by Charles Dickens)

maps NOUN charts of the night sky ❑ *Let maps to others, worlds on worlds have shown* (*The Good-Morrow* by John Donne)

mark VERB look at or notice ❑ *Mark but this flea, and mark in this* (*The Flea* by John Donne)

maroons NOUN A maroon is someone who has been left in a place which it is difficult for them to escape from, like a small island ❑ *if schooners, islands, and maroons* (*Treasure Island* by Robert Louis Stevenson)

mast NOUN here mast means the fruit of forest trees ❑ *a quantity of acorns, dates, chestnuts, and other mast* (*Gulliver's Travels* by Jonathan Swift)

mate VERB defeat ❑ *Where Mars did mate the warlike Carthigens* (*Doctor Faustus Chorus* by Christopher Marlowe)

mealy ADJ Mealy when used to describe a face meant pallid, pale or colourless ❑ *I only know two sorts of boys. Mealy boys, and beef-faced boys* (*Oliver Twist* by Charles Dickens)

middling ADV fairly or moderately ❑ *she worked me middling hard for about an hour* (*The Adventures of Huckleberry Finn* by Mark Twain)

mill NOUN a mill, or treadmill, was a device for hard labour or punishment in prison ❑ *Was you never on the mill?* (*Oliver Twist* by Charles Dickens)

milliner's shop NOUN a milliner's sold fabrics, clothing, lace and accessories; as time went on they specialized more and more in hats ❑ *to pay their duty to their aunt and to a milliner's shop just over the way* (*Pride and Prejudice* by Jane Austen)

minching un' munching PHRASE how people in the north of England used to describe the way people

from the south speak ❑ *Minching un' munching!* (*Wuthering Heights* by Emily Brontë)

mine NOUN gold ❑ *Whether both th'Indias of spice and mine* (*The Sun Rising* by John Donne)

mire NOUN mud ❑ *Tis my fate to be always ground into the mire under the iron heel of oppression* (*The Adventures of Huckleberry Finn* by Mark Twain)

miscellany NOUN a miscellany is a collection of many different kinds of things ❑ *under that, the miscellany began* (*Treasure Island* by Robert Louis Stevenson)

mistarshers NOUN mistarshers means moustache, which is the hair that grows on a man's upper lip ❑ *when he put his hand up to his mistarshers* (*Tess of the D'Urbervilles* by Thomas Hardy)

morrow NOUN here good-morrow means tomorrow and a new and better life ❑ *And now good-morrow to our waking souls* (*The Good-Morrow* by John Donne)

mortification NOUN mortification is an old word for gangrene which is when part of the body decays or 'dies' because of disease ❑ *Yes, it was a mortification–that was it* (*The Adventures of Huckleberry Finn* by Mark Twain)

mought VERB mought is an old spelling of might ❑ *what you mought call me? You mought call me captain* (*Treasure Island* by Robert Louis Stevenson)

move VERB move me not means do not make me angry ❑ *Move me not, Faustus* (*Doctor Faustus 2.1* by Christopher Marlowe)

muffin-cap NOUN a muffin-cap is a flat cap made from wool ❑ *the old one, remained stationary in the muffin-cap and leathers* (*Oliver Twist* by Charles Dickens)

mulatter NOUN a mulatter was another word for mulatto, which is a person with parents who are from different races ❑ *a mulatter, most as white as a white man* (*The Adventures of Huckleberry Finn* by Mark Twain)

mummery NOUN mummery is an old word that meant meaningless (or pretentious) ceremony ❑ *When they were all gone, and when Trabb and his men – but not his boy: I looked for him – had crammed their mummery into bags, and were gone too, the house felt wholesomer.* (*Great Expectations* by Charles Dickens)

nap NOUN the nap is the woolly surface on a new item of clothing. Here the surface has been worn away so it looks bare ❑ *like an old hat with the nap rubbed off* (*The Adventures of Huckleberry Finn* by Mark Twain)

natural ■ NOUN a natural is a person born with learning difficulties ❑ *though he had been left to his particular care by their deceased father, who thought him almost a natural.* (*David Copperfield* by Charles Dickens) ■ ADJ natural meant illegitimate ❑ *Harriet Smith was the natural daughter of some-body* (*Emma* by Jane Austen)

navigator NOUN a navigator was origi-nally someone employed to dig canals. It is the origin of the word 'navvy' meaning a labourer ❑ *She ascertained from me in a few words what it was all about, comforted Dora, and gradually convinced her that I was not a labourer – from my manner of stating the case I believe Dora concluded that I was a navi-gator, and went balancing myself up and down a plank all day with a wheelbarrow – and so brought us together in peace.* (*David Copperfield* by Charles Dickens)

necromancy NOUN necromancy means a kind of magic where the magician speaks to spirits or ghosts to find out what will happen in the future ❑ *He surfeits upon cursed necro-mancy* (*Doctor Faustus chorus* by Christopher Marlowe)

negus NOUN a negus is a hot drink

made from sweetened wine and water ❑ *He sat placidly perusing the newspaper, with his little head on one side, and a glass of warm sherry negus at his elbow.* (*David Copperfield* by Charles Dickens)

nice ADJ discriminating. Able to make good judgements or choices ❑ *consequently a claim to be nice* (*Emma* by Jane Austen)

nigh ADV nigh means near ❑ *He'll never know how nigh he come to getting lynched* (*The Adventures of Huckleberry Finn* by Mark Twain)

nimbleness NOUN nimbleness means being able to move very quickly or skilfully ❑ *and with incredible accuracy and nimbleness* (*Treasure Island* by Robert Louis Stevenson)

noggin NOUN a noggin is a small mug or a wooden cup ❑ *you'll bring me one noggin of rum* (*Treasure Island* by Robert Louis Stevenson)

none ADJ neither ❑ *none can die* (*The Good-Morrow* by John Donne)

notices NOUN observations ❑ *Arch are his notices* (*The Prelude* by William Wordsworth)

occiput NOUN occiput means the back of the head ❑ *saw off the occiput of each couple* (*Gulliver's Travels* by Jonathan Swift)

officiously ADV kindly ❑ *the governess who attended Glumdalclitch very officiously lifted me up* (*Gulliver's Travels* by Jonathan Swift)

old salt PHRASE old salt is a slang term for an experienced sailor ❑ *a 'true sea-dog', and a 'real old salt'* (*Treasure Island* by Robert Louis Stevenson)

or ere PHRASE before ❑ *or ere the Hall was built* (*The Prelude* by William Wordsworth)

ostler NOUN one who looks after horses at an inn ❑ *The bill paid, and the waiter remembered, and the ostler not forgotten, and the chambermaid taken into consideration* (*Great Expectations* by Charles Dickens)

ostry NOUN an ostry is an old word for a pub or hotel ❏ *lest I send you into the ostry with a vengeance* (*Doctor Faustus 2.2* by Christopher Marlowe)

outrunning the constable PHRASE outrunning the constable meant spending more than you earn ❏ *but I shall by this means be able to check your bills and to pull you up if I find you outrunning the constable.* (*Great Expectations* by Charles Dickens)

over ADV across ❏ *It is in length six yards, and in the thickest part at least three yards over* (*Gulliver's Travels* by Jonathan Swift)

over the broomstick PHRASE this is a phrase meaning 'getting married without a formal ceremony' ❏ *They both led tramping lives, and this woman in Gerrard-street here, had been married very young, over the broomstick (as we say), to a tramping man, and was a perfect fury in point of jealousy.* (*Great Expectations* by Charles Dickens)

own VERB own means to admit or to acknowledge ❏ *It's my old girl that advises. She has the head. But I never own to it before her. Discipline must be maintained* (*Bleak House* by Charles Dickens)

page NOUN here page means a boy employed to run errands ❏ *not my feigned page* (*On His Mistress* by John Donne)

paid pretty dear PHRASE paid pretty dear means paid a high price or suffered quite a lot ❏ *I paid pretty dear for my monthly fourpenny piece* (*Treasure Island* by Robert Louis Stevenson)

pannikins NOUN pannikins were small tin cups ❏ *of lifting light glasses and cups to his lips, as if they were clumsy pannikins* (*Great Expectations* by Charles Dickens)

pards NOUN pards are leopards ❏ *Not charioted by Bacchus and his pards* (*Ode on a Nightingale* by John Keats)

parlour boarder NOUN a pupil who lived with the family ❏ *and somebody had lately raised her from the condition of scholar to parlour boarder* (*Emma* by Jane Austen)

particular, a London PHRASE London in Victorian times and up to the 1950s was famous for having very dense fog – which was a combination of real fog and the smog of pollution from factories ❏ *This is a London particular . . . A fog, miss* (*Bleak House* by Charles Dickens)

patten NOUN pattens were wooden soles which were fixed to shoes by straps to protect the shoes in wet weather ❏ *carrying a basket like the Great Seal of England in plaited straw, a pair of pattens, a spare shawl, and an umbrella, though it was a fine bright day* (*Great Expectations* by Charles Dickens)

paviour NOUN a paviour was a labourer who worked on the street pavement ❏ *the paviour his pickaxe* (*Oliver Twist* by Charles Dickens)

peccant ADJ peccant means unhealthy ❏ *other peccant humours* (*Gulliver's Travels* by Jonathan Swift)

penetralium NOUN penetralium is a word used to describe the inner rooms of the house ❏ *and I had no desire to aggravate his impatience previous to inspecting the penetralium* (*Wuthering Heights* by Emily Brontë)

pensive ADV pensive means deep in thought or thinking seriously about something ❏ *and she was leaning pensive on a tomb-stone on her right elbow* (*The Adventures of Huckleberry Finn* by Mark Twain)

penury NOUN penury is the state of being extremely poor ❏ *Distress, if not penury, loomed in the distance* (*Tess of the D'Urbervilles* by Thomas Hardy)

perspective NOUN telescope ❏ *a pocket perspective* (*Gulliver's Travels* by Jonathan Swift)

phaeton NOUN a phaeton was an open carriage for four people ❏ *often* *condescends to drive by my humble abode in her little phaeton and ponies (Pride and Prejudice by Jane Austen)*

phantasm NOUN a phantasm is an illusion, something that is not real. It is sometimes used to mean ghost ❑ *Experience had bred no fancies in him that could raise the phantasm of appetite (Silas Marner by George Eliot)*

physic NOUN here physic means medicine ❑ *there I studied physic two years and seven months (Gulliver's Travels by Jonathan Swift)*

pinioned VERB to pinion is to hold both arms so that a person cannot move them ❑ *But the relentless Ghost pinioned him in both his arms, and forced him to observe what happened next. (A Christmas Carol by Charles Dickens)*

piquet NOUN piquet was a popular card game in the C18th ❑ *Mr Hurst and Mr Bingley were at piquet (Pride and Prejudice by Jane Austen)*

plaister NOUN a plaister is a piece of cloth on which an apothecary (or pharmacist) would spread ointment. The cloth is then applied to wounds or bruises to treat them ❑ *Then, she gave the knife a final smart wipe on the edge of the plaister, and then sawed a very thick round off the loaf: which she finally, before separating from the loaf, hewed into two halves, of which Joe got one, and I the other. (Great Expectations by Charles Dickens)*

plantations NOUN here plantations means colonies, which are countries controlled by a more powerful country ❑ *besides our plantations in America (Gulliver's Travels by Jonathan Swift)*

plastic ADJ here plastic is an old term meaning shaping or a power that was forming ❑ *A plastic power abode with me (The Prelude by William Wordsworth)*

players NOUN actors ❑ *of players which upon the world's stage be (On His Mistress by John Donne)*

plump ADV all at once, suddenly ❑ *But it took a bit of time to get it well round, the change come so uncommon plump, didn't it? (Great Expectations by Charles Dickens)*

plundered VERB to plunder is to rob or steal from ❑ *These crosses stand for the names of ships or towns that they sank or plundered (Treasure Island by Robert Louis Stevenson)*

pommel ◼ VERB to pommel someone is to hit them repeatedly with your fists ❑ *hug him round the neck, pommel his back, and kick his legs in irrepressible affection! (A Christmas Carol by Charles Dickens)* ◼ NOUN a pommel is the part of a saddle that rises up at the front ❑ *He had his gun across his pommel (The Adventures of Huckleberry Finn by Mark Twain)*

poor's rates NOUN poor's rates were property taxes which were used to support the poor ❑ *'Oh!' replied the undertaker; 'why, you know, Mr Bumble, I pay a good deal towards the poor's rates.' (Oliver Twist by Charles Dickens)*

popular ADJ popular means ruled by the people, or Republican, rather than ruled by a monarch ❑ *With those of Greece compared and popular Rome (The Prelude by William Wordsworth)*

porringer NOUN a porringer is a small bowl ❑ *Of this festive composition each boy had one porringer, and no more (Oliver Twist by Charles Dickens)*

postboy NOUN a postboy was the driver of a horse-drawn carriage ❑ *He spoke to a postboy who was dozing under the gateway (Oliver Twist by Charles Dickens)*

post-chaise NOUN a fast carriage for two or four passengers ❑ *Looking round, he saw that it was a post-chaise, driven at great speed (Oliver Twist by Charles Dickens)*

postern NOUN a small gate usually at the back of a building ❑ *The little servant happening to be entering the*

213

fortress with two hot rolls, I passed through the postern and crossed the drawbridge, in her company (*Great Expectations* by Charles Dickens)

pottle NOUN a pottle was a small basket ❏ *He had a paper-bag under each arm and a pottle of strawberries in one hand . . .* (*Great Expectations* by Charles Dickens)

pounce NOUN pounce is a fine powder used to prevent ink spreading on untreated paper ❏ *in that grim atmosphere of pounce and parchment, red-tape, dusty wafers, ink-jars, brief and draft paper, law reports, writs, declarations, and bills of costs* (*David Copperfield* by Charles Dickens)

pox NOUN pox means sexually transmitted diseases like syphilis ❏ *how the pox in all its consequences and denominations* (*Gulliver's Travels* by Jonathan Swift)

prelibation NOUN prelibation means a foretaste of or an example of something to come ❏ *A prelibation to the mower's scythe* (*The Prelude* by William Wordsworth)

prentice NOUN an apprentice ❏ *and Joe, sitting on an old gun, had told me that when I was 'prentice to him regularly bound, we would have such Larks there!* (*Great Expectations* by Charles Dickens)

presently ADV immediately ❏ *I presently knew what they meant* (*Gulliver's Travels* by Jonathan Swift)

pumpion NOUN pumpkin ❏ *for it was almost as large as a small pumpion* (*Gulliver's Travels* by Jonathan Swift)

punctual ADJ kept in one place ❏ *was not a punctual presence, but a spirit* (*The Prelude* by William Wordsworth)

quadrille ◼ NOUN a quadrille is a dance invented in France which is usually performed by four couples ❏ *However, Mr Swiveller had Miss Sophy's hand for the first quadrille* (*country-dances being low, were utterly proscribed)* (*The Old Curiosity Shop* by Charles Dickens) ◼ NOUN quadrille was a card game for four people ❏ *to make up her pool of quadrille in the evening* (*Pride and Prejudice* by Jane Austen)

quality NOUN gentry or upper-class people ❏ *if you are with the quality* (*The Adventures of Huckleberry Finn* by Mark Twain)

quick parts PHRASE quick-witted ❏ *Mr Bennet was so odd a mixture of quick parts* (*Pride and Prejudice* by Jane Austen)

quid NOUN a quid is something chewed or kept in the mouth, like a piece of tobacco ❏ *rolling his quid* (*Treasure Island* by Robert Louis Stevenson)

quit VERB quit means to avenge or to make even ❏ *But Faustus's death shall quit my infamy* (*Doctor Faustus 4.3* by Christopher Marlowe)

rags NOUN divisions ❏ *Nor hours, days, months, which are the rags of time* (*The Sun Rising* by John Donne)

raiment NOUN raiment means clothing ❏ *the mountain shook off turf and flower, had only heath for raiment and crag for gem* (*Jane Eyre* by Charlotte Brontë)

rain cats and dogs PHRASE an expression meaning rain heavily. The origin of the expression is unclear ❏ *But it'll perhaps rain cats and dogs tomorrow* (*Silas Marner* by George Eliot)

raised Cain PHRASE raised Cain means caused a lot of trouble. Cain is a character in the Bible who killed his brother Abel ❏ *and every time he got drunk he raised Cain around town* (*The Adventures of Huckleberry Finn* by Mark Twain)

rambling ADJ rambling means confused and not very clear ❏ *my head began to be filled very early with rambling thoughts* (*Robinson Crusoe* by Daniel Defoe)

raree-show NOUN a raree-show is an old term for a peep-show or a fairground entertainment ❏ *A raree-show is here, with children gathered round* (*The Prelude* by William Wordsworth)

recusants NOUN people who resisted authority ❏ *hardy recusants* (*The Prelude* by William Wordsworth)

redounding VERB eddying. An eddy is a movement in water or air which goes round and round instead of flowing in one direction ❏ *mists and steam-like fogs redounding everywhere* (*The Prelude* by William Wordsworth)

redundant ADJ here redundant means overflowing but Wordsworth also uses it to mean excessively large or too big ❏ *A tempest, a redundant energy* (*The Prelude* by William Wordsworth)

reflex NOUN reflex is a shortened version of reflexion, which is an alternative spelling of reflection ❏ *To cut across the reflex of a star* (*The Prelude* by William Wordsworth)

Reformatory NOUN a prison for young offenders/criminals ❏ *Even when I was taken to have a new suit of clothes, the tailor had orders to make them like a kind of Reformatory, and on no account to let me have the free use of my limbs.* (*Great Expectations* by Charles Dickens)

remorse NOUN pity or compassion ❏ *by that remorse* (*On His Mistress* by John Donne)

render VERB in this context render means give. ❏ *and Sarah could render no reason that would be sanctioned by the feeling of the community.* (*Silas Marner* by George Eliot)

repeater NOUN a repeater was a watch that chimed the last hour when a button was pressed – as a result it was useful in the dark ❏ *And his watch is a gold repeater, and worth a hundred pound if it's worth a penny.* (*Great Expectations* by Charles Dickens)

repugnance NOUN repugnance means a strong dislike of something or someone ❏ *overcoming a strong repugnance* (*Treasure Island* by Robert Louis Stevenson)

reverence NOUN reverence means bow. When you bow to someone, you briefly bend your body towards them as a formal way of showing them respect ❏ *made my reverence* (*Gulliver's Travels* by Jonathan Swift)

reverie NOUN a reverie is a daydream ❏ *I can guess the subject of your reverie* (*Pride and Prejudice* by Jane Austen)

revival NOUN a religious meeting held in public ❏ *well I'd ben a-running' a little temperance revival thar' bout a week* (*The Adventures of Huckleberry Finn* by Mark Twain)

revolt VERB revolt means turn back or stop your present course of action and go back to what you were doing before ❏ *Revolt, or I'll in piecemeal tear thy flesh* (*Doctor Faustus 5.1* by Christopher Marlowe)

rheumatics/rheumatism NOUN rheumatics [rheumatism] is an illness that makes your joints or muscles stiff and painful ❏ *a new cure for the rheumatics* (*Treasure Island* by Robert Louis Stevenson)

riddance NOUN riddance is usually used in the form good riddance which you say when you are pleased that something has gone or been left behind ❏ *I'd better go into the house, and die and be a riddance* (*David Copperfield* by Charles Dickens)

rimy ADJ rimy is an adjective which means covered in ice or frost ❏ *It was a rimy morning, and very damp* (*Great Expectations* by Charles Dickens)

riper ADJ riper means more mature or older ❏ *At riper years to Wittenberg he went* (*Doctor Faustus chorus* by Christopher Marlowe)

VIRGINIA WOOLF

rubber NOUN a set of games in whist or backgammon ❏ *her father was sure of his rubber* (*Emma* by Jane Austen)

ruffian NOUN a ruffian is a person who behaves violently ❏ *and when the ruffian had told him* (*Treasure Island* by Robert Louis Stevenson)

sadness NOUN sadness is an old term meaning seriousness ❏ *But I prithee tell me, in good sadness* (*Doctor Faustus 2.2* by Christopher Marlowe)

sailed before the mast PHRASE this phrase meant someone who did not look like a sailor ❏ *he had none of the appearance of a man that sailed before the mast* (*Treasure Island* by Robert Louis Stevenson)

scabbard NOUN a scabbard is the covering for a sword or dagger ❏ *Girded round its middle was an antique scabbard; but no sword was in it, and the ancient sheath was eaten up with rust* (*A Christmas Carol* by Charles Dickens)

schooners NOUN A schooner is a fast, medium-sized sailing ship ❏ *if schooners, islands, and maroons* (*Treasure Island* by Robert Louis Stevenson)

science NOUN learning or knowledge ❏ *Even Science, too, at hand* (*The Prelude* by William Wordsworth)

scrouge VERB to scrouge means to squeeze or to crowd ❏ *to scrouge in and get a sight* (*The Adventures of Huckleberry Finn* by Mark Twain)

scrutore NOUN a scrutore, or escritoire, was a writing table ❏ *set me gently on my feet upon the scrutore* (*Gulliver's Travels* by Jonathan Swift)

scutcheon/escutcheon NOUN an escutcheon is a shield with a coat of arms, or the symbols of a family name, engraved on it ❏ *On the scutcheon we'll have a bend* (*The Adventures of Huckleberry Finn* by Mark Twain)

sea-dog PHRASE sea-dog is a slang term for an experienced sailor or pirate

❏ *a 'true sea-dog', and a 'real old salt,'* (*Treasure Island* by Robert Louis Stevenson)

see the lions PHRASE to see the lions was to go and see the sights of London. Originally the phrase referred to the menagerie in the Tower of London and later in Regent's Park ❏ *We will go and see the lions for an hour or two – it's something to have a fresh fellow like you to show them to, Copperfield* (*David Copperfield* by Charles Dickens)

self-conceit NOUN self-conceit is an old term which means having too high an opinion of oneself, or deceiving yourself ❏ *Till swollen with cunning, of a self-conceit* (*Doctor Faustus chorus* by Christopher Marlowe)

seneschal NOUN a steward ❏ *where a grey-headed seneschal sings a funny chorus with a funnier body of vassals* (*Oliver Twist* by Charles Dickens)

sensible ADJ if you were sensible of something you are aware or conscious of something ❏ *If my children are silly I must hope to be always sensible of it* (*Pride and Prejudice* by Jane Austen)

sessions NOUN court cases were heard at specific times of the year called sessions ❏ *He lay in prison very ill, during the whole interval between his committal for trial, and the coming round of the Sessions.* (*Great Expectations* by Charles Dickens)

shabby ADJ shabby places look old and in bad condition ❏ *a little bit of a shabby village named Pikesville* (*The Adventures of Huckleberry Finn* by Mark Twain)

shay-cart NOUN a shay-cart was a small cart drawn by one horse ❏ *'I were at the Bargemen t'other night, Pip;' whenever he subsided into affection, he called me Pip, and whenever he relapsed into politeness he called me Sir; 'when there come up in his* *shay-cart Pumblechook.'* (*Great Expectations* by Charles Dickens)

shilling NOUN a shilling is an old unit of currency. There were twenty shillings in every British pound ❑ *'Ten shillings too much,' said the gentleman in the white waistcoat.* (*Oliver Twist* by Charles Dickens)

shines NOUN tricks or games ❑ *well, it would make a cow laugh to see the shines that old idiot cut* (*The Adventures of Huckleberry Finn* by Mark Twain)

shirking VERB shirking means not doing what you are meant to be doing, or evading your duties ❑ *some of you shirking lubbers* (*Treasure Island* by Robert Louis Stevenson)

shiver my timbers PHRASE shiver my timbers is an expression which was used by sailors and pirates to express surprise ❑ *why, shiver my timbers, if I hadn't forgotten my score!* (*Treasure Island* by Robert Louis Stevenson)

shoe-roses NOUN shoe-roses were roses made from ribbons which were stuck on to shoes as decoration ❑ *the very shoe-roses for Netherfield were got by proxy* (*Pride and Prejudice* by Jane Austen)

singular ADJ singular means very great and remarkable or strange ❑ *'Singular dream,' he says* (*The Adventures of Huckleberry Finn* by Mark Twain)

sire NOUN sire is an old word which means lord or master or elder ❑ *She also defied her sire* (*Little Women* by Louisa May Alcott)

sixpence NOUN a sixpence was half of a shilling ❑ *if she had only a shilling in the world, she would be very lilkely to give away sixpence of it* (*Emma* by Jane Austen)

slavey NOUN the word slavey was used when there was only one servant in a house or boarding-house – so she had to perform all the duties of a larger staff ❑ *Two distinct knocks, sir, will produce the slavey at any*

time (*The Old Curiosity Shop* by Charles Dickens)

slender ADJ weak ❑ *In slender accents of sweet verse* (*The Prelude* by William Wordsworth)

slop-shops NOUN slop-shops were shops where cheap ready-made clothes were sold. They mainly sold clothes to sailors ❑ *Accordingly, I took the jacket off, that I might learn to do without it; and carrying it under my arm, began a tour of inspection of the various slop-shops.* (*David Copperfield* by Charles Dickens)

sluggard NOUN a lazy person ❑ *'Stand up and repeat "'Tis the voice of the sluggard,"' said the Gryphon.* (*Alice's Adventures in Wonderland* by Lewis Carroll)

smallpox NOUN smallpox is a serious infectious disease ❑ *by telling the men we had smallpox aboard* (*The Adventures of Huckleberry Finn* by Mark Twain)

smalls NOUN smalls are short trousers ❑ *It is difficult for a large-headed, small-eyed youth, of lumbering make and heavy countenance, to look dignified under any circum-stances; but it is more especially so, when superadded to these personal attractions are a red nose and yellow smalls* (*Oliver Twist* by Charles Dickens)

sneeze-box NOUN a box for snuff was called a sneeze-box because sniffing snuff makes the user sneeze ❑ *To think of Jack Dawkins — lummy Jack — the Dodger — the Artful Dodger — going abroad for a common twopenny-halfpenny sneeze-box!* (*Oliver Twist* by Charles Dickens)

snorted VERB slept ❑ *Or snorted we in the Seven Sleepers' den?* (*The Good-Morrow* by John Donne)

snuff NOUN snuff is tobacco in powder form which is taken by sniffing ❑ *as he thrust his thumb and fore-finger into the proffered snuff-box of the undertaker: which was an* *ingenious little model of a patent coffin.* (*Oliver Twist* by Charles Dickens)

soliloquized VERB to soliloquize is when an actor in a play speaks to himself or herself rather than to another actor ❑ *'A new servitude! There is something in that,' I soliloquized (mentally, be it understood; I did not talk aloud)* (*Jane Eyre* by Charlotte Brontë)

sough NOUN a sough is a drain or a ditch ❑ *as you may have noticed the sough that runs from the marshes* (*Wuthering Heights* by Emily Brontë)

spirits NOUN a spirit is the nonphysical part of a person which is believed to remain alive after their death ❑ *that I might raise up spirits when I please* (*Doctor Faustus* 1.5 by Christopher Marlowe)

spleen ■ NOUN here spleen means a type of sadness or depression which was thought to only affect the wealthy ❑ *yet here I could plainly discover the true seeds of spleen* (*Gulliver's Travels* by Jonathan Swift) ■ NOUN irritability and low spirits ❑ *Adieu to disappointment and spleen* (*Pride and Prejudice* by Jane Austen)

spondulicks NOUN spondulicks is a slang word which means money ❑ *not for all his spondulicks and as much more on top of it* (*The Adventures of Huckleberry Finn* by Mark Twain)

stalled of VERB to be stalled of something is to be bored with it ❑ *I'm stalled of doing naught* (*Wuthering Heights* by Emily Brontë)

stanchion NOUN a stanchion is a pole or bar that stands upright and is used as a building support ❑ *and slid down a stanchion* (*The Adventures of Huckleberry Finn* by Mark Twain)

stang NOUN stang is another word for pole which was an old measurement ❑ *These fields were intermingled with woods of half a stang* (*Gulliver's Travels* by Jonathan Swift)

starlings NOUN a starling is a wall built around the pillars that support a bridge to protect the pillars ❑ *There were states of the tide when, having been down the river, I could not get back through the eddy-chafed arches and starlings of old London Bridge* (*Great Expectations* by Charles Dickens)

startings NOUN twitching or night-time movements of the body ❑ *with midnight's startings* (*On His Mistress* by John Donne)

stomacher NOUN a panel at the front of a dress ❑ *but send her aunt the pattern of a stomacher* (*Emma* by Jane Austen)

stoop VERB swoop ❑ *Once a kite hovering over the garden made a stoop at me* (*Gulliver's Travels* by Jonathan Swift)

succedaneum NOUN a succedaneum is a substitute ❑ *But as a succedaneum* (*The Prelude* by William Wordsworth)

suet NOUN a hard animal fat used in cooking ❑ *and your jaws are too weak For anything tougher than suet* (*Alice's Adventures in Wonderland* by Lewis Carroll)

sultry ADJ sultry weather is hot and damp. Here sultry means unpleasant or risky ❑ *for it was getting pretty sultry for us* (*The Adventures of Huckleberry Finn* by Mark Twain)

summerset NOUN summerset is an old spelling of somersault. If someone does a somersault, they turn over completely in the air ❑ *I have seen him do the summerset* (*Gulliver's Travels* by Jonathan Swift)

supper NOUN supper was a light meal taken late in the evening. The main meal was dinner which was eaten at four or five in the afternoon ❑ *and the supper table was all set out* (*Emma* by Jane Austen)

surfeits VERB to surfeit in something is to have far too much of it, or to overindulge in it to an unhealthy degree ❑ *He surfeits upon cursed* necromancy (*Doctor Faustus chorus* by Christopher Marlowe)

surtout NOUN a surtout is a long close-fitting overcoat ❏ *He wore a long black surtout reaching nearly to his ankles* (*The Old Curiosity Shop* by Charles Dickens)

swath NOUN swath is the width of corn cut by a scythe ❏ *while thy hook Spares the next swath* (*Ode to Autumn* by John Keats)

sylvan ADJ sylvan means belonging to the woods ❏ *Sylvan historian* (*Ode on a Grecian Urn* by John Keats)

taction NOUN taction means touch. This means that the people had to be touched on the mouth or the ears to get their attention ❏ *without being roused by some external taction upon the organs of speech and hearing* (*Gulliver's Travels* by Jonathan Swift)

Tag and Rag and Bobtail PHRASE the riff-raff, or lower classes. Used in an insulting way ❏ *'No,' said he; 'not till it got about that there was no protection on the premises, and it come to be considered dangerous, with convicts and Tag and Rag and Bobtail going up and down.'* (*Great Expectations* by Charles Dickens)

tallow NOUN tallow is hard animal fat that is used to make candles and soap ❏ *and a lot of tallow candles* (*The Adventures of Huckleberry Finn* by Mark Twain)

tan VERB to tan means to beat or whip ❏ *and if I catch you about that school I'll tan you good* (*The Adventures of Huckleberry Finn* by Mark Twain)

tanyard NOUN the tanyard is part of a tannery, which is a place where leather is made from animal skins ❏ *hid in the old tanyard* (*The Adventures of Huckleberry Finn* by Mark Twain)

tarry ADJ tarry means the colour of tar or black ❏ *his tarry pig-tail*

(*Treasure Island* by Robert Louis Stevenson)

thereof PHRASE from there ❏ *By all desires which thereof did ensue* (*On His Mistress* by John Donne)

thick with, be PHRASE if you are 'thick with someone' you are very close, sharing secrets – it is often used to describe people who are planning something secret ❏ *Hasn't he been thick with Mr Heathcliff lately?* (*Wuthering Heights* by Emily Brontë)

thimble NOUN a thimble is a small cover used to protect the finger while sewing ❏ *The paper had been sealed in several places by a thimble* (*Treasure Island* by Robert Louis Stevenson)

thirtover ADJ thirtover is an old word which means obstinate or that someone is very determined to do want they want and can not be persuaded to do something in another way ❏ *I have been living on in a thirtover, lackadaisical way* (*Tess of the D'Urbervilles* by Thomas Hardy)

timbrel NOUN timbrel is a tambourine ❏ *What pipes and timbrels?* (*Ode on a Grecian Urn* by John Keats)

tin NOUN tin is slang for money/cash ❏ *Then the plain question is, an't it a pity that this state of things should continue, and how much better would it be for the old gentleman to hand over a reasonable amount of tin, and make it all right and comfortable* (*The Old Curiosity Shop* by Charles Dickens)

tincture NOUN a tincture is a medicine made with alcohol and a small amount of a drug ❏ *with ink composed of a cephalic tincture* (*Gulliver's Travels* by Jonathan Swift)

tithe NOUN a tithe is a tax paid to the church ❏ *and held farms which, speaking from a spiritual point of view, paid highly-desirable tithes* (*Silas Marner* by George Eliot)

towardly ADJ a towardly child is

dutiful or obedient ❑ *and a towardly child* (*Gulliver's Travels* by Jonathan Swift)

toys NOUN trifles are things which are considered to have little importance, value, or significance ❑ *purchase my life from them bysome bracelets, glass rings, and other toys* (*Gulliver's Travels* by Jonathan Swift)

tract NOUN a tract is a religious pamphlet or leaflet ❑ *and Joe Harper got a hymn-book and a tract* (*The Adventures of Huckleberry Finn* by Mark Twain)

train-oil NOUN train-oil is oil from whale blubber ❑ *The train-oil and gunpowder were shoved out of sight in a minute* (*Wuthering Heights* by Emily Brontë)

tribulation NOUN tribulation means the suffering or difficulty you experience in a particular situation ❑ *Amy was learning this distinction through much tribulation* (*Little Women* by Louisa May Alcott)

trivet NOUN a trivet is a three-legged stand for resting a pot or kettle ❑ *a pocket-knife in his right; and a pewter pot on the trivet* (*Oliver Twist* by Charles Dickens)

trot line NOUN a trot line is a fishing line to which a row of smaller fishing lines are attached ❑ *when he got along I was hard at it taking up a trot line* (*The Adventures of Huckleberry Finn* by Mark Twain)

troth NOUN oath or pledge ❑ *I wonder, by my troth* (*The Good-Morrow* by John Donne)

truckle NOUN a truckle bedstead is a bed that is on wheels and can be slid under another bed to save space ❑ *It rose under my hand, and the door yielded. Looking in, I saw a lighted candle on a table, a bench, and a mattress on a truckle bedstead.* (*Great Expectations* by Charles Dickens)

trump NOUN a trump is a good, reliable person who can be trusted ❑ *This lad Hawkins is a trump, I perceive* (*Treasure Island* by Robert Louis Stevenson)

tucker NOUN a tucker is a frilly lace collar which is worn around the neck ❑ *Whereat Scrooge's niece's sister – the plump one with the lace tucker: not the one with the roses – blushed.* (*A Christmas Carol* by Charles Dickens)

tureen NOUN a large bowl with a lid from which soup or vegetables are served ❑ *Waiting in a hot tureen!* (*Alice's Adventures in Wonderland* by Lewis Carroll)

turnkey NOUN a prison officer; jailer ❑ *As we came out of the prison through the lodge, I found that the great importance of my guardian was appreciated by the turnkeys, no less than by those whom they held in charge.* (*Great Expectations* by Charles Dickens)

turnpike NOUN the upkeep of many roads of the time was paid for by tolls (fees) collected at posts along the road. There was a gate to prevent people travelling further along the road until the toll had been paid. ❑ *Traddles, whom I have taken up by appointment at the turnpike, presents a dazzling combination of cream colour and light blue; and both he and Mr Dick have a general effect about them of being all gloves.* (*David Copperfield* by Charles Dickens)

twas PHRASE it was ❑ *twas but a dream of thee* (*The Good-Morrow* by John Donne)

tyrannized VERB tyrannized means bullied or forced to do things against their will ❑ *for people would soon cease coming there to be tyrannized over and put down* (*Treasure Island* by Robert Louis Stevenson)

'un NOUN 'un is a slang term for one – usually used to refer to a person ❑ *She's been thinking the old 'un* (*David Copperfield* by Charles Dickens)

undistinguished ADJ undiscriminating or incapable of making a distinction between good and bad things ❑

their undistinguished appetite to devour everything (*Gulliver's Travels* by Jonathan Swift)

use NOUN habit ❑ *Though use make you apt to kill me* (*The Flea* by John Donne)

vacant ADJ vacant usually means empty, but here Wordsworth uses it to mean carefree ❑ *To vacant musing, unreproved neglect* (*The Prelude* by William Wordsworth)

valetudinarian NOUN one too concerned with his or her own health. ❑ *for having been a valetudinarian all his life* (*Emma* by Jane Austen)

vamp VERB vamp means to walk or tramp to somewhere ❑ *Well, vamp on to Marlott, will 'ee* (*Tess of the D'Urbervilles* by Thomas Hardy)

vapours NOUN the vapours is an old term which means unpleasant and strange thoughts, which make the person feel nervous and unhappy ❑ *and my head was full of vapours* (*Robinson Crusoe* by Daniel Defoe)

vegetables NOUN here vegetables means plants ❑ *the other vegetables are in the same proportion* (*Gulliver's Travels* by Jonathan Swift)

venturesome ADJ if you are venturesome you are willing to take risks ❑ *he must be either hopelessly stupid or a venturesome fool* (*Wuthering Heights* by Emily Brontë)

verily ADV verily means really or truly ❑ *though I believe verily* (*Robinson Crusoe* by Daniel Defoe)

vicinage NOUN vicinage is an area or the residents of an area ❑ *and to his thought the whole vicinage was haunted by her.* (*Silas Marner* by George Eliot)

victuals NOUN victuals means food ❑ *grumble a little over the victuals* (*The Adventures of Huckleberry Finn* by Mark Twain)

vintage NOUN vintage in this context means wine ❑ *Oh, for a draught of vintage!* (*Ode on a Nightingale* by John Keats)

virtual ADJ here virtual means powerful or strong ❑ *had virtual faith* (*The Prelude* by William Wordsworth)

vittles NOUN vittles is a slang word which means food ❑ *There never was such a woman for givin' away vittles and drink* (*Little Women* by Louisa May Alcott)

voided straight PHRASE voided straight is an old expression which means emptied immediately ❑ *see the rooms be voided straight* (*Doctor Faustus 4.1* by Christopher Marlowe)

wainscot NOUN wainscot is wood panel lining in a room so wainscoted means a room lined with wooden panels ❑ *in the dark wainscoted parlor* (*Silas Marner* by George Eliot)

walking the plank PHRASE walking the plank was a punishment in which a prisoner would be made to walk along a plank on the side of the ship and fall into the sea, where they would be abandoned ❑ *about hanging, and walking the plank* (*Treasure Island* by Robert Louis Stevenson)

want VERB want means to be lacking or short of ❑ *The next thing wanted was to get the picture framed* (*Emma* by Jane Austen)

wanting ADJ wanting means lacking or missing ❑ *wanting two fingers of the left hand* (*Treasure Island* by Robert Louis Stevenson)

wanting, I was not PHRASE I was not wanting means I did not fail ❑ *I was not wanting to lay a foundation of religious knowledge in his mind* (*Robinson Crusoe* by Daniel Defoe)

ward NOUN a ward is, usually, a child who has been put under the protection of the court or a guardian for his or her protection ❑ *I call the Wards in Jarndcye. The* *are caged up with all the others.* (*Bleak House* by Charles Dickens)

waylay VERB to waylay someone is to lie in wait for them or to intercept them ❑ *I must go up the road and waylay him* (*The Adventures of Huckleberry Finn* by Mark Twain)

weazen NOUN weazen is a slang word for throat. It actually means shrivelled ❑ *You with a uncle too! Why, I knowed you at Gargery's when you was so small a wolf that I could have took your weazen betwixt this finger and thumb and chucked you away dead* (*Great Expectations* by Charles Dickens)

wery ■ ADV very ❑ *Be wery careful o' vidders all your life* (*Pickwick Papers* by Charles Dickens) ■ *See* wibrated

wherry NOUN wherry is a small swift rowing boat for one person ❑ *It was flood tide when Daniel Quilp sat himself down in the wherry to cross to the opposite shore.* (*The Old Curiosity Shop* by Charles Dickens)

whether PREP whether means which of the two in this example ❑ *we came in full view of a great island or continent (for we knew not whether)* (*Gulliver's Travels* by Jonathan Swift)

whetstone NOUN a whetstone is a stone used to sharpen knives and other tools ❑ *I dropped pap's whetstone there too* (*The Adventures of Huckleberry Finn* by Mark Twain)

wibrated VERB in Dickens's use of the English language 'w' often replaces 'v' when he is reporting speech. So here 'wibrated' means 'vibrated'. In *Pickwick Papers* a judge asks Sam Weller (who constantly confuses the two letters) 'Do you spell it with a 'v' or a 'w'?' to which Weller replies 'That depends upon the taste and fancy of the speller, my Lord' ❑ *There are strings . . . in the human heart that had better not be wibrated* (*Barnaby Rudge* by Charles Dickens)

wicket NOUN a wicket is a little door in a larger entrance ❑ *Having rested*

here, for a minute or so, to collect a good burst of sobs and an imposing show of tears and terror, he knocked loudly at the wicket (*Oliver Twist* by Charles Dickens)

without CONJ without means unless ❑ *You don't know about me, without you have read a book by the name of The Adventures of Tom Sawyer* (*The Adventures of Huckleberry Finn* by Mark Twain)

wittles ■ NOUN vittles is a slang word which means food ❑ *I live on broken wittles–and I sleep on the coals* (*David Copperfield* by Charles Dickens) ■ *See* wibrated

woo VERB courts or forms a proper relationship with ❑ *before it woo* (*The Flea* by John Donne)

words, to have PHRASE if you have words with someone you have a disagreement or an argument ❑ *I do not want to have words with a young thing like you.* (*Black Beauty* by Anna Sewell)

workhouse NOUN workhouses were places where the homeless were given food and a place to live in return for doing very hard work ❑ *And the Union workhouses? demanded Scrooge. Are they still in operation?* (*A Christmas Carol* by Charles Dickens)

yawl NOUN a yawl is a small boat kept on a bigger boat for short trips. Yawl is also the name for a small fishing boat ❑ *She sent out her yawl, and we went aboard* (*The Adventures of Huckleberry Finn* by Mark Twain)

yeomanry NOUN the yeomanry was a collective term for the middle classes involved in agriculture ❑ *The yeomanry are precisely the order of people with whom I feel I can have nothing to do* (*Emma* by Jane Austen)

yonder ADV yonder means over there ❑ *all in the same second we seem to hear low voices in yonder!* (*The Adventures of Huckleberry Finn* by Mark Twain)